B

THE OTHER LOVE

Briony Moore is jilted just days before her marriage when her fiancé decides his new job abroad is more important than her. Seeking solace and oblivion in work, she becomes secretary to Hew Vanner, the explorer and writer. Hew's heart had been broken like Briony's by tragic circumstances, but in the idyllic surroundings of his home in the Lake District, Hew and Briony find a common bond—the other, enduring love.

THE OTHER LOVE

Briony Moore is jilted nine days before her marriage when her fiancé decides his new job abroad is more important than her. Seeking solace and oblivion in work, she becomes secretary to Hew Vannel, the explorer and writer. Hew's heart had been broken like Briony's by tragic circumstances, but in the idyllic surroundings of his home in the Lake District, Hew and Briony find a common bond — the other, enduring love.

THE OTHER LOVE

The Other Love

by

Denise Robins

Dales Large Print Books
Long Preston, North Yorkshire,
England.

British Library Cataloguing in Publication Data.

Robins, Denise
The other love.

A catalogue record for this book is
available from the British Library

ISBN 1-85389-957-7 pbk

First published in Great Britain by Hutchinson & Co. (Publishers) Ltd., 1952

Published in Large Print 1999 by arrangement with Patricia Clark

Dales Large Print is an imprint of
Library Magna Books Ltd.
Printed and bound in Great Britain by
T.J. International Ltd., Cornwall, PL28 8RW.

TO
CONNIE AND WILLIE

ONE

Briony Moore's small cousin David was, of course, the hit of the afternoon. While they were all finishing tea, his mother brought him downstairs in his page's suit of pale blue satin with the frills of lace on collar and wrists. With his golden curls and laughing, long-lashed eyes he looked so adorable that everybody stopped eating and drinking, to stare at him.

'Oh, the angel!' the two bridesmaids chorused. They were Elizabeth Moore, another older cousin, and Penelope Taylor who was Briony's dearest friend and who had been at school with her.

Mrs Moore, family teapot suspended in mid-air, also smiled fondly at little David. He was her nephew's son and the only boy to be born in the Moore family for a long time, so, of course, he always created a sensation. Mrs Moore liked him particularly because something about him reminded her of Briony at the same age, although she had always had a decidedly red tint in the gold of her hair. But those eyes, that exquisite skin, short chiselled nose and vivid air of general health and beauty were Moore characteristics.

While the rest of the family congratulated

David's mother, and they all petted him, Mrs Moore continued to pour out tea. Every now and then she stole a happy look at the bride-to-be.

Briony was her only child and she was going to be a great loss, the mother thought with a sigh. As well as being lovely to look at, she was such a *nice* girl. Kind and generous like her father and with none of his pleasant vagueness. Briony had a strong will and first-class memory. Geoffrey Moore had been a charming, good-looking young man in the regular Army when Lorna married him. Ill-health—the result of an old war wound—had forced him to retire, but he had bought a partnership in a firm of builders and had done very well here in Reigate, where they had finally settled.

The present-day situation prevented them from being rich but they were 'quite comfortable' as Lorna Moore liked to put it and had this nice little house and garden. They had been able to give Briony a good education.

Briony had chosen a secretarial career for herself. She had always been an ardent reader and collected books since she was a schoolgirl. One of her ambitions, she used to tell everybody, laughingly, was to become private secretary to a famous author and so live in the world of books.

Then, just as she had become thoroughly proficient and on the point of advertising for the sort of job she wanted—Clive Dormer came into her life.

Now, in a week's time, Briony was going to be married to Clive. With something of a shock Lorna Moore looked at her 'ewe lamb' this afternoon and thought:

'This time next week she won't be sitting here ... our Briony ... Her bedroom will be empty. The house will be horribly quiet and tidy, instead of full of the sound of her gay voice, and her young friends. She will be Mrs Clive Dormer ... down in Cornwall on her honeymoon, and Geoff and I will be alone, so *very* much alone!'

The mother's heart ached suddenly with the realization of all that she was going to lose once she handed this dear daughter over to the stranger who had come into their midst. She was glad, because Briony was so much in love with Clive. Yet anxious at times because six months ago she hadn't even known him. She met him at a party in London last Christmas.

They had nothing against Clive. He was an attractive boy—aged twenty-six—five years older than Briony, which was just right. Slight, dark-haired, vivacious, a good foil for Briony's fairness. He held a Manchester University degree in engineering, and was the only son of a Midlands solicitor. His mother had died when he was born and he had been brought up by an aunt who was now also deceased.

It appeared that when his father died, Clive would have a little money of his own. There seemed every prospect of his getting a bigger job than the small one he held, in the near future. This was not yet settled, and the Moores had wanted Briony to wait for it. But Clive had insisted on a June wedding. Lorna and Geoffrey Moore, like so many modern parents, soon found that they had no real say in the matter. Briony had just come home one day and said:

'Oh, Mummy, isn't it *terrific?* ... Clive and I are going to get married the last day of June because it is *his* birthday and he says I shall make such a gorgeous present so you can just wrap me in tissue paper and hand me to him, tied up with silver ribbon!'

Typical of Briony—eager—gay—impetuous, so very young.

No use suggesting that the couple should wait until they knew each other better. Briony was of age and Clive seemed quite sure that the new job he was after was as good as settled.

He had told Briony last night that he expected to hear at any moment where he was being sent, and when, then they could start looking for a home.

'Thank God our child is so happy,' Lorna Moore's reverie continued. Bri really did look beautiful this afternoon, flushed with excitement, her eyes dancing. It had been 'present-showing day'. All their friends had come in to see the lovely things which Lorna had arranged on the dining-room table. The young couple were doing very well. It had made quite a 'show'. Briony had already written thirty or forty 'thank-you' letters. The cake was ordered. The dress was being sent home tomorrow. She had had a final fitting first thing this morning and looked, the mother thought, so beautiful that it had made her want to weep. Tall and straight and slender in her white bridal gown; red-gold head veiled with the Limerick lace which had been loaned by Aunt Caroline. Lorna's sister, Caroline Shaw, older than herself, and a spinster, lived up in the Lake District, where she ran a small antique shop. She was coming down from Seascale for the wedding to stay with them. She had always been particularly fond of Briony.

'Oh, Mummy, what an afternoon we've had!' came Briony's fresh happy voice. 'Are you *exhausted?*'

'Completely,' said Lorna, nodding a short-curled head which was only just beginning to grow grey. She was at forty-five still a good-looking, youthful woman.

'Liz and Penelope are absolute scavengers, they have finished all the cake!' giggled Briony.

The two bridesmaids protested, joining in the giggle. David snatched a chocolate biscuit which his mother took away from him at once because of the blue satin suit, whereupon he set up a yell, and was carted upstairs again.

'I hope he doesn't behave like that on my wedding day,' said Briony more solemnly, then flung herself back on the sofa and momentarily closed her eyes.

'Isn't life *superb!*' she added in a rapturous voice.

Mrs Moore finished her tea and stood up.

'It's nice to know that you find it so, my darling, and I wish I had ten more daughters and ten more weddings to organize in spite of the work. They create such a gay atmosphere for everyone.'

Briony unclosed her eyes and smiled dreamily at her mother.

'I feel more than gay,' she said, 'and I must be the luckiest girl in the world. All that we have got to pray for now is that this gorgeous weather will last. Liz ... Penny ...' she addressed her cousin and her friend, 'let's go out in the garden and have a cigarette. And if that is the postman at the door, Mummy, will you be a darling and hide whatever he brings. I couldn't open another present today. Keep the parcels for tomorrow when Clive comes down ... we'll open them together.'

The three girls walked through the french windows on to the lawn. It was perfect June weather. The lawn looked dry for want of rain but the herbaceous border, which was Mr Moore's special pride, was vividly beautiful—full of colour. The first roses were out. The striped deck-chairs under the chestnut tree looked especially inviting. Briony and her chosen bridesmaids retired to these chairs for what they called a 'good gossip'.

Gay! Briony decided that the word could not really describe her own feelings. They were blissful. It was wonderful to be young and strong and beloved and just about to be married to the most marvellous man in the world. To have that lovely trousseau all packed in a trunk upstairs, ready for the honeymoon ... Mummy and Daddy had been wonderfully generous ... provided her with all that she needed. Clive had bought the wedding ring, and had it inscribed with the date of the wedding, and something personal, which was to be a secret he said, until he put it on her finger. Their rooms were booked in one of the most glamorous hotels on the Cornish coast. They were to spend the first week there then go on to the Scilly Isles. After that there would be the thrill of coming back, finding a home and furnishing it, and settling down to life as a married couple.

Briony thought with poignant tenderness of Clive. Her heart throbbed with the strong passionate conviction that she was making the absolutely right choice.

It had been a case of love at first sight. Never to be forgotten was that thrilling evening at the Savoy. Penelope was responsible for her meeting with Clive. It had been her twenty-first birthday party.

Her brother, Peter, had brought Clive along. Peter was also an engineer. It amused Briony now to remember that when she had first been introduced to Clive and danced with him, she had been rather cool and off-hand with him. He was so good looking and full of charm and she had been so fascinated by him, that it had had the effect of making her hold herself aloof. She was terrified that he would see how strongly he affected her. Now she knew that he (so he said) had felt the same way about her. He had had many girlfriends, but did not intend to marry until he was over thirty. But Briony had 'knocked him flat'. She had been in white that night, a white spangled net dress 'off the shoulders', and with the full crinoline type of skirt. Her hair was arranged in a bunch of red-gold curls over one ear. She had worn long white gloves and silver sandal shoes.

'My crinoline girl!' Clive had called her. That Victorian touch of coldness, of shyness, belying the warmth in Briony's grey-blue eyes, had intrigued him vastly.

After that, he had scarcely missed a weekend in the Moores' Reigate home, and not long afterwards he and Briony had become officially engaged.

As she sat talking with the other girls, it struck Briony that one of the most amazing things about an engagement was the fact that although the two concerned seemed to know each other intimately, they did not really know each other at all. They were bound to discover all kinds of new and wonderful things about each other after they were married. Some of them *un*attractive perhaps! He would produce faults ... inevitably ... since he was only human, although at the moment she could find absolutely nothing wrong with Clive except that he was unpunctual and a little inclined to exaggerate. Once or twice she had thought, too, that he was on the vague side, and liable to forget some of the important things he said, or meant to do. However, he never forgot to tell her that he loved her! That was what counted with a girl in love. And he was oh! so charming and so clever. She was sure he would succeed at any job he took up. Daddy, himself, said that Clive was very intelligent. He was always nice to Mummy, too, and he played wonderful tennis and was a *marvellous* dancer. What more could a girl want? They would not be frightfully well off to begin with but few young couples of their age could expect to be, at first. And if matrimony meant cooking and housework and all the rest of it ... what did it matter, Briony thought, if one had a husband like Clive?

Mrs Moore called playfully from the french windows.

'Am I to hide a *letter* from Clive as well as your parcels?'

'Don't you *dare!*' cried Bryony, and darted out of her deck-chair and rushed to her mother.

'This will be to say what time he is coming down tomorrow,' she added breathlessly.

Mrs Moore smiled and began to clear up the tea things. What it was to be in love! Even though it was over twenty-two years ago she could remember feeling the same feverish happiness at the sight of a letter in Geoffrey's handwriting.

Then she turned her head quickly and looked at her daughter. Briony had given a sharp exclamation. The mother saw that all her lovely rose pink colour had drained from her cheeks. She was milk white. Mrs Moore put down the tea-tray.

'Bri! What on earth is the matter, darling?'

The girl did not answer. It was obvious that she had received some kind of a shock. Her eyes which had been so full of happiness a few minutes ago had gone suddenly blank, with dilated pupils.

'What is it, darling?' repeated her mother, terrified.

Briony shook her head. She seemed unable to speak. The muscles of her throat worked. Mrs Moore saw that the slim body was shaking. Then blindly Briony held out the letter that she had just read.

Mrs Moore found her glasses, put them on and hurriedly glanced through the letter.

Her heart sank as she took in its meaning. She, herself, was conscious of shock. This was calamity. She could hardly believe what she read, but it was there in black and white

... in Clive Dormer's small rather cramped handwriting .... there to be seen and believed, shocking and incredible though it was.

Briony, my darling, how much I hate to write this letter I can never tell you. I have already written three letters and torn them up. I wondered if it might be better to come down as arranged tomorrow and tell you the news myself. Then I decided that I could not face you, for if I did I might break down and revoke my own decision. I love you so much. I can hardly bear it. Yet the decision is one I have got to make for both our sakes.

Briony, we can't get married next week. We must cancel the whole thing. I know it is leaving it pretty late. It means sending back all the presents and that sort of thing. It's pretty awful but it has got to be done. I have already cancelled my part of the arrangements because I am leaving England on Monday. Briony, it's my job. My whole career is at stake. From the bottom of my heart I beg you to forgive me and try to understand. It isn't that I have stopped loving you. I've never met any other girl that I wanted to marry and you are wonderful and I still want you to marry me if you don't mind waiting. But it means a three years' wait for both of us. It's pretty grim when you think of all our dreams and plans. I can't allow myself to remember Land's End and all I am going to miss next week. But there it is. Oh, Briony, try to forgive me and tell me you understand ...

Mrs Moore skipped through a few more paragraphs of this (as she afterwards described it to her husband *'nauseating stuff')*, and went on to facts. There was one salient fact that stood out in the whole letter. Clive had been offered a wonderful job in the engineering world, but it was open only to *an unmarried man*. It was to be abroad, and it carried a big salary—magnificent prospects. Fine for Clive! Tempting bait for any ambitious young man and Clive *was* ambitious. Briony's father had recognized that fact. But none of them had imagined that so overmastering was his desire for fame and fortune that he would put it in front of his marriage.

A positively devastating selfishness leaped nakedly from the four pages of Clive's letter. It was meant to be a form of apology—he continually reassured Briony that he loved her. But it was in fact the revelation of a man's absorbing interest in *himself* to the exclusion of anybody or anything else.

It must have taken Clive hours to concoct. It twisted and turned. He seemed conscious of his own guilt; ashamed of it. Euphemistically he talked about 'only postponing the wedding'. After his three years' term was up, he said, he would find a way of getting Briony out to him. Or, perhaps, before that he would find a bigger and better job which would enable him to send for her.

It ended with an appeal to her to forgive,

but never to forget him, and to assure her that he was 'hurting himself' far more than her by this decision. But the said decision was irrevocable. He finished by begging her to send him away with her good wishes and still to wear his ring.

Mrs Moore finished the letter and looked at her daughter, her whole being flooded with resentment against Clive. She could see what the letter had already done to her darling. The girl's face was a mask of pain and bewilderment. Her teeth chattering, Briony now spoke:

'He can't *ever* have loved me as I loved him. He *can't* or he couldn't have done this to me. Oh Mummy, we were going to be married *next week*. Everything is arranged. Mummy, tell me it is not true!'

Mrs Moore shook her head dumbly. Sensible woman though she was, this was too much. She was at a loss to know what to say or how to comfort her girl. But somewhere at the back of her brain a small voice was beginning to remind her that right from the start she had mistrusted Clive. He was too good looking—had too much charm, not enough stability. He had been spoiled by that aunt who had brought him up in place of his mother and who, along with his silly doting old father, had always let him have his own way. He had never really been good enough for Briony. Her loyal, honest, deeply affectionate Bri, who would have died rather than do a thing like this.

Briony was speaking again in an anguished voice which cut the mother to the quick.

'I can't understand it ... I *can't.* He was just as thrilled as I was about our marriage when I saw him the day before yesterday. I suppose he had not had the job offered him then. And he hasn't even waited to talk things over with me. He says he has cancelled everything. He's going abroad on Monday and without *me.* For three whole years. Oh, *Mummy ...!*' Suddenly, wildly, Briony called to the two girls who were laughing and chatting under the chestnut tree.

'Hi! you two ... Liz ... Pen ... you had better come and help pack up the wedding presents. They have all got to go back. I am not going to get married after all. Isn't it a *joke?*'

Her voice cracked. The other girls started to come across the lawn, their faces bewildered. Briony turned and rushed out of the dining-room and up the stairs. The house reverberated with the sound of a door banging. Her bedroom door.

Lorna Moore stood very still, holding Clive's letter in one hand, the other pressed against her lips which were quivering. She felt quite sick. It seemed impossible that anything like this could happen to Briony ... to any of her family. They had all been so happy always and especially today. All those presents in there ... little David in his page's suit ... Briony's wedding dress ... over one hundred guests invited to the church; the reception all arranged. Oh, how *dreadful!*

Then she pulled herself together and tried to answer the questions the two girls were hurling at her. Yes, something *had* happened ... she could explain now ... yes, the wedding would not now take place ... poor Briony was very upset, naturally ... but she didn't want anything said to anybody in the district. Please go home now, dears, she told them, but don't take anything for *granted* or start any rumours. Briony would telephone them and tell them more later on ...

So Elizabeth and Penelope left. Full of disappointment, anxious for Briony—they left the house which a short while ago had been so full of bliss. There now hung over it a black threatening cloud.

David and his mother also left. Nobody knew anything except that the wedding was 'off', because Briony had had bad news. The birds went on singing merrily in the green trees and the close of the beautiful June day was tranquil and heavenly. But from Briony's bedroom came the sound of heartbroken sobs. And the girl who had thought that she was going to get married next week to the most wonderful man in the world, lay face downwards on her bed, drenching the pillow with the most bitter tears she was ever likely to shed.

TWO

'You had better have a strong drink before I tell you the news, Geoff,' said Lorna Moore as her husband entered the house and greeted her with the usual kiss and genial smile.

'Glorious day—' he began.

She broke in and told him exactly what had happened about Briony and Clive.

The smile was wiped from Mr Moore's face. He did not have the 'strong drink' but he had a long soft one and while he sat in the cool sitting-room, drinking and listening to what his wife had to say, the most bitter anger and resentment on behalf of his young daughter welled up in him.

'Well, I'm blowed!' he exclaimed. 'But I never liked that young man, *never*. There was always something about him that I *didn't* like. I accepted him because Bri wanted me to.'

'Same here,' said Briony's mother.

She had recovered from the shock of Clive's letter, but not from the knowledge that Briony was still upstairs, locked in her bedroom, crying her eyes out. Her child's hurt was *hers*. It all seemed so humiliating as well as miserable for the poor darling. She had virtually been 'jilted'! That 'wait for me' business with a three years' limit was a lot of bunkum.

Mr Moore agreed. He had much more to say and said it vigorously.

'Young whippersnapper! He can't do this to our girl. Where's our ABC, Lorna! I am going to see and settle Mr Clive.'

That was where Briony came in—she had entered the room so quietly that her parents did not notice the door handle turn. They looked at her. She was very pale and her eyes were red rimmed but she was quite calm now. Her lips were a tight line.

'No, Daddy. No, thank you,' she said. 'You are not to do anything of the sort.'

Geoffrey Moore approached her, his kindly face puckered and his heart torn at the sight of her face. She was so sadly changed from the radiant Briony whom he had seen at the breakfast table this morning. His lovely girl! Lovelier even than her own mother had been at the same age, and Lorna had been hard to beat, he thought. Dammit, why must one live to see one's child broken up and tortured? If he could put a bullet into Clive Dormer at this moment ...

Then Briony gave him a touching little smile and patted his shoulder.

'Don't look so worried, Daddy. I'll work this thing out my own way. I am not the first girl to be jilted, you know.'

'Won't you let me go and see him?'

'Absolutely not. He's sailing on Monday. Let him sail.'

The father's heart swelled. The child had pride. Briony added:

'And no waiting three years for *me*. If Clive had loved me he would not have asked me to wait all that time, nor walked out on me at the last moment. It's ... it's just *hellish* ...' her voice broke but she instantly recovered herself.

Mr Moore sighed. Lorna Moore said:

'Well, I am glad you look at it like that. I should hate you to wait for him. Now I suggest that you go up to Aunt Caroline's until the gossip blows over.'

'No,' said Briony, red-gold head tilted high. 'No running away for me. I shall stay here and look for a job and just tell everyone that Clive and I parted ... by mutual consent ...'

Mrs Moore looked doubtful. Mr Moore approved. The shadows on the lawn lengthened. The June day drew to its close. An agonizing close for Briony. She had many letters to write ... explanations to give to friends ... wires for Mummy and herself to send ... cancellations of the church service and other things for Daddy to do. *(Don't look at that shining new trunk full of new clothes. Don't think about the honeymoon in Cornwall. Try to put it all in the background and forget ... call it a bad dream ... wake up to reality no matter how hard. But oh, Clive, Clive!...)*

It was horribly difficult to forget that attractive, charming person with his winning smile and strong arms, and all the passionate love that had existed between them. How incredible to find that he loved her so little that he could leave her for money and ambition! No matter what she suffered, she felt that she would *die* rather than eat humble pie at Clive's hands and let him think that she was willing to sit down and *wait.*

She wrote to him. Posted the letter with red-hot pain searing her heart but an indomitable determination to abide by what she had written.

It was just *Good-bye, Clive.* She made no attempt to try and make him change his mind. She was too sensible for *that.* She knew that his request that she should wait had been just a feeble effort to soften the blow. He would sail on Monday, whatever she said.

I wish you the best of luck, Clive. That was how she ended the letter.

After posting the letter she walked back into the house through the soft June night and felt that she never wanted to see the stars, smell the roses or think of summer in her life again.

The next few days were hard ... much harder than she had imagined they could be. For a while there was much to do packing up presents and cancelling preparations. She was kept busy. Despite her mother's protests and father's anxiety, she wore herself out, physically, in the endeavour to dull the mental pain. Monday came ... the day on which Clive was to sail ... that was another black day with remembrance piercing her heart. He was going ... out of her life. It was hard to carry on—be proud, wear a façade of indifference for the world to see.

Clive did not answer her letter. Perhaps it was as well. It did at least show her that she had been right to break entirely with him and not lay herself open to further insult and disillusion.

But breaking point was bound to come. And in the end, a much thinner Briony retired to her bed with a temperature. The doctor called it 'summer flu', but her mother knew that Briony's illness was more of the mind than of the body. Devotedly she nursed her daughter. She said to her husband:

'It is so awful that Briony hasn't got anything really to *do* to take her mind off that abominable young man. It is so quiet for her here with just us. What she wants is a big cheerful household. One can't afford to go abroad nowadays, otherwise I would have taken her to France or something, the poor sweet. I wish we could persuade her to go up to Caroline. The sea air would do her good and she was always interested in the shop and knows a lot about old glass and china.'

Mr Moore agreed. And the time came

when Briony also agreed. She could no longer stay in Reigate. She knew too many people. It was so hurtful to meet her friends and read the sympathy in their eyes and realize that she was an object of pity. Everybody was kind but there must always be the not-so-kind. Heaven alone knew what rumours were going about as to *why* the bridegroom had walked out on the bride at the eleventh hour! Perhaps, she told herself with wry humour (thank goodness she still had a sense of humour) they whispered that Clive had found out just in time that she *drank,* or that there was *insanity* in the family, or some vile thing. People would say anything. *She must get away*.

So the day came when Briony took the train up to the Lake District. There was a double incentive now to go up to dear Aunt Caro who had written to say that she had a bad attack of asthma (from which she suffered); so bad indeed that she had had to close down the 'Treasure Shop'. And it was just at the height of the season when there were many visitors in Seascale. She really needed someone to help her out.

If Briony came, Aunt Caro said, she might look round for a permanent job. She knew her proud independent young niece and was quite sure that Briony would not want to stay at home after this catastrophe.

Her parents, always understanding, bade Briony good-bye with all their love and told her that the house would be lonely without her but she must do just what she wanted. They only wanted her to find peace and happiness.

As Briony travelled up north and looked out at the fair English countryside (they were enjoying a perfect spell of weather) she wondered what life could offer her now. By this time, Clive was well on his way to Nigeria. She would never see him again. That was all over. But in her heart it wasn't over, because although he had proved unworthy, she was not a person who could transfer her affections easily, or who loved lightly. She felt, as she put it, when she had talked to Penelope, *'all withered inside'*.

Pen, trying to be comforting, had replied:

'You'll meet someone else one day, darling. You are much too pretty and attractive to stay alone long.'

But Briony thought that Pen was wrong. All her life she would be haunted by silly little memories of Clive. The way his greenish hazel eyes crinkled up when he laughed ... a trick he had of smiling at her slantways ... of brushing her lips with his just before he kissed her ... of flicking the ash from his cigarette with the tip of his little finger ... all his individual fascination ... all so unforgettable ... and *unrepeatable.* Of that she was sure. She would never find such another lover and never love again.

But she was glad she had been persuaded into going up to Seascale once she got there.

Auntie Caro was just the right person for her to be with. She was not quite as sentimental as Mummy. She had been hurt, herself ... Briony knew all about Aunt Caro's one big affair which had ended in her fiancé being taken from her in the First World War. She had been a good-looking girl then and *he* in the Navy. He had been brutally murdered—machine-gunned by the enemy whilst floundering in the water after his ship had been blown up. And that, thought Briony, must have been pretty good hell for Aunt Caroline who had never put anybody in his place. But at least he had not run away from her. He had died a hero's death. Briony began to see that death could be kinder than desertion.

Aunt Caro was a sensible, friendly person. No longer attractive—grey-haired and angular, she wore thick stockings, awful clothes and comic hats. But she had a heart of gold and a wide knowledge of antiques. Everybody in Seascale knew the 'Treasure Shop', and Miss Shaw who ran it. And she knew exactly how to deal with heartbreak like Briony's. She ignored it. She was delighted to see her. Briony was definitely her favourite, and old Alice who had been Caroline's cook-housekeeper for the last twenty years had nursed Miss Briony when she was a tiny baby and was also very fond of the girl.

Briony was given a great welcome by the two elderly women, with a merciful absence of sympathy or pity. Miss Shaw said:

'Glad you've come, child. Now you can open up the shop for me and get those Yanks to buy up my stock and fill up my coffers. They are pretty empty what with taxation, and my poor "divs." falling right and left!'

Briony settled down remarkably well in the little ivy-covered Victorian house which was close to the sea front. Many of her school holidays had been spent in Seascale. She liked the sea and she used to adore the lakes. On a beautiful day she used to cycle to Wast Water—her favourite—and climb Scafell Pike, where the scenery was wild and splendid. She had had her bicycle sent up this time and planned to do some cycling while she was here.

She opened the 'Treasure Shop' up for Aunt Caroline and did quite a brisk trade the first week, at the end of which her aunt had recovered sufficiently to 'take over' again.

Briony at least reached one definite conclusion. She would not go back to Reigate—to the south which was filled with memories of Clive. She would try and find a good secretarial job up here. Perhaps even a residential post because although she knew she was welcome in her aunt's house, it might be better to be independent, and for her to live away from the family.

On her last day alone in the 'Treasure Shop', she busied herself by cleaning one or two pieces of Georgian silver while she waited for closing time.

She loved this tiny shop with its little leaded-light window in which Miss Shaw displayed her rarest treasures. Americans, of course, adored the place. It was old and oak-beamed—a wing, in fact, of a Tudor house, the rest of which was a café. Miss Shaw had the two small rooms; one at the back which was used as a small office and stock room.

There was a bit of 'junk' lying round, but most of the stuff was lovely ... Miss Shaw often went to sales and travelled quite a distance in order to pick up treasures. There was one large showcase full of exquisite china and Waterford glass. Antique bureaus and tables were covered with rich china bowls, plates and jugs. There were books, pieces of tapestry, one or two Persian rugs. Embroidered shawls, Bristol glass, carved boxes, a colourful variety of things to delight a connoisseur.

Into the shop this afternoon suddenly came a tall man. He was so big that his presence seemed to blot out the sun. He crashed the door ... so that the little bell jangled ... in rather an uncivil, rough way, Briony thought.

She glanced up disapprovingly. Then what colour she had acquired since she arrived in Seascale, vanished from her cheeks. Her heart gave a nervous jerk.

The customer was exactly like Clive. Seen thus in half shadow with his back against the sunlight, he might have been a taller, broader Clive. The same thick brown hair with the suggestion of a wave in it. The same narrow handsome eyes and straight proud nose. Then he spoke ... and the colour slowly stole back into Briony's cheeks. Her heart beats slowed down. Of course he wasn't *really* like Clive. And now as he drew nearer, she could see that he was without Clive's charm. He scowled. Curtly he said:

'What sort of books do you sell? Got anything by Peter Fleming?'

She found herself stuttering.

'No ... nothing modern at all ... only a few old rare editions. We don't really stock novels ... I mean biographies ... so sorry ...'

(That trick of resemblance to Clive was still there to hurt, to worry her ... and she felt so nervous that she dropped the piece of silver she had been cleaning onto the counter.) The man frowned harder as though irritated by the noise. Briony apologized.

He turned round and almost knocked over a little pie-crust table, clutched at the Toby jug which stood on it as he steadied it, and muttered:

'No room to move in here!'

'Surly boor,' she thought. Clive would have smiled and apologized. Who was this man? A visitor, presumably. She had never seen him in Seascale before. Now he cast her a quick glance and grunted:

'I haven't see *you* here before ...'

She told him that the 'Treasure Shop' belonged to her aunt, Miss Shaw. Then she asked if he was a visitor, or did *he* live here?

No, he didn't live in Seascale, he said. He hated the place. He had driven here from a lonelier part of the district. He hated crowds, hated the fact that he could not move in this shop and was annoyed that she had not got the book he wanted. Grunting 'Good evening', he left as abruptly as he had come. Briony closed down the shop and walked home, shaking her head and telling herself that she had seldom come across a more surly individual. How ridiculous that he should look at *all* like the man she had loved and lost; and how aggravating that he had ever entered her shop because that chance meeting had upset her ... shown her that she was still all too vulnerable to hurt.

Then she forgot about the rude man who wanted a book by Peter Fleming. She spent the evening searching the local newspapers to ascertain if there was any kind of job that she could consider.

She answered two advertisements—each asking for a resident secretary; one in a hotel which she really did not fancy, the other from a private house near Wasdale Head. Well, Wast Water at least was her favourite lake, the loneliest, the loveliest of them all. She hoped the advertiser would be interested in her letter.

The morning brought her news from Clive's

father. An unexpectedly kind and sympathetic note. Disapproving of the way Clive had let her down just before the wedding; in fact deploring the whole thing.

That, of course, reopened the old wound thoroughly. She had met Clive's father and had not particularly liked him. Clive's looks and charm must have been inherited from his mother. William Dormer so far as she could remember had been a dried-up little man who wore a beard, and had rather a pettish fussy manner; he had seemed to her as dried up and dreary as his office. But he had shown quite a lot of interest in Briony, his future daughter-in-law. He had been nice to her. And he was obviously shocked by his son's behaviour. The gentle tone of his letter to Briony reduced her to tears.

It also made her realize, all the more, how much she wished to escape from sympathy. She *must* harden up. She must, in fact, get down quickly to some strenuous absorbing work.

THREE

When the answers from the advertisers came for Briony, Aunt Caroline advocated the one from the local hotel.

'Certainly not the other!' she declared.

'The other' was a terse, rather untidily written note from a man who signed himself *H.G. Vanner.* The address was Monks Farm, near Wasdale Head. He required, he said, a first-class shorthand-typist; temporarily to 'live in', as he was engaged on an important book and wished to work at all odd hours. His housekeeper, Mrs Berry, would look after her and provided they got through the requisite amount of work, she could have every evening and Sundays to herself.

To Briony this sounded interesting. Had she not in the good old days always wanted to work for an author? But Miss Shaw had nothing good to say for Mr Vanner.

'He is a mystery man. I've heard of him. Hew Gordon Vanner. Personally I have never met him, but my friend, Mrs Scott—you know, our dentist's wife—once met him. Mr Scott took a tooth out for him. Raging toothache may have accounted for his rudeness, but both the Scotts thought him impossible!'

'Perhaps it's my surly stranger who came into the "Treasure Shop",' suggested Briony.

Aunt Caroline went on to say that nobody in the Lake District knew much about Mr Vanner, except that he had recently returned from abroad and bought Monks Farm which was a derelict old farmhouse. He had done it up rather patchily. He went nowhere and had no one in his house.

But Aunt Caroline might have saved her

breath, for whatever the snag was in the post offered by Mr H.G. Vanner, it intrigued her niece because of its very mystery.

Aunt Caroline had a friend who ran a local garage. This kindly gentleman volunteered to drive Briony to Monks Farm for an interview, the next morning.

The moment she saw the place she was further intrigued but a little depressed. True, the fine weather had broken and it was raining, and what is more mournful than one of the lakes in bad weather? Half-way down a hill overlooking the wild wonderful Lake Wast Water which could be so beautiful in the sunlight, stood a low-built, grey stone house with a white portico over which clustered a profusion of tangled creepers. The architecture was early Georgian. At one time it must have been a wonderful place, Briony reflected, but now it looked in poor repair. The paint was peeling off windows and doors. The garden, which was laid out in a succession of terraces leading down toward the lake, was utterly neglected. Flowers, vegetables, fruit bushes rioted together.

Smith drove Briony up to the front door. The garden was encircled by a brick wall. The house was almost obscured from the main road by tall trees. In the dripping rain, it presented a grim spectacle. The old woman who opened the door to Briony was as grim as her surroundings, Briony thought. Gaunt-looking, with snow-white unkempt hair, and small eyes, blinking in a face like seamed brown leather. Grudgingly, she admitted Briony and showed her into a small cold room. The furniture here was good Briony decided, and some of the glass and china on the shelves better than anything in the 'Treasure Shop'. But nothing was well arranged. The whole place had an air of neglect, of decay which struck chill at Briony's soul.

'The job is off!' Briony mentally decided. 'I should go mad here!'

Then the door opened and—as she had suspected—in walked the man whom she had already met and who had been so uncivil in the 'Treasure Shop' yesterday.

This morning more than ever, his resemblance to Clive was startling. But he was not as well groomed. Mr Vanner wore old grey flannels and a blue sports shirt. His dark hair fell untidily across his forehead. His brown powerful arms were bare. Briony noticed that at least he was *clean.* His hands were well kept and his tanned cheeks had been well shaven. The shabbiness did not so much matter. He returned her scrutiny with some irony.

'Oh—so it's *you!*' he said.

'Yes,' she said, with a slight flush, 'and it's quite obvious that you won't want me as your secretary any more than I shall want to come.'

He raised his brows as though this direct statement was a challenge.

'May I ask why?'

She answered and with a bluntness which further challenged him. He could not stand the meek or servile and this girl obviously had spirit. He was even amused when she informed him that he had shown, by his abrupt manner in her aunt's shop yesterday, that he had no use for her.

'I have no use for any woman,' he said with a dry laugh.

'In that case,' said Briony with a flash of her eyes, 'you had better advertise for a male secretary. I'll say good-bye, Mr Vanner.'

Suddenly a rather sheepish look of pleading came into his eyes.

'Don't go, and please don't take offence at my manners, I've been living in the wilds and I'm unused to civilized society,' he said in a grudging voice and motioned her to a chair. 'Sit down and have a cigarette and let's discuss things quietly. I really *do* most urgently need someone who can take dictation straight on to the machine—which you stated in your letter you can do. I've got to deliver 80,000 words to my publisher in three months, and I do not see myself doing it, without expert help.'

Briony hesitated, then accepted the chair and the cigarette. After all she had come to apply for the post—so why run away? And *why* must her heart plunge when she saw a ghost of a smile crinkle Mr Vanner's eyes just as they used to crinkle Clive's? How ever could she work for anyone who reminded her so forcibly of her lost love, and her torturing sorrow?

Hew Gordon Vanner had an abrupt unpleasant way with him, but he was *trying*, she could see, to be pleasant. He was telling her now about this book that he had agreed to write; a book about social conditions in strange places. He had travelled all over the world. Fascinating names fell from his lips ... the names of remote cities ... deserts ... jungles ... civilizations unknown to her. He seemed to have culled a terrific amount of information combined with hundreds of photographs from which he wanted to compile a series of books. It was to be his life's work. He had to be quiet ... away from crowds while he wrote. And he must have somebody to work with who would aid and not annoy him.

He began to pace up and down the room while he talked. He walked gracefully for so big a man, Briony thought; padding like a caged tiger. Perhaps he was a genius ... that might account for his 'queerness', and yet every time he turned to look at her with that effort of a smile, he was pure Clive, and made her hold her breath.

Hew! Suitable name for such a rough-hewn man who must have Scottish blood in his veins (afterwards she was to find that it was so; his mother was a daughter of the Highlands). Certainly, Briony thought, he would look marvellous in a kilt; he had such long straight legs.

Hew Vanner, completely unconscious of the impression he was making on this girl, or why, found himself in the unusual position of being suppliant to a female. He hated to ask favours of anybody, least of all 'females'. But if this girl's typing was good as she said, he *must* persuade her to come here. He must lose no more time before he commenced his precious work.

He hardly noticed the fact that Miss Moore was beautiful, although Mrs Berry, announcing her arrival, had muttered that 'the young lady was too young and frivolous looking' for the job. He never took much notice of old Berry. She had been his nurse and still called him 'Master Hew'. The only 'frivolous' thing Hew Vanner could see about this girl was her wonderful red-gold hair, and she couldn't help that. It wasn't dyed. She was sensibly dressed in a flannel suit and jumper, and wore sensible-looking shoes. Also he noted that hers were useful-looking hands, without polish on the nails. He detested the red varnish which so many girls used.

Hew Vanner had never really recovered from an unfortunate childhood. The only child of an Oxford Don and his Scots mother—his fate had been ill-starred from the time that the mother died and his father was literally seduced into marrying again by the daughter of a local publican. A pretty painted creature who had married the man so many years older than herself only because she had wanted a respectable name and security.

She had hated the small Hew as much as he had hated her stepping into his mother's shoes. He had had a good education—his father had insisted on that—but his holidays were bitterly unhappy. His stepmother had made them so, with feminine malice, because the Don spent the money on his son which *she* wanted. As Hew grew up, it was only to watch his father's gradual deterioration and finally his death. He had been broken by the heartless little hussy he had married. She passed out of Hew's life, then. (She might be alive still for all he knew or cared!)

At the time of his father's death he had almost completed his own education. But he was never to forget what he had suffered at *her* hands, nor forgive her for destroying his father. He grew to manhood having no use for women or their wiles. He trusted nobody, and the prettier the woman, the less he trusted her, which was, of course, an obsession. Unfortunately he had become shy and reticent, very much of an introvert. He was often rude when he did not mean to be, and so had made more enemies than friends. Those who really came to know Hew Vanner, worshipped him, for he was a man of dauntless courage and innate generosity. Time and time again he had denied himself to help those in need.

Fortunately a small legacy from one of his mother's Scottish brothers had enabled him to go abroad after he finished with the war, in which he had done a good job with the Commandos. Always he had wanted to travel and investigate conditions in remote places. He had managed to do this.

The one time of his life when he might have found the key to real happiness and a fuller life was during the last year of the war when he had fallen in love.

The girl, Anne Graham, was the daughter of his commanding officer. He had met her on leave and gradually fallen in love with her. She was gentle and lovely, and the very type to bring out all that was best and affectionate in him. For she, in her turn, had loved Hew. She had never exactly said so because he gave her no chance. He had scrupulously refused to marry while the war was on, and perhaps be killed and leave a young widow and a child.

But he had known that she had loved him. It had lain in her eyes and in all the letters she had written him while he was fighting in France and Germany. And there had been one or two unforgettable evenings with her when he had kissed her, known the heaven of a beloved woman's passion and tenderness. He had returned to his unit as happy as a schoolboy—a Hew with renewed faith in womankind. Companionship with Anne completely reversed his opinion of her sex and wiped out the memory of his unattractive stepmother. He had meant to ask Anne to marry him the moment the fighting was over. He knew that her answer would be 'yes'. On VE Day he had gone into action with her photograph in his tunic pocket over his heart.

And then the awful news had reached him in a letter from a mutual friend. Unbelievable and horrible. He was aware that his C.O. had gone back on leave. Nicest and bravest of men, Colonel Graham had led Hew on many a dangerous expedition in the Commandos and come out unscathed. But he was doomed to die with his wife and daughter in what was possibly the last V2 raid on London.

There came an unforgettable morbid evening not long afterwards, when Hew, haunted and agonized, stood in front of what had once been the Graham house in St John's Wood, and saw only rubble and ashes. It had been blown to pieces. Nothing left but the frail ghost of his gentle and deeply loved Anne. Hew could only hope that she had been hurled into Eternity without suffering—not knowing.

In those ashes, he buried his last hopes of happy love. He began to believe that he was foredoomed to misery and disappointment. There and then he vowed that no other love should enter his life.

It took him a long time to get over the shock of Anne's death, but, of course, in time her memory grew a little dimmer and the pain less hard to bear. He flung himself heart and soul into his life as an explorer. He could not find happiness. He was too bitter; too frustrated. But there was an antidote to be found in action and danger and a satisfaction in his writing. The first book he ever published, which was about Burma, had a compelling sincerity in it and a strange disturbing strength which emanated from the man himself and quickly brought him a market. But adventure could not be pandered to *ad infinitum.* He must now—at the age of thirty-two—settle down entirely to writing, and earn his living.

So he had bought—cheaply for nowadays—this derelict farm in the Lake District, and established himself and his old nurse in the farm house in which he put what was left of his parents' furniture.

Old Berry idealized him. She had been his one friend when he was a small boy, and broken her heart when his stepmother had turned her out. After that she, herself, had married. Now a widow, she was willing to devote the rest of her life to 'Master Hew'. But she wasn't good for him and Hew knew it. She had become jealous and rather possessive, and they had blazing rows which irritated him.

How would this young girl fit in here? Would her parents even allow her to come?

He stopped his restless pacing and glowered down at Briony from his great height.

'Well? Have I scared you away? Is it all off?'

Suddenly to her own surprise she answered in the negative.

'No. I'm not easily scared.'

'Could you live here for a bit so that we could work all hours? Berry ... my old nurse ... would look after you and stop tongues from wagging.'

Her cheeks burned.

'I don't take any notice of wagging tongues so long as I know I am in the right.'

He was impressed by that and said so.

'An admirable philosophy. Well, I won't eat you and I won't ask anything except that you should be punctual and do your job well. I'll feed you, and pay you whatever salary you think fair. I am on the telephone and your aunt can ring you up morning, noon and night to make sure you haven't been murdered.'

That made her smile. In spite of his gruffness, Hew had a sense of humour, she decided.

She temporized.

'Hadn't you better see if I can take your dictation at the required speed?'

'Follow me,' he said.

She followed him through the old cold house, and into a room at the back which had French windows—possibly put in at a much later date—leading on to a small garden where somebody had made an attempt to keep the grass cut and grow a few flowers. Beyond, she could see down to the lake—which was smooth and shining—a gunmetal hue. The tall mountain range of Scafell was veiled in weeping rain. The sky was banked with dark clouds. The scene was wild and sinister and magnificent. It stirred her strangely. She thought:

'It really is terrific here ... just not in this world! It makes my home in Reigate and Aunt Caroline's little house in Seascale seem so paltry.'

Somehow Hew Vanner was like those hills, and that vast sheet of water ... mournful, sinister yet magnificent.

When she found that she could type easily to his dictation, and that her work satisfied him, she also found herself agreeing to come and 'try the job'.

He looked genuinely pleased and relieved.

'Tomorrow, then,' he said, 'and get that fellow to drive you over so that you are here by nine o'clock. I like to start work early. I'll pay for your car.'

She looked around her. Nothing but book shelves, piled untidily with every kind of book ... a desk ... a couple of armchairs ... some framed photographs of natives and animals (Hew, himself, with a group of pygmies, towering above them), a huge tiger skin was splayed in front of the fireplace on a polished pine floor, and there was a small table at which she would type.

She was suddenly fascinated by the idea of coming here as this man's personal secretary. *Was it that* or was it because of his fugitive resemblance to Clive? As though she enjoyed biting on an aching tooth?...

Whatever it was, Briony left Monks Farm having promised faithfully to return to it tomorrow ... and stay.

She began to giggle a little to herself at the preposterous idea. What *would* Mummy and Daddy say? Certainly Mrs Berry was a chaperone, but what a reluctant one! Seeing Briony off, Mrs Berry had croaked at her:

'Better not bring more than a suitcase ... you won't stay long with *him*. He can't abide girls ...'

Briony smiled.

'I couldn't care less!' she answered pertly. And thought about the incomprehensible Hew Vanner with his jungle trophies, his photographs, his roughness, and ... in contrast ... that strange look of Clive about the dark thick hair, and the brilliant greenish eyes.

Briony returned to Seascale feeling as though something tremendous was about to happen in her life; feeling, in fact, far less flat and miserable than when she had first come up north.

She ran into her aunt's house eager to tell her story, when she noticed the orange envelope of a telegram, lying on the hall table. It was addressed to her and redirected from Reigate.

The contents of that telegram stunned her. The message was so simple and yet so staggeringly unexpected. It was from Clive. *Clive whom she had thought on his way to Nigeria.* But the telegram had been sent from London. It read:

Travelling north tonight must see you meet me off train Seascale 11.56 a.m. Clive.

FOUR

Briony stood in the little hall clutching that telegram and trying to calm the mad beating of her heart, as she realized what it meant.

Clive hadn't gone to Nigeria after all.

Must see you. Those three words caused a kind of inner revolution in Briony and shattered the peace that she had been gradually acquiring. Her first natural reaction was one of terrific hope; of excitement. He wanted to see her. He was coming up here and would arrive in the morning. She would look upon him again. She would hear his voice, touch him, know that he was once again in the circle of her existence. The man whom she had loved so completely and whom she had thought never to see again.

Trembling from head to foot, Briony hid her flushed face in her hands.

'Clive, oh Clive!' she said in a strangled little voice.

Aunt Caroline came into the hall and saw her standing like that.

'My dear, what's wrong? Was there bad news in your wire? I didn't open it—but I was afraid—'

'No, no, Auntie—it isn't *bad* news. On the contrary, I assure you!'

Miss Shaw, staring at her niece, saw now that Briony was not crying but that her face was hot and pink with excitement and her eyes as bright as stars. Miss Shaw blinked through her tortoise-shell glasses.

'Then you've come into a fortune. Good. You shall share it with your old aunt.'

The cool collected voice with the amused note did much to restore Briony's composure. She put an arm through her aunt's and walked with her into the sitting-room but she was still trembling.

'Aunt Caro, what do you think? Here—read this.'

Miss Shaw sat down, changed her spectacles for the kind she wore for reading small print, and scanned the wire. An instant's silence. She could feel Briony's bright luminous eyes devouring her as though wanting her to share her thrill. But Aunt Caroline did nothing of the kind. She was far too practical and too far-seeing. Many years of loneliness, with her emotions well under restraint, had, she thought, better equipped her to deal with this sort of crisis than this highly sensitive and emotional girl. She loved Briony so devotedly that she had no intention of siding with her on the wrong track. She handed back the telegram and said quietly:

'The young man has appalling cheek.'

Briony's expression changed.

'Cheek?' she echoed the word in some dismay.

'Yes. To send such a wire—a peremptory order to you to meet his train as though nothing had happened. Yet he walked out on his wedding in the most disgraceful fashion.'

Briony stared down into her aunt's calm grey eyes and felt, suddenly, like a pricked balloon. The old wild love for Clive had been sweeping her away. But sensible Aunt Caroline had reached out into the dangerous current and drawn her back to shore, to safety again. She bit hard at her lower lip. Some of her rose colour faded.

'Oh but something must have happened to make him change his mind.'

'Quite so. But does that mean that you are going to change *yours?* Are you the sort of girl who is willing to be dropped and then picked up again like a glove which Mr Dormer has decided he might, after all, like to wear?'

Briony swallowed. Her lashes fluttered.

'Oh!' she said as though she had been hit in the face.

Aunt Caroline rose and put both hands on

her niece's slender shoulders.

'I'm very, very fond of you, Briony. I want you to be happy. But I do not think that happiness can lie for you in the hands of a man who has just jilted you—then for some unknown reason decided to re-enter your life. It savours altogether too much of the potentate giving or withdrawing favours to suit his own whims. However—' she broke off significantly.

Then Briony drew breath. She was herself again. Pride came to the rescue. She knew that every word that Aunt Caro said was true. She remembered the agony, the humiliation she had suffered at Clive's hands. All those returned presents, those cancelled arrangements—those letters of explanation ... no ... Unforgivable! She tore the telegram to pieces. Then she said slowly:

'Of course, we don't know why Clive is coming up to see me, and until I've seen him I had better not make any vital decisions—or sit in judgment.'

Miss Shaw looked at Briony anxiously.

'Supposing he *has* decided that he wants you after all—surely you won't ... surely you couldn't ...' again she broke off.

Said Briony:

'I can't for a moment imagine reopening things with Clive. He hurt me too much. And nothing can ever excuse what he did or the way he did it.'

'Ah! Now you are talking sense, my dear.'

'But I think I had better meet him,' said Briony, 'I must ... I must find out why he wants to see me so urgently.'

Miss Shaw remained silent. Personally, she reflected, if any young man had done to her what Clive did to Briony, nothing would have induced her to give him the satisfaction of a meeting. But Briony was tender-hearted—always had been. Always the first to forgive and forget, even as a small child, bless her. Miss Shaw could not resist a last word of advice.

'Be sensible, darling. Don't let your generous heart run away with your head—whatever he says.'

Briony gave a short laugh and her cheeks flamed again. Already she was beginning to feel nervous at the mere thought of meeting Clive.

'Don't worry, I'll take care of that,' she said.

Then she tried to forget Clive and the astounding and unexpected wire and to tell her aunt the result of this morning's interview with Mr Hew Vanner. She described the house, the man and the job.

'It *was* the gruff creature who came into the "Treasure Shop"—and I agree with your friend, Mrs Scott, that he is a bit of a mystery, but terribly interesting, Aunt Caro. A sort of walking encyclopaedia about strange lands. And such photographs, such books—'

She launched into further description of

Monks Farm, and its occupants. The grumpy queer old nurse.

'I agreed to take the job and be there by nine o'clock tomorrow—' she finished and then put a hand to her mouth, 'oh, goodness! I won't be able to go now I have got to meet this train.'

And, her mind carried her farther: *Perhaps I won't want the job after all, perhaps I won't want to work for anybody if Clive has changed his mind ... if he still loves me—still wants to marry me* ... She tried desperately not to let such ideas enter her head, to keep the flag of pride hoisted high. *To hate him.* To prepare herself for their meeting and tell him exactly what she thought of him. And yet if she were going to do that, why meet him at all? Well, she didn't know where he was, so she couldn't contact him and put him off. And if she didn't meet the train he'd go straight to Aunt Caro's house. He knew where she was.

Oh, if only that wire had never come! She had been quite pleased to accept the job at Wasdale, and reorganize her life. And now it was as though a bomb had burst and shattered it into pieces again.

Miss Shaw had never felt more concerned about her cherished niece. Certainly she did not want her to take Clive Dormer back—if indeed it was his intention to try and get her back. Neither did she think the job with Mr Vanner sounded quite right. That lonely farmhouse and the old housekeeper—no—she didn't think Briony's parents would care much for it. Mr Vanner sounded so aggressive and overbearing—surely not a nice person to work for?

But Briony must lead her own life—Caroline Shaw disapproved of older people who try too hard to organize the lives of the young. They must learn by their own experience and use their own judgment within reason. So she said no more just now. And as Briony did not mention Clive again, Miss Shaw did not mention him either.

But Briony thought about little else for the rest of that day.

She felt thoroughly upset, and passed from one mood to another. First of all she was madly thrilled at the mere thought of seeing Clive, then shrank from it and thought up all the awful things that she would say to him. Later, she decided that she would be icily cold and say nothing. And then wondered if she would retire to her bed and announce that she was too ill to see anybody. Or run away and drive over to Wasdale Head to take up her secretarial post, disappear in Monks Farm. Let Clive call at Holly Cottage, Aunt Caro's home, in vain.

By the end of that day, Briony felt, as she put it to herself, 'a trifle potty'. She really did not know what to think or do, but it seemed positive that she must meet that infernal train and find out why Clive had come.

She decided to telephone to Mr Vanner and explain that she could not be with him by nine o'clock.

She then found that the telephone at Monks Farm was out of order. That was a blow because it was now too late to send a wire. How awful of her! She had promised to get there. He would be absolutely furious. He had laid such stress on the fact that she must be punctual. Oh, well, after she had seen Clive, she would either try to get the Monks Farm number again, or go over to see Mr Vanner and explain, in person.

She did not sleep well that night. She kept thinking about Clive and trying to make up her mind how to greet him; also to guess what was in his mind; why he had not sailed for Nigeria after all.

If she had wanted to look her best, that sop to her vanity was denied her. It turned out to be a pouring wet day; one of those mornings of grey driving rain common in the Lake District. So she had to go to the station wearing a blue mackintosh which had a little hood buttoned under her chin and carrying an umbrella. Scarcely glamorous, she thought. But why want to be glamorous for the man who had treated her so badly? Why not remember how bitterly he had hurt her, and remain indifferent? Yet, there she was on the platform, half an hour before the train was due. And feeling a little ashamed because she knew that Aunt Caroline was scornful about it. She hadn't said a word, but Briony had sensed the scorn. Aunt Caroline was so much more stronger-minded and proud.

Briony found it hard to be proud in love. She had *loved* Clive. She had built her whole world around him; dedicated her life to him before he had delivered that knock-out blow.

Perhaps when she saw him again she would hate him, she decided, and find it no hardship to turn her back on him. Or would her very bones melt at the sight of his face—at the sound of that gay voice, at the touch of those cool slim fingers that used to caress her hair and send such delicious tremors right through her? Would he just say that he was sorry, sweep her off her feet and beg her to consider another wedding, immediately?

Briony was a nervous wreck by the time that train steamed into the station.

There he was—the all-too-familiar figure. Carrying a dispatch case, Clive hurried along towards her, lifting a hand in greeting. He had seen her, too. Her throat felt dry. Her knees started to shake. Funnily enough, as he drew nearer she found herself comparing him with Hew Vanner. Clive was much slimmer and not nearly as tall as Hew. Clive had a *weaker* face ... that seemed quite obvious, this morning. A more girlish, if a more attractive, mouth. But then Hew Vanner's features were as though carven from granite. But seeing Clive again, Briony was not surprised that she had thought the two men alike.

Clive removed his hat. He was close to her now.

'Hallo, Briony,' he said in a low voice.

The old, caressing voice. (That was certainly more pleasant than Hew's.) The old look of warmth and tenderness in the handsome eyes. (How was it that he could ever have treated her so badly, yet still look at her like that?) His manner was constrained—a trifle self-conscious; as though he was uncertain of his reception.

Now that he was actually before her, she felt curiously calm, and mistress of herself. Her trembling ceased. She said:

'Hallo, Clive, where do you want to go?'

He frowned. 'I don't quite know. What do you suggest?'

'Home—to Holly Cottage?'

He twisted his lips. He had an uncomfortable remembrance that when he had met Aunt Caroline, soon after his engagement to Briony, he had not liked her much, because *she* had not liked him. He had thought her ugly and rather difficult. He liked women—no matter of what age—to look nice and to succumb, at once, to his charm. Miss Shaw had *not* succumbed. If he could remember right, she had penetrating eyes. He didn't like analytical people who could see through him.

'No, I want to speak to you where there is no chance of interruption,' he said.

'Well, it's nearly twelve and we could have an early lunch at the Kestral Café,' she suggested. 'It's fairly good there and never very full so early.'

'That'll do,' said Clive.

They walked to the Kestral Café, which had been newly opened and was not far from Seascale Station.

It was small, *pseudo*-Tudor, full of the type of imitation oak, willow-pattern china and cheap brass which would grate on antique lovers, like Aunt Caroline. But it was clean. At this hour they had the room to themselves.

It was still pouring. Clive and Briony took off their drenched mackintoshes and hung them up. Now they seated themselves at one of the small tables, and looked at each other.

She thought: 'He hasn't changed at all. He's just as attractive as ever although he looks a bit tired and worried. So he ought to be.' And she also thought with a pang that it was rather sad that everything about him should be so familiar to her. That pin-stripe suit in which she had so often seen him; even the red-spot tie and carefully chosen handkerchief to match—she had helped him to buy *them*. Clive was always particular about his clothes. Yet he was a stranger to her today. He had made himself a stranger by his unspeakable, inexplicable conduct.

The man looked through narrowed lids at the girl's lovely face. Lovelier than ever, with its deeper tan and that glory of red-gold hair. And without the mackintosh, her figure looked exquisite. She wore a short grey flannel skirt and white cotton shirt, and a pale blue cardigan. He remembered that cameo brooch on the front of her collar, too.

'What a frightful day!' muttered Briony.

'Frightful,' he agreed.

The waitress—a pallid-looking little blonde—mooched up to them concealing a yawn.

'There's a change in the menu,' she said affectedly. 'Mrs Quinley says she's sorry the butcher's let her down over the meat, so there's only corned beef and salad.'

Briony gave a rather hysterical little laugh. How unglamorous that sounded—and she happened to remember that Clive loathed corned beef. But they both said that they didn't mind what they had.

It was quite a few minutes before Clive seemed able to explain his appearance and himself, and quite obvious that he was very nervous and uncertain of himself, which, Briony reflected, he had never been in the past. He used to be full of self-confidence.

He said:

'I suppose you must wonder why on earth I'm here instead of on the high seas.'

'Yes. It does want some explaining,' she said, and fixed her gaze on her plate. Suddenly she couldn't bear to look at him. Half of her, the human, romantic side, she supposed, longed to break down this barrier of embarrassment and to feel his arms go round her and his lips on hers in one of those passionate hungry kisses which used to make her so completely his. She could hardly swallow the food she raised to her lips. She called desperately on the other, stronger half of her which was proud and practical and which bitterly resented what he had done, and despised him.

Then he began to speak. All his plans had changed, he said. The firm he was going to work for had asked him to postpone the actual trip to Nigeria till the end of July. He was working now partly at the head office in London, and some of the time at the other branches. One of them was at Barrow-in-Furness. He was going to Barrow after he left Seascale this afternoon.

'I had to see you first,' he said. 'I would have come before but quite honestly, I did not know how to face you. I realized what you must feel about me, Briony, I behaved atrociously. I admit it ... but there are extenuating circumstances ...'

He broke off stammering, and gulped at a glass of water. She looked up at him. She could see that he was distressed, but somehow she had no wish to help him out. Let him get on with the story, she thought, and set her lips and waited for him to continue.

He had a lot to say and said it rather badly, jumbling the words.

He repeated what he had written in his

letter when he had first broken with her. The necessity to put off his marriage until he had got out to Nigeria and paved the way. His ambition ... his desire to take the big job that had been offered, and make a lot of money ... solidify his position while the going was good. Times were bad. The world was in a chaotic condition, it would have been madness to turn down what was a unique chance. Surely she could see that ... understand his point of view ... it wasn't that he had ever stopped wanting to marry her.

'I asked you to wait for me, didn't I?' he said, warming up to his subject, his face flushed and those extraordinary greenish eyes of his appealing to her, 'it was you who kicked me out. I didn't want the break to be so final.'

She listened to it all, her heart throbbing, and her mind confused. She admitted that she had been the one to say good-bye for good and all.

'But you can't blame me, Clive,' she said. 'Look at the way you behaved. Everything was all set for our wedding. You just wrote and said that it must be indefinitely postponed. No girl would have accepted that without a very much more serious reason than you gave me.'

He leaned across the table.

'Briony, darling, I know it was unpardonable. After I sent the letter I cursed myself. I deplored it. It was cowardly. That was the whole trouble! I was afraid to face you. I should have come down to see you and talk it over, but I was so afraid of the very thing you actually did. That you might turn on me altogether. I did not *want* that.'

She made a gesture of bewilderment.

'I don't understand. If you really loved me, why cancel our wedding like that?'

'I did it because of the job—which was for you—I wanted to get it at all costs and make a success for you,' he argued.

Her eyes challenged him.

'I find that hard to believe. I think it was just your own personal ambition for yourself.'

'No, any man who is worth while should be ambitious for his wife.'

'That's all very well. But nobody was going to understand it. Certainly neither my parents nor my friends. It just looked as though you ... you found out you didn't *want* to marry me,' she ended with a catch in her voice.

'Briony, darling, I'm terribly sorry. Sorry isn't the word. I haven't been happy since. I went through hell on what was to have been our wedding day.'

'What do you think it was like for me?' she asked in a low voice.

'It's all been damnable,' he muttered, 'and not what I intended.

'What did you intend?'

'That we should carry on with our engagement.'

She twisted her lips and put down her knife and fork. She could not eat.

'Wasn't that horribly selfish of you—to want me to wait interminably?'

'But, Briony, it wasn't my fault. My firm would not give the job to a married man,' he argued.

'You keep harping on this job. But I thought that our marriage—our being together—was the most important thing to you—just as it was to me. I was quite willing to marry the Clive who had a small job and smallish salary.'

'That was very sweet of you and I appreciate it, but—'

'Oh, don't let's go on like this!' she broke in. 'You haven't really explained anything satisfactorily. But even if I try to understand that it was just terrific ambition that prompted your conduct, Clive, I don't see why you have come to see me *now.*'

'Because I want you to become engaged to me again,' he said, 'because I still love you with all my heart and I find that I can't go on without you.'

Her heart plunged. He said those words with such passion and conviction it could not fail to touch her when she had once loved him so much.

'Oh, Clive,' she whispered.

He looked quickly round the little café. The waitress had passed through to the kitchen. They were alone.

'Give me your hand,' he said.

She gave it hesitatingly. He took it and covered it with both of his.

'Briony, Bri, *darling,* I've been through hell since I wrote you that letter,' he exclaimed, 'you'll never know.'

'Well, you hurt me abominably,' she cried, 'and I don't understand why you are here today. Your job's still on—you're still going to Nigeria, aren't you?'

'Yes, but why shouldn't we still belong to each other? Don't you love me enough to wait for me?'

Her hand quivered in his.

'So you still ask me to wait?'

'I don't *want* it—but it's inevitable, if I'm to get this job.'

Her heart-beats quickened but this time more in anger than in love.

'You still think it fair to ask a girl to wait when she has been so near to her marriage? You insist upon putting your work first?'

'But, Briony—'

'What do you think?' she broke in hotly. 'What can you know of a girl's feelings if you think she can get as far as *we* got to being married, then shove it all on one side and tell everybody the wedding must be postponed for years? It would make me look an absolute fool.'

'Darling—'

'Do you really expect me to believe that you love me so much you can't live without me?' she interrupted again. 'Because I don't. I know that if you had really loved me, nothing would have induced you to cancel our wedding.'

'I swear I do love you,' he said.

For an instant she looked with doubt, with frayed emotions at his handsome fascinating face. How strong his attraction for her still was! The very clasp of his fingers weakened her resolves to be proud and firm. Let Aunt Caro be contemptuous—let everybody sneer—she still loved him, heaven help her!

Then Clive said:

'If you want to know, it was father who really opened my eyes as to what I *had* done. I stayed with him this week. He was awfully attached to you, you know. The old boy gave it to me hot and strong.'

That was a mistake on Clive's part. A piece of information which had a bad effect upon Briony. Scarlet, indignant, she snatched her fingers away.

'So it was your *father* who sent you up here. You didn't come of your own accord.'

'Yes, I did. He didn't send me—he just hoped that I'd come.'

'No, he sent you! I can well believe it. He *was* fond of me, he wrote me a very sweet letter. Perhaps you are afraid he might cut you out of his will if you don't marry me ...' She gave an hysterical laugh.

'That's a rotten thing to say!' protested Clive.

'Well, don't you admit that he made you come up to see me?'

'No, I don't! I merely agreed with him when he said that I had lost the most wonderful girl in the world.'

A little mollified, Briony said:

'Well, what have you come to do, except to ask me to wait, and I just won't.'

Clive bit his lips. His long fingers nervously crumbled a roll of bread. Never had he wanted Briony more during all the days of their engagement. In his egotistical way he had been much in love with her and he still was. Physically he had never met a girl to compare with her. She attracted him vitally. He was, furthermore, intrigued by the fact that she was now difficult to get. Clive was the type to desire most a thing that was denied him. This new spirited Briony was even more alluring, than the soft pliable young girl whom he had so nearly married. But he felt like a man torn in two. Love and desire on the one hand, and ambition on the other. He hovered between them.

She seemed to sense what he was thinking.

'If I tell you that I am willing to start life with you on very little money—as we agreed—are you willing to chuck up this job in Nigeria which is open only to an unmarried man?' she asked him.

And while she waited for his answer she felt as though it was her whole soul depended on it. His agreement was vital. She could forgive him what he had done in the name of ambition if real sincere love had driven him back to her, and he was willing to make the sacrifice.

Anxiously her big eyes watched the changing expressions on his face. Then his brow cleared as though he had reached a solution of the problem. He gripped her hand again.

'I know! I've got it! *We'll get married secretly before I sail.* We won't tell anybody—even your people or my father. But you'll be my wife and you'll know that I belong to you. But I won't need to let the firm know about it.'

Briony went dead cold. It was as though her heart stopped beating for a moment and then began to pump again with slow heavy throbs of bitter disappointment.

Of all the disgraceful propositions for a man to make! ... this seemed the worst. Fresh proof of his colossal egotism, his conceit, his lack of regard for her feelings.

Once more she pulled away her hand. Her face was quite white. She said:

'So you wouldn't want anybody to know that I was your wife! You'd be afraid to acknowledge me!'

'Afraid only of losing the job and making money for *you*. You're putting the wrong construction on things again, Briony.'

She stood up. She was trembling. And she was terribly angry. In this moment there was no place in her heart for fresh sorrow. She was too furious with him.

'I'm sorry you ever bothered to come up to Seascale to see me,' she said. 'You've wasted your time.'

'Briony, sit down; you haven't finished your lunch.'

'I couldn't care less.'

She crossed the room, reached for her mackintosh and began to put it on.

He followed her, his face flushing.

'Look here, Briony—I don't see why you should be so upset. Why shouldn't we get married and—'

'Please don't insult me any further.'

'But, good heavens, where is the insult?'

'If you don't see it—you don't. But I do. I think it is insulting for a man who is supposed to love me to cancel one wedding and then suggest another which must be kept a deadly secret. No man who loved a girl could want to put her in such a vile position.'

'You're pretty difficult!' he exclaimed.

'And you're utterly selfish and unscrupulous,' she said, 'you want the best of both worlds—me and your ambition. Well, you can have your ambition, but not me—that's all.'

Now he seized her arms and drew her suddenly and violently against him.

'I shall have you. I shall never give up trying to get you back,' he said between his teeth, 'you may not understand my wish to make a success in life and you may not want to help me to get it. But I intend to *be* a success and to marry you, too.'

'Let go of me, please. I never want to see you again, Clive.'

'Oh yes, you do,' he said and pulled her against him and kissed her violently on the mouth.

That kiss was almost her undoing. It roused so many heartbreaking memories of the passion they had shared and which had been so glorious. But she pulled herself out of his embrace and marched past him, her eyes furious. She drew the back of her hand across the lips that he had bruised.

'I *hate* you, Clive.'

'No, you don't, you still love me as much as I love you,' he said, following her to the door.

'Well, I don't intend to marry you secretly; I don't intend to marry you at all, so please never try to see me again,' she said in a strangled voice.

Now he caught her arm and pleaded with her.

'For lord's sake don't be so hard, Briony. Don't you see that I have been trying to find a way out ... so that we can get married and I can give you everything you want, as well?'

'*I* only wanted your love, Clive.'

'You've got it ... but—'

'It's that '*but*' which is finishing us,' she broke in, 'please let me go.'

'I shall come back, Briony, I swear here and now that I will make you change your mind—I shall get what you call "the best of both worlds".'

She shook her head. She was almost at breaking point. She did not want to continue the discussion and risk further humiliation. No matter how strong Clive's attraction still was for her, she did not *want* to forgive him. He was not worth her love.

She walked out of the shop into the rain. The wind tore down the street and drove the raindrops into her face. But she did not put up her umbrella. She even began to run as though she was afraid that Clive might follow, break down her resistance and get her back on his own terms.

She knew that she would never respect herself if she let him persuade her into accepting that last outrageous proposal.

When she got back to Holly Cottage she rushed in, slammed the front door, ran up to her bedroom and began to cry.

FIVE

It wasn't long before Briony's natural elasticity of mind and body cured her of her wish to go on crying. She went to the telephone and called Hew Vanner's number.

Fortunately Aunt Caroline was at the 'Treasure Shop'. No need to tell her, yet, of the fresh humiliation which Clive had heaped upon her. Aunt Caro would only think (even if she didn't say it) serve you right, my girl, for meeting that train.

She remembered her job. More than ever she wanted that job—the preoccupation. But would Hew Vanner take her, now?

The number was still out of order.

'Well,' said Briony to herself, 'here goes—all I can do is to go along to Wasdale Head and make my apologies.'

She took the car which she had hired yesterday.

Even in the weeping rain, this countryside was gorgeous, she thought. Her tired, tear-reddened eyes gazed at the stormy darkness of the lake, at the towering magnificent mountains—the grey screes and black crags. So frowning, so formidable, and yet so splendid. It only wanted the sun to break through those ragged billowing clouds to make the whole place green and sparkling again. But somehow the angry, stormy scene which greeted her as she drove down the hill to Monks Farm, fitted in better with her present mood.

And what would Hew be like? As angry and formidable as those crags, no doubt.

Old Mrs Berry muttered and grumbled as she admitted Briony, who was told to wait in that same room in which she had been interviewed yesterday. Hew Vanner walked in. Sleeves rolled up, pipe in the corner of his mouth, he greeted her with a sarcasm which he made no attempt to conceal.

'Just as I thought. The young lady who will be right on the job at nine a.m. turns up at two o'clock. Admirable.'

With heightened colour, Briony said:

'I can explain—'

'So can I,' interrupted Hew, in a sharp biting voice, 'just that the job does not attract you sufficiently, and it was not worth your while to put off some trivial appointment in order to get here on time. *In spite* of the fact that I told you how important it was for me to start work on time this morning.'

His rudeness, instead of annoying her, had the reverse effect. Her heart was so sore that she was in the mood to welcome a fight. Even pleased with rough treatment. She tossed back her head.

'And are you a crystal gazer, Mr Vanner? Has it been revealed to you that my appointment was so trivial? Or was the crystal so obscure that you could not see me trying to get through to you on the phone with my apologies, only to be told twice that the line was out of order?'

His frown disappeared. He looked mildly discomfited.

'Oh, well' he said, and ran his hands irritably through his thick untidy hair, 'yes—that *is* so. I remember now. I never use the phone but Berry said the men were coming out to repair it this afternoon.'

'Then perhaps you'll take back what you've said.'

'I still don't know why you were phoning to break your appointment with me, do I?'

'That,' said Briony, 'is my own personal business. Even if I am to become your secretary, Mr Vanner, I am not compelled to tell you all my private affairs.'

He looked at her with grudging admiration. He wondered if the girl knew how attractive she looked with the raindrops sparkling on that vivid disturbing hair of hers. Certainly she wasn't afraid of him and he liked that. He could not have stood a servile crawling type. 'Yes, Mr Vanner ... No, Mr Vanner ...!' Heaven forbid!

He swung on his heel.

'Keep your affairs to yourself, my dear girl, I am not interested, but you said you would be here at nine o'clock, and I accepted your word.'

'I would have come,' she snapped, 'but I just couldn't. Something cropped up which made it quite impossible. I was *not* having my hair permed by the way, it's naturally curly.'

Suddenly he grinned.

'I accept the fact. Now let's get down to work. You have already wasted three good hours.'

She gave a sigh of relief. She was quite surprised to find how relieved she was that he still intended to employ her. She had not realized until now how desperately she needed the distraction. Whatever happened she must forget Clive. Every now and then during her drive out to Wast Water her heart had given a throb of panic at the memory of Clive's violent embrace, his threat to pursue her—make her change her mind. She wouldn't. She wouldn't wait for Clive. Not a day. Not an hour after what he had said.

'Come on!' Hew's voice interrupted impatiently. 'Have you given Berry your luggage?'

'I am afraid I haven't brought any.'

'Why not?'

'I—well, something happened at home which won't interest you even if I tell you—but it drove everything else out of my mind and I haven't had time to discuss this job fully with my aunt.'

'So you are going to waste more of my time?' he barked.

'Really, Mr Vanner—'

'Oh, come on into the study and let's get down to some of this dictation,' he interrupted in a tone of exasperation.

She blinked. There was not much change to be got out of *this* surly brute. His likeness to Clive was less disturbing today, since she had seen Clive again. One was smooth and beguiling, almost feline and *dangerous*. But this one was safe—rock-like—rough as those dark crags across the stormy water. More trustworthy, surely. Anyhow, she wasn't afraid of Hew, but she *was* afraid of Clive, and her old passion for him which made her so weak.

She found herself settling down in Hew's study. A few seconds at the typewriter and she could use it efficiently. A half hour of his dictation and she could follow him with the speed that he demanded. He paced up and down the room while he began the first chapter which embraced his first long voyage out to the Transvaal. Not as a passenger on an expensive liner, but on a little cargo boat. Just as one would expect him to travel ... a rough passage, no comforts, right down to nature, and studying everything and everybody that came his way.

She became absorbed in the work. She forgot that lamentable lunch with Clive. She forgot everything but the sound of Hew's vibrant voice and the compelling way in which he told his story. Up and down he paced like a jungle animal, pausing every now and then to glance over her shoulder at what she had typed. Once, when she could not keep up with him, he was unexpectedly patient and repeated what he had said. He spelt difficult names for her and when she apologized for her ignorance, said:

'I don't expect you to know things like that—how could you?'

She worked for three hours without stopping, although sitting up so long, straight, tense, at the machine finally made her back ache. Her fingers grew sore, almost numb. But she had no intention of asking for breathing space. She was going to show this man what she could do.

By the end of the afternoon she had developed more than a little admiration for him as a story-teller; for his wonderful powers of observation and attention to detail; and above all, for his deep impassioned love of the countries in which he travelled; of flowers and trees, animals and birds. What was there that he did not know? He seemed to be completely at home with all living, breathing things.

He, on his part, began to have a grudging but very wholesome respect for his new secretary.

Now and again he forgot his work and paid attention to that straight young back and the quickly moving fingers. She was tireless and she was intelligent, and he had managed to get more writing done with her than he had ever thought possible.

When at last he stopped, it was late in the afternoon. The rain had stopped. The sun had broken through the clouds above Scafell and touched the dark grey waters of the lake to living gold. In the garden it was fresh and sparkling. A solitary thrush filled the air with liquid silver song.

Hew was horrified to find how late it had grown.

'Hey, it's time you had a breather!' he

grunted, and held out his hand for the manuscript.

She turned round in her chair. He was even more dismayed to see that she was very pale and that her eyes were red-rimmed, even bloodshot.

'You look exhausted!' he said contritely.

'I'm okay.'

He stood up and pulled at an old-fashioned bell.

'I'll get Berry to make you a cup of tea. I'm afraid I have been very selfish. You must be worn out.'

She smiled. Tired she certainly was, but she welcomed the fatigue. It dulled her susceptibilities. She had actually been so absorbed in the work that she had not given a thought to her personal troubles since she arrived.

Hew went out of the room because nobody answered the bell. He stayed out quite a time. Briony stretched her cramped limbs, walked to the French windows and opened them wide. Seen thus half in shadow, half in sunlight, the garden was mysteriously beautiful. It saddened and yet enchanted her. She loved the fruit trees in the tangled orchard. The old stone wall. And the scent of old-fashioned roses in the drenched garden was so delicious that she stood sniffing the air appreciatively. Her tired eyes were closing.

When she turned back, she found Hew Vanner, himself, carrying in a tray with tea on it and a currant cake.

'Berry is in one of her tantrums, because the telephone men have brought mud into her kitchen,' he said.

Briony was surprised to see how much more youthful and human that granite face was when Hew Vanner smiled. In fact she began to like him much better than she had done yesterday, and to realize that the rude dominating man with the bitter tongue could equally be a charming companion when he chose.

He treated her now as though she were an honoured guest—pouring out her tea; apologizing for the dry cake.

She ate a large slice quite hungrily.

She wondered what this man would say if she could describe to him that awful lunch in the Kestral Café in Seascale. Her half-eaten corned beef and salad; that scene with Clive. She could just imagine Hew despising a man like Clive and telling her to forget him and get down to some more hard work.

She found herself speculating about Hew's own emotional life, if he had ever had one! Ordinarily speaking she could not associate him with a woman ... or romance. He was scarcely a romantic figure. Yet when he smiled ... when he had handed her her tea with that quite boyish and even shy smile just now ... a completely different Hew had presented himself. Quite a friendly person—with some charm. Now she began to believe that Clive had had *too much* charm. All the goods in the shop-window—empty—shallow—behind the façade.

Hew took her empty cup and placed it on the tray.

'I've got an idea for a better end to that chapter we've just done. Could you bear to do another hour, do you think, or would it be too much for you?'

She at once agreed to carry on with the typing, but at six o'clock she interrupted him.

'Forgive me, Mr Vanner. I really must stop and get home. The car ought to be here. I told the driver to come back, and my aunt will be wondering where I am.'

Hew Vanner rubbed the back of his ear and avoided her gaze as though embarrassed.

'I've taken care of that,' he said, 'I hope you won't mind, but I sent the chap back to Seascale, with a note asking your aunt if she would kindly pack up a bag for you and let the driver bring it along here later on. I said you wouldn't get back to Seascale this evening.'

She stared at him, open-mouthed.

'You said what?'

He repeated what he had written and added:

'I explained that I was on some very important work and that you had agreed to stop and help me. I told her that you would phone her later as the men were here mending the wires.'

Her colour rose.

'And when did you do all this, Mr Vanner?'

'While Berry was making the tea. I dare say you'll think it a trifle high-handed of me but to tell you the truth I am so impressed by your efficiency, you've given me the thirst to work on my book and I want to start again really early in the morning. I didn't want to risk you getting held up.'

Under normal circumstances Briony might have been furious. But somehow this afternoon she found herself amused. Certainly Mr Hew Vanner knew what he wanted and got it. And when she considered the matter, she decided that it might be better for her to stay out here in this lonely farmhouse and not go back to Seascale tonight. Clive, after her rejection of him, was quite capable of trying to get at her at Holly Cottage and break down her resistance. She could avoid that by staying here, and even if he found out where she was and arrived at Monks Farm—determined to get his own way—Hew would make a good watch dog. He wouldn't stand any nonsense from Clive.

As she stood thinking about it all, the black misery of the whole affair with her one-time promised husband, swept down upon her. Real overwhelming misery that gripped her by the throat. Clive had taken everything lovely and bright from her life. All the fun and laughter—all the passionate happiness—all her secret dreams. It wasn't going to be much fun just working for her living, alone, with nothing to look forward to.

Her face puckered. Hew Vanner, watching her shrewdly, suddenly caught the glint of unshed tears in the eyes of this beautiful girl who had come to work for him. And it was as though he *knew* ... as though he was filled with an almost mystic understanding and wishful to give her courage. For he said:

'You know, Miss Moore, there is an infallible cure for what women like to call "a broken heart". Work, work and *more work*. Come along—let's make some notes for the end of that chapter, shall we?'

SIX

Those words were exactly what Briony needed. She swallowed back her misery. She blinked back the tears. Somehow Hew Vanner's whole attitude renewed her strength and determination to put the past behind her. And with this came the wish to hide her humiliation from this man. She said, in a hard defiant young voice:

'I am quite willing to go on working, but I don't quite understand what you mean about a "broken heart".'

He cocked an eyebrow, turned from her and seated himself at his desk and began to fill a pipe. If she did not wish to confide in him—that was her affair. He wasn't one to try and pry into other people's secrets. He did not really know what had made him make that remark. He knew nothing at all about the girl's personal life. And he was rather annoyed with himself for meddling. Why should he surmise that she was suffering from an unhappy love affair? Queer how at times he had an almost psychic knowledge about people he was with. He had done it before and hit the nail on the head. He was sure he had hit it this time but he had no intention of driving it in any farther. Gruffly he answered her:

'Haven't the least idea and to use that delightful and popular phrase—I couldn't care less!'

That was what Briony needed. Anything but sympathy. She felt relieved and reseated herself at the typewriter. With a rather red face she tackled him again.

'Still—I don't think you had any right to send that message to my aunt without consulting me.'

He shrugged and without even looking at her, said:

'Oh, my dear girl, I dare say I do a lot of things I have no right to do. "Doing the right thing" can be so boring and is so often a waste of time. You have every right to be annoyed—but you know why I did it. However, if you want to go home—go now and get it over. Cancel all the arrangements.'

Briony clenched her hands and gave an angry tug at the roller of the typewriter. It made the little bell clang at the end.

'And don't break my one and only machine,' added Hew wryly.

Really, she thought, he was an impossible man. He asked for a fight. Why must he be so pugnacious? But he seemed to be able to take the wind out of one's sails no matter who was right and who was wrong. She could not help being amused—and interested—which went a long way towards curing her so-called "breaking heart" in this moment. But she could not help wondering what on earth Aunt Caroline must be thinking. With the man fetching her luggage—no word from her personally—the sooner Briony got on to the telephone and explained the situation, the better. Otherwise Aunt Caro might imagine that this extraordinary man had murdered her and flung her body into the lake!

This idea made her giggle. Now Hew Vanner swung round and stared at his newly made secretary. A few moments ago he had thought she was going to cry and here she was laughing to herself. He was darned if he could understand women, but he was less harassed by her laughter than by the hint of tears.

'Can I share the joke?' he asked mildly.

Briony laughed a little more and shook her head at him.

'I don't think you would appreciate it, Mr Vanner.'

'Well, are you staying here or are you going home?'

Briony took a chance.

'I'm staying,' she announced firmly.

He was quite astonished to find how much that reply satisfied him. He had enjoyed every moment that he had worked with this girl. His mind was teeming with further ideas. He stuck his pipe between his teeth.

'Good—then let's get on with the job.'

'Do you mind if I try and phone my aunt first of all—in case she doesn't quite understand your—er—lack of conventionality?'

Now Hew's brilliant eyes sparkled with unusual humour. He liked the direct challenging way that this girl had with her. She was full of 'guts', he thought. He could still swear that something had happened in her life to upset her badly, otherwise she wouldn't have wanted to come out into the wilds like this and do this job. There couldn't be much fun in it—and, after all, she was young and attractive. Yes, for all his lack of interest in 'females' he could see her attraction and especially when the hot red blood ran up under that translucent skin of hers and she tossed back those golden-red curls. Most effective and perfect colouring!

'Go along then—the phone's in the hall,' he said, 'and tell Miss Shaw she is at liberty to come and see you any time she wants except working hours, *and* as long as she does not expect me to entertain her, *and* as long as you don't ask anybody else here, because I am extremely anti-social, and that is all there is to it,' he added significantly.

With this warning ringing in her ears, Briony went to the telephone. The line was once more in working order.

Aunt Caroline's voice sounded anxious.

'My *dear* Briony, I am glad you have phoned. Mr Smith is actually here now with the car and I have just read Mr Vanner's note. I thought it was most extraordinarily high-handed of him and I was certainly not going to send your things until you had confirmed it.'

Briony looked in the direction of the study door and smothered a laugh.

'I know. Well, I can't say much, Aunt Caro. The phone is in the hall. It must all seem rather odd, but my employer is an odd man.'

'Then you can't possibly stay there,' began Miss Shaw firmly.

'Oh, but I assure you he isn't as odd as all *that,*' broke in Briony, 'and I am well chaperoned by that old nurse of his who is the housekeeper here. And you need have no fears about me because I assure you he is interested *only* in making me slog on the typewriter until I drop.'

'We-e-ll!' came from Miss Shaw.

'Yes, I am all right really, darling,' Briony assured her, 'and I think I shall quite enjoy being here. The work is most interesting and Mr V says please come out and see me when you want, and after all I am within cycling distance. Tell Smith to bring out my bike as well as my suitcase. Mr V can't dictate *all* day long, and I shall get a few hours off to cycle into Seascale.'

Miss Shaw, having decided not to interfere with her niece's life, capitulated.

'Well, as long as you are quite sure it is all it should be—'

'Oh, Aunt Caro, it's more than that, if you only knew what he was like,' Briony giggled into the telephone in as low a tone as possible.

'Then I'll give Smith the suitcase. What do you want?'

Briony thought rapidly. Another cotton frock ... her slacks ... a couple of jumpers ... a blouse or two ... her framed photograph of Mummy and Daddy, and, yes, she promised her aunt that she would write home this evening and let Reigate know where she was and what she was doing.

Poor Auntie! She obviously didn't want to take the responsibility. So Briony removed it from her.

Her last words were:

'If by any chance *Clive* communicates with you—don't tell him where I am.'

'Is he likely to?' her aunt asked.

Briony considered this. It was quite on the cards, she thought, Clive was obstinate. He wouldn't want to lose something that he made up his mind to get. He *might* try and rout her out, she said. So would Aunt Caro just be on her guard, should he do so.

'Leave that to me—I'll soon tackle *him,*' said Aunt Caroline drily.

Briony hung up the receiver and returned to the study.

'Well,' said Hew Vanner, glancing up from his manuscript, 'has your aunt any objections?'

'None, now that I have explained the situation,' said Briony, 'and my things are coming over with the car shortly.'

Hew pulled a pound note out of his pocket and tossed it to her.

'What's this for?' she asked, catching it.

'Expenses. Pay the car—both ways, please.'

'Thanks,' she said, and decided that was one more good point about Mr Vanner. He was not mean to his employees.

They worked for another hour. Once again the difficult, irascible man became the brilliant entertaining adventure-loving creature who fascinated her and drew her so completely out of herself.

It was Mrs Berry who interrupted them, an hour later.

'The car's at the door and the driver wants to see Miss Moore.'

Hew sat back in his chair and flung

his notebook on to the desk. He growled something about 'interruptions' and abruptly told Briony to go.

'I'll carry on when I get back if you like,' she said.

'Haven't you had enough?'

'Well, I could manage another hour—'

Mrs Berry, who was watching them with deep disapproval in her eyes, folded her arms over her chest and pursed her lips.

'Maybe you would like supper brought in and laid in here for two,' she said, and cackled.

Hew scowled at her.

'Don't be an old fool, Berry.'

She tossed her head and then as Briony's slim young figure vanished, said:

'So *she* is going to sleep here tonight, is she?'

'Yes, and every night until I have finished my book.'

'Well, you take care, Master Hew.'

'Of what, pray, idiot?' he asked with dry affection. He was fond of this old woman who had been one of his family since he could remember, but she irritated him vastly at times and this was one of them.

'Having young women in the house,' she said, 'much better for you to take on a daily secretary. Mark my words, *this* will lead to trouble.'

'Really, Berry, I don't know what you are insinuating, but you exasperate me,' he snapped, 'and considering we live miles from anywhere, I don't quite know how you imagine I'd ever find a daily typist.'

'There's buses.'

'Nonsense.'

'There's cars.'

'And who's going to pay for them? I am trying to economize. And don't forget it. And what's all the fuss, anyhow? Don't you want an extra one to cook and do for, you lazy old woman?'

Mrs Berry snorted.

'Master Hew, I'd work my fingers to the bone for you and well you know it. But when you start having young women in the house with paint on their faces and dyed hair, I wouldn't like to say what might happen. I trust you, Master Hew, but I don't trust such young girls and little doubt she is looking for a husband and—'

Here Hew sprang to his feet. He had lost his temper.

'Get out of here, you doddering old fool! I've never heard such unmitigated tripe. Miss Moore is *not* husband-hunting, and even if she *is,* I'm old enough and wise enough to take care of myself, and I don't want you or anybody else to run my life for me. Neither, in fact, is her hair dyed. No, go on, beat it!'

Mrs Berry eyed him through narrowed lids, gave her cackling laugh and departed. She was quite used to these passages-at-arms with her one-time charge. But she had no smile for Briony who was just coming in through the front door with her suitcase, followed by Smith, wheeling in the bicycle. She was filled with the most bitter jealousy. She did not want anybody else in the house with her and 'Master Hew'. However, she dared not openly revolt. She did not want to be sent away and she knew just how far she could drive Hew. She was a privileged person but she was still a paid servant and aware of it. She cast a malevolent glance at the girl. Briony met it with a slight sinking of the heart. She was not quite sure why the old housekeeper should be so antipathetic.

'Would you like to show me my room?' she asked.

'It isn't ready yet,' muttered Mrs Berry, 'and I am in the middle of preparing the evening meal.'

'Well, if I can help at all—please don't hesitate to ask me, Mrs Berry.'

'I want no help, thanks, and I don't like interference in my kitchen.'

Briony raised her brows, shrugged her shoulders and passed the old woman without another word. It seemed that she could not expect a friendly attitude from *her*.

She said to Hew:

'Your housekeeper seems to resent me coming here.'

'Take no notice of her,' said Hew, 'she is always like that with strangers.'

'Well, I told her I would help if I could—I don't mind what I do.'

'You are not engaged for domestic work,' said Hew abruptly, 'you are here as my secretary.'

Well, thought Briony later that evening, when a reluctant Mrs Berry showed her up to her room; being in Monks Farm as Mr Hew Vanner's secretary certainly promised to be an uncommon sort of job. Like most jobs it had its drawbacks as well as its assets. She liked the actual work. She quite admired Hew Vanner when he wasn't being rude or difficult. But—he had called himself anti-social—and he was so with a vengeance. She need expect no entertainment from *him* once the dictation was over. And Mrs Berry maintained a depressingly unbending attitude of hostility.

Once the summer day had ended and darkness began to fall, veiling the sad beauty of the lake and the towering majesty of Scafell Pike, the house developed a gloom and silence which threatened to dampen anybody's spirits. It quenched some of Briony's fiery determination to put the romantic side of life away from her, and concentrate entirely on her job.

She was only human ... and there was something not quite human about Hew Vanner or his housekeeper. Or the house, she decided.

She had now had time to examine the place

at leisure. First of all her bedroom. A huge and rather frightening room with a bathroom next door, with a rusty, mahogany-framed old bath.

The old farmhouse was L-shaped. One side downstairs was devoted to the kitchens and huge sculleries, and what had once been a still-room, and the old dairies. Over these, the bedrooms had been shut up. Then there were the living-rooms, with four bedrooms overhead. One was occupied by Hew; a smaller one by Mrs Berry. Farther along the corridor was this big guest room which had been allotted to the 'resident secretary'. Briony, used to her own bright home in Reigate, or her dear little bedroom in Holly Cottage, would have liked cosier quarters, but thought it might appear ungrateful to complain. Hew had obviously given her the grandest of the bedrooms. It had a huge double bed with an old-fashioned maple-wood top and bottom, a gigantic maple wardrobe with a mirror in the centre, a dressing table to match and a washstand bearing a Victorian-looking floral china basin and jug, which made Briony giggle. It had obviously been there for the last thirty or forty years, and no one had bothered to remove it.

The whole house was in a poor state of repair. There was a damp patch on the ceiling of Briony's room which, she thought, humorously, would have sent Mummy into fits. At one time there had been a Victorian paper on walls which had been more recently painted over in an awful shade of salmon pink, which clashed with the grass green carpet. This was moth-eaten, although it must once have been a very expensive one. Two square-paned windows framed in green chenille curtains, looked out upon the glory of Wast Water. On fine days the view would be superb. But Briony, after unpacking her suitcase, felt small and lost and lonely in her gigantic room; gingerly she turned down the bed clothes and wondered if she ever dare to climb into that enormous bed. There was no electricity. The house was lit by Calor gas. She had no bedside lamp, which meant no reading in bed, she told herself ruefully.

Everything was clean enough. Mrs Berry had a passion for cleanliness. But there was an air of desolation and decay about the whole place. At a later date, Briony was to learn that most of the bedroom furniture had been there when Hew bought Monks Farm. His own possessions were for the most part downstairs. There were one or two lovely pieces, Briony noted as she made her tour of inspection over which Aunt Caroline would have gloated. All the stuff in that long, low ceilinged dining-room was genuine Chippendale. The drawing-room was never used, because Hew sat in his study. It was cold and felt damp even on a summer's night, with that musty smell that emanates from closed-in spaces.

But there was a glorious grey stone fireplace to admire with the white tudor rose in scrolls on it, and a big wrought-iron basket grate and dogs, calling for log fires. A French walnut cabinet full of treasures—wonderful ivories—innumerable *objets d'arts*—collected at some time or other by Hew, on his travels. A handsome Georgian card table. Two fine oils in carved Italian frames. A pair of gilt ormolu candelabra; a wonderful Louis Quatorze mirror over the fireplace. Somebody—perhaps Hew's mother—had had excellent taste in her time, and his father, the Don, had probably collected some good pieces in the day when they were a reasonable price.

So here it all was now—an amazing assortment filling the old neglected farmhouse. The whole place, Briony reflected, screamed for attention to detail. It wanted a woman's touch—flowers—a little comfort—that touch of 'homeliness', none of which was provided by Mrs Berry. And such things as a leaking roof, or bells that wouldn't ring, or taps that didn't run, seemed hardly to be noticed by Hew Vanner who, Briony decided, was like a man walking in a trance. He lived in a world of his own.

Her first dinner in that house was an embarrassing meal, to say the least of it. She sat on one side of the long polished table, which had an old-fashioned damask table cloth spread over it, and Hew on the other. She had taken the trouble to change into a dark silk dress. He was washed and his hair brushed, but he wore the same old clothes. He seemed, at least, to notice her own efforts because he glanced at her when she entered the room and grunted:

'H'm! You won't find me in a dinner jacket, I'm afraid. We're not very formal at Monks Farm.'

Briony coloured and laughed.

'I'm scarcely in evening dress, but I had to have a wash and change.'

He made no further comment. As she seated herself, he took his own chair. He seemed to be brooding about something and made only cursory answers when she attempted polite conversation. Finally she gave it up. They ate in silence, served by Mrs Berry who put the dishes down on the table with an expression of complete disapproval. But it was a well-cooked meal of Cumberland ham and fresh vegetables from the garden, followed by damson tart and cream. No rationing up here apparently, thought Briony, and wished that her father were present. Poor old Daddy who so loved good ham and hadn't tasted one like this since the war.

Briony, with healthy appetite, ate what she was given, but refused the second helping of ham which Hew carved for himself. Then he rang the bell for Mrs Berry.

'Where the devil's that bottle of wine? It

must be chilled by now, Berry.'

She looked out of the corners of her small eyes at Briony.

'I didn't think you would want it *tonight.*'

'Why not? The only thing we've got in this house that's worth offering anybody is the wine cellar, and as we bought it, we might as well make use of it.'

Mrs Berry shrugged her shoulders and returned with a tall slender bottle of hock and one glass.

He glowered at her.

'Why only one?'

She made a clicking sound with her false teeth.

'Is the *seketary* drinking wine, then? Your cellar won't last long, and you supposing to economize.'

Briony's cheeks flamed. She began to say that she was not used to wine. But Hew seemed to be infuriated by the old woman's attitude. He snarled at her:

'Bring another glass at once, Berry. And allow me to decide on the economies I wish to make in this house.'

The old woman departed, muttering.

'Really, Mr Vanner, I never take wine—' began Briony.

He cut in:

'Well, please take a glass with me this evening, if only to teach that old woman her manners. Does she think that I would drink alone without even offering you a glass?'

Then Briony laughed.

'I don't take any notice of her. She's not used to anyone else in the house. I quite understand.'

'She's a pig-headed old fool.'

'Well, I would much rather not cause any trouble,' said Briony.

Hew made no further remark. The second wine glass was brought—they were wonderful cut-glass Georgian goblets, Briony noticed, and fingered hers with respect, storing up the memory of all that she would have to describe to Aunt Caroline. She sipped a little of the wine just to please Hew, but she felt that he was not helping to make her popular with the old nurse. And he refused to allow her to offer to help wash up.

'Go into the kitchen at your peril,' he said with a twisted smile, 'she'll only bite your head off. Leave her alone and let her get on with it.'

'I don't feel I ought to make more work. This is a huge place for one old woman to do.'

'I think that is my affair,' said Hew calmly.

Briony's heart beat a little faster, but she held her tongue.

There was certainly nothing friendly or gay in Monks Farm—no feeling that she was really welcome. Hew Vanner only wanted her as a machine to which he could dictate. It was, to say the least of it, a depressing atmosphere.

And now, what? Would Hew shut himself up in his study? If so, she would have to retire to that huge frightening bedroom and climb into that great forbidding bed. Almost she regretted her decision to remain. Almost ran to the telephone and phoned Smith in Seascale for the car to take her back to Aunt Caroline's darling friendly cottage.

Then pride stepped in. She told herself not to be silly. She had come here to *work* and not for entertainment, dash it all!

'I had better say good-night—' she began awkwardly.

Hew paused in the act of lighting the inevitable pipe, and glanced at her through a cloud of blue smoke.

'Bed at this hour?'

Briony cleared her throat.

'There's nothing else to do. It's a bit late for a walk.'

'Do you usually take a walk after dinner?'

'I don't know exactly—I mean—I might do at home—one of us always used to take the dog for a walk when we had one. I rather wish there were a dog here,' she added.

'I had one at first—a rather nice mongrel—but he ran off and was caught in a trap and had to be destroyed,' said Hew shortly. 'I didn't try to replace the poor little beggar.'

'What a shame!'

He frowned, then glanced again at the slim figure in the blue silky dress, at the lamplight on her red-gold hair. It seemed strange to see a girl like this in his lakeside home which had been so deadly quiet and lonely—so bereft of feminine society except for the unglamorous figure of old Berry. He had really quite enjoyed seeing Miss Moore at his dinner table. But he was embarrassed. Hew knew what to do with a secretary—but not with a young and charming girl who had tonight suddenly and mysteriously taken on the form of a guest whom he ought to try and entertain. Damn it, he couldn't be bothered. She must find her own entertainment in her leisure hours. At the same time—he, himself, felt that he had worked enough for one day. He wasn't going to sit in this study any longer. To his own surprise he suggested taking Briony for a stroll.

'We might go down the hill as far as the lake and then turn back.'

She was equally surprised, and a little doubtful.

'You've no need—' she began.

'I know that,' he cut in almost rudely, 'and if you don't want to take a walk with me you have no only to say so!'

'I would like it,' she stammered.

'Then you had better get on some sensible shoes,' he said, glancing down at her light blue sandals.

What a bear he was, she thought, but turned promptly and went upstairs to put on thick shoes and find her coat.

Old Mrs Berry peered out of the door

five minutes later and saw the two figures walking away from the farmhouse. The tall, straight figure or her beloved 'Master Hew'; the slender and unfamiliar one of the girl. The housekeeper's features contorted and her sunken eyes became like boot buttons, black and snapping under their bushy white brows.

'So that's the way of it! Off gallivanting the very first night she's here. I knew it! I *knew*. And it will come to no good. He'll rue the very day he got a seketary here.'

So saying, she slammed the door; turning sharply back into the hall and trod on the tail of the slinking tabby cat which had followed her from the kitchen. It set up a blood-curdling yowl and rushed away, like a streak of lightning. She followed it, looking like an old witch, muttering to herself.

SEVEN

One week later, Briony sat at a little writing-table which she had fixed up for herself in her bedroom, finishing a letter to her parents.

She was close to an open window. It was a humid, uncomfortable kind of afternoon. A fine grey slanting rain veiled the lake and the lush green countryside. The mountains were obscured by low-lying cloud. Yesterday had been brilliant, so this was a disappointment. Briony had planned to take Aunt Caroline for a picnic. But she had just telephoned to say that it would be useless to come out to Wast Water in such weather, and Briony had settled down to a lone afternoon of correspondence.

Her employer was in London today. Much as he hated it, Hew had been forced by business to go up and spend twenty-four hours in the City, and see both his lawyers and his bank.

As Briony bent over her writing pad, she decided that she was not altogether writing truthfully. She hated hypocrisy but she could not have told her mother or her father what she was really feeling about things. She did not think they would understand. Would they not—like her aunt—think it was time she had forgotten the old deep love for the man whom she had been going to marry? Would they not be surprised and disappointed at her lack of pride—or was it a lack of will-power? But she just could not put Clive right out of her thoughts, as she had hoped to do.

She had that sort of nature. When Briony loved, it was with the whole of her heart. She had literally adored the charming and handsome young man who had been such a gay amusing companion as well as the perfect lover. No matter what she did, she automatically wondered what *his* reaction would have been ... what *he* would have thought or said about a certain situation; a book; or a tune. She remembered that once she had cut out some verses and sent them to him.

'I have no thought but owes to thee its being
Thou art my world and all things turn to
  thee
Deep in my heart with love's devotion seeing,
I love thee now unto Eternity.'

That famous song set to Grieg's immortal music, *Ich Liebe Dich*. That was the name of the original song which Briony had heard and remembered always. Both she and Clive had bought a gramophone record of it. They each played it when apart and told each other at what time. So foolish; so sentimental! But they had wanted to synchronize the song. That was how it had been with them. And with that white-hot fervour of youthful passion burning her up—all roads in her mind leading towards that one great day when she should become his wife—it had been such a terrible shock to Briony when Clive had abandoned her.

She had plenty of time in which to think, here in Monks Farm. For when she was not actually taking Hew's dictation or re-typing a manuscript, there was nothing much to do but read or write or go for walks. *And think.* There had been too much time for thinking about Clive. The longer she was separated from him, the more vivid the remembrance of all the little things they had both shared. Not once but many times, she had lain in the great big bed in this great big bedroom crying herself to sleep. She tried in vain to harden her heart; to recall only that shameful lunch in Seascale when he had asked her to marry him in secret and she had been so angry. She tried to hate him and failed. And hated herself instead—because of the even more shameful longing which now and then gripped her, to send for him; tell him that she would marry him on any terms, because she wanted him back so terribly.

She wished that she were more matter of fact and unsentimental. Like her cousin Pen who laughed a lot and skimmed over the surface of things. Nothing ever went very deep with Pen. She had had several boy friends; one whom Briony had once thought Pen loved devotedly. But when the affair ended, Pen had shed a few tears, then a week later found another love. If only she, Briony, could be like *that.* How much easier life would be!

She had hoped to find forgetfulness in her work. While she was actually with Hew Vanner, she was, indeed, absorbed. Every morning she went eagerly to her typewriter. Sometimes she allowed him to go on dictating until she was so tired that she could hardly sit upright. But that absorption was only temporary. When it was over she would start to think of Clive again and all that she had missed. She would remember his face (the faint insistent likeness to Hew didn't help her to forget), and she would hear his voice saying:

'I still love you with all my heart and I find that I can't go on without you.'

She found herself debating this again and again. How could it be true? How could he still love her and yet put ambition first? Was it *really* only for her that he wished to do well in life? Had she been too hard on him? Then his final words:

'I shall never give up trying to get you back.'

She remembered those uneasily. Had he meant them? Would he come and try his luck again? And would she have the strength to resist a second time? Somehow she *knew* that she had been right to send him away. Yet that humiliating deep-rooted desire to fling herself into his arms again, remained.

This, then, was Briony's confused and unhappy state of mind at the end of her first week at Monks Farm. But nobody knew. Certainly not Hew Vanner. In his presence she was just a practical, cool young woman. Briony had decided that Hew was hard and self-centred and interested in nothing but his writing; his travels, his past adventures. Human beings just did not matter to him! He was kind enough to her—he often apologized for making her work too long and too hard.

He was polite at the meals which they shared. He took her out for a stroll most evenings. He was quite talkative—but always on the subject of Nature—the countryside. Never personal. He had even made himself charming to Miss Shaw when she had come to see Briony (out of sheer curiosity as that good lady had admitted).

She had asked to see some of his treasures and he had shown them with apparent pleasure and afterwards announced to Briony that 'Aunt Caroline was an intelligent woman', a compliment from *him!* Miss Shaw, on her part, had left Monks Farm feeling slightly more relieved about her niece being there. Mrs Berry she thought a 'stupid, jealous old woman', but Mr Vanner was 'extremely interesting and very definitely a gentleman' and that meant a lot, coming from Aunt Caroline.

All the same Briony was unhappy and that was why she felt a hypocrite as she wrote home:

You need have no worries about your little Bri. She is fine and feeding off the fat of the land here. Mr Vanner goes out with a gun now and then. He is friendly with the local farmers. We had wild duck for dinner last night. And we never lack butter or ham or eggs or even cream. You must both come up and stay at the Wast Water Hotel. It's all so beautiful.

And Mummy, please stop worrying about Mr

V. falling for me. You see me through rose-coloured spectacles. Your 'beautiful Bri' to him is just a recording machine. And except when we are working I don't think he realizes that I am in the house, but I am perfectly happy. The book is grand and we've done nearly 20,000 words in one week which is terrific. As soon as it is finished I expect I shall be shot out of Monks Farm and will be looking for another job ...

She finished this letter and sealed it. She had meant to write to her Cousin Liz, but could not settle down to it. Liz had just become engaged to a young officer in the Air Force. They were going to be married in August and then her fiancé, Squadron-Leader Derek Forbes, expected to be posted to Malta. Liz had just sent a rapturous letter announcing the news and asking Briony if she would be a bridesmaid.

Ironic, Briony thought. The positions reversed. Elizabeth was to have been *hers*. What a pang it gave Briony to remember all those preparations during the blissful days just before the wedding that never came off. Not very long ago—yet it seemed a century. Another life.

Briony put down her pen and gazed despondently around her room. Even after a short week, it had taken on a slightly more cheerful appearance. A big bowl of roses by her bed, picked from the tangled garden which nobody bothered to cultivate.

Her photographs, her favourite books on the mantelpiece. Her own little wireless. Hew Vanner loathed radio and there wasn't one in the house so she had asked permission to bring hers here. His answer had been typical:

'Have what you like in your own room, my dear girl. If you like all the drivel you hear on the air, you are welcome to it.'

Briony, who could never resist an argument, had said:

'Oh, come! There are some wonderful concerts on the radio and some most interesting talks.'

He had given his dry smile and said:

'I like good music and I don't mind listening to intelligent conversation, but *not* on the wireless.'

'How difficult you are!' she had said, and then apologized quickly, adding: 'Perhaps I shouldn't say such things to my employer.'

That had made him laugh loudly, which he rarely did, and in quite a friendly way he had added:

'You *do* amuse me, you funny little thing.'

Which had sent her out of the room with scarlet cheeks, feeling like a small child who has been ridiculed.

They were always arguing. Most times Briony got the worst of it. And nothing she could do, could put her right with Mrs Berry. It was all jealousy with the old woman, of course, and Briony knew it. She was sorry. It was unpleasant living in the house with somebody who so openly hated the sight of you, and for the last day or two Mrs Berry had started a new campaign; with sly cunning she tried to upset Briony by neglecting to do her bedroom, as though defying Briony to complain. Which, of course, she did not do. Nothing would have induced her to run down the old nurse to her beloved 'Master Hew'. So Briony took to sweeping and dusting her own room, and nothing was said about it.

How restless she felt this wet muggy afternoon! It was better when the sun was out. Better when Hew was at home so that she could get down to some work, but she had got the typing right up to date and there was absolutely nothing to do today. She put on her mackintosh, walked to the post-office, and sent off her letter to Reigate.

As she turned back and began to stroll down the hill looking over the yellow lichened roof tops of Monks Farm, she heard the horn of a car just behind her. She stood aside to let it pass. But the driver drew up alongside her.

EIGHT

Briony's first thought was—*what a peach of a car?* It had one of those long graceful bodies of the sporting variety. A black drop-head coupé—hood down at the moment—with a beautiful polish on everything. The driver was a very good-looking man with particularly broad shoulders, a tan that suggested the tropics, and a pair of sea-blue eyes that twinkled behind large horn-rims. He had fair thick hair cropped so close that it stood up, after the fashion of Americans. He wore an American sports shirt and lumber jacket and for a moment Briony thought indeed he might have come from the States. But when he spoke his voice was wholly English. It had a breezy note in it which matched his personality.

'I beg your pardon,' he greeted her, 'but I wonder if you can tell me the way to Monks Farm. Mr Vanner's place.'

She smiled and pointed to the roof tops of the farmhouse down the hill.

'You're just on it. But I am afraid he is not at home.'

The stranger looked disappointed. The powerful car throbbed and hummed beside him. He took a large silk handkerchief out of his pocket and mopped his face. He looked hot. Briony thought she had never seen a fair man so dark brown. Most blonds of his type turned red. Unusual and rather attractive, she thought, with those intensely blue eyes and goldenish hair. She rather liked the look of him.

'Don't tell me I have come all this way to see old Van and he's away!' exclaimed the stranger.

'Only for a day. He should be back fairly soon.'

'He'd better be. He invited me up here for the week-end.'

Now Briony stared.

'Oh, goodness! Then he must have forgotten. He never said a word to me or to Mrs Berry, his housekeeper.'

The stranger took a packet of cigarettes from his pocket and offered her one. She shook her head. He tapped his cigarette on a thumb-nail and regarded her speculatively.

'Well, as a matter of fact, Van did not specify which week-end, but I've got a standing invitation.'

'I see. Mind you, I don't even know when he will be back,' added Briony.

'Well, I'm not budging from here till I've seen him,' said the young man and laughed. Briony was to become familiar with that rich chuckling laugh which was most infectious. This man—he must be over thirty—exuded good nature and energy, she thought, and had a youthful freshness about him which might have belonged to a schoolboy. But another thing she was to discover was the wary brain and common sense behind that schoolboy façade. He was an extraordinary mixture.

Now he was introducing himself.

'My name's Forrester—Dick Forrester. I've known Van all my life. We were at Oxford together and, later, on many expeditions. I expect you have heard him talk about his travels.'

'I have indeed,' said Briony, and added: 'I am Briony Moore. Mr Vanner's secretary.'

'You live at Monks Farm?'

'Yes.'

Dick Forrester whistled and looked over the rim of his glasses with something more than a twinkle in those very blue eyes of his.

He had thought when he first stopped the car to ask his way, that he must surely have hit upon the prettiest girl in the Lake District. Unlike Hew Vanner, although a bachelor, he felt no antipathy towards the opposite sex. On the contrary he was rarely without a girlfriend of some kind. He had every intention of settling down to married life once he had got over this *'wanderlust'*—an urge for travel—exploring—adventure which was now his whole life. Rather like a sailor, who liked to have a 'girl in every port', he was a bit of a philanderer. But a nice one. As generous to women as he was charming; immensely popular with them. His experienced eye had at once noted the grace and perfection of Briony's slender figure when she was walking down the hill. Now he thought he had never seen a more intriguing face framed in that wonderful red-gold hair. As for those long silky lashes ... he chuckled to himself: 'Ye gods! Old Van with a secretary like this! What a change for the old boy who says he has neither time nor place for women!'

'I say! Things *are* looking up!' said Dick Forrester aloud.

Briony stared.

'I don't think I understand.'

'Never mind,' said Dick. 'But if you're Van's secretary, you're just the girl I want. You'll look after me very nicely until he does come back.'

Briony coloured, then laughed. There was something so frank and irresistible about this friend of Hew's—she couldn't take offence at anything he said. He invited her to step into the car.

'Let me drive you in state to the front door in my new toy. My Bentley Mark VI. Like her?'

'I think she's a dream,' sighed Briony who had a taste for lovely cars.

'And I think you are a dream,' Dick Forrester thought, but dared not say so aloud. He threw an admiring glance at the slenderest of ankles as Briony stepped on to the running board.

'Do you think I might be permitted to stay until old Van turns up?' he asked as he drove her up to the house.

'You'll have to ask Mrs Berry. She is the boss. Quite a bit of a dragon. Not a bad old soul at heart but—well, she isn't very welcoming,' Briony grinned.

'Mrs Berry being the sole member of the staff, I presume.'

'Exactly. Hew's old nurse.'

Dick gave a rich chuckle and that amusing provocative glance at Briony over his horn-rims.

'Leave her to me. I'm a genius at handling staff. And I fancy I know her. Seen her in our Oxford days.'

'I'll give you full marks if you can handle *her,*' said Briony.

But handle the old nurse he did. When Mrs Berry, peering at him with her short-sighted eyes, sniffed and observed that it was impossible to offer him a room without Mr Vanner's permission, Dick gave her his most winning smile and adopted a tone of appeal, succulent enough to melt even the heart of a withered, irritable old woman. And he reminded her that they had met once before when she went up to Oxford to visit Hew.

'Come, you wouldn't turn me away, would you? I've driven hundreds of miles to see my old friend. Now, be a darling, Berry, and find me a bed. An attic will do, I'm a chap who can sleep on anything, even a plank. There's many a night old Van and I have laid ourselves down on the good earth or rolled ourselves up in a bit of sacking and slept the clock round. Find me a corner, there's a pet. I've so often heard Van talk of you. Old Nanny Berry—eh? His one and only girl-friend, he used to call you.'

A slow smile relaxed the corners of Mrs Berry's disapproving mouth. Briony stared. It was the first time she had ever seen a smile on Berry's gloomy countenance. It was easy to see that she was flattered and even delighted by Dick. She capitulated.

'Well, there is *one* room, but it is not particularly comfortable. The bed is very hard. However, I dare say Mr Hew would want you to have it. I seem to remember you at Oxford, sir. There are some photographs of you in this house, too.'

'I bet there are,' said Dick. 'Me, with the lions and tigers, or standing on a bison's head, or kneeling on a rhino, and so on. Bags of glamour ...' he chuckled and grinned at Briony. 'Think Van will be back tonight?' he asked her.

'I just don't know,' she said, 'but I am sure he would like to find you here if and when he comes.'

'Good,' said Dick and looked relieved. 'Now, we must park the Bentley. I am not leaving my new love out in the wind and the rain. Got a garage?'

They had. An apology for one but it was a roof to go over the Bentley. But Dick decided not to garage her just then.

'You might like to try her out,' he suggested to Briony, 'I like to show her off. I only got back from the Far East a week ago. For years I have promised myself a millionaire's car. And here she is. It almost broke me, but I've got her. And I'm never going to let her go. When I sail on my next expedition, she can be jacked up and wait for me. This is actually my first visit to the English Lakes. I want to do a bit of routing round. Do you know I have seen half the lakes in the world. In South America. Africa. Australia. But never the ones in my own country. Shocking, isn't it?'

They laughed together. Briony's spirits, which had been so low before, rose steadily. Over a cup of tea she sat listening to Dick Forrester, enthralled as she was when Hew talked to her. They were both men with a thirst for voyage and discovery; the perpetual urge to conquer new fields. Cut to the same pattern. Gold mines of knowledge; ready to share some of their exciting and absorbing experiences with others. But in every other way they were different. For whereas Hew Vanner was so reserved and shut within himself, Dick Forrester had a frank open nature and no inhibitions. He made Briony feel that she knew him well within an hour. By the time that day ended they were 'Briony' and 'Dick' to each other. And she was giggling as she had not giggled since her broken engagement. Dick was so funny. He had a fund of amusing stories which included many tales about the friend whom he called 'old Van'.

It was easy to see that he had an immense admiration for Hew. Van was *'tremendous'*; that was the word Dick used. A rare being. He had the courage of a lion, and yet the gentleness of a lamb. He would never give up, no matter how hard the chase, or dangerous the hazards. His knowledge of animals, in whatever country he crossed, was astounding. One never felt anything but safe in his hands.

'We've had some crashing good times together,' Dick told Briony. They were still talking after the evening meal, sitting in the lamp-light in Hew's study. 'And we've been in some tight spots. On two occasions I owe my life to Hew. Did I tell you earlier on about that time when the black mamba—the most deadly snake—nearly got me, and old Van shot it—shot the damned thing just as it was about to strike. I tell you—' and out came the full story of the black mamba. To be followed by others. Briony listened, breathless with interest. She felt a queer personal pride in hearing Hew's virtues extolled by another fine, brave man. The pair of them, she thought, were of the hunter type, Alan Quartermaine—whom Rider Haggard wrote about, in *King Solomon's Mines*. Either of them might have played the role. There was something unique about this atmosphere in which she now found herself. These two, Hew and Dick, made men like Clive seem extraordinarily petty and weak—somehow worthless. She began to feel spiritually strengthened—refreshed in Dick's presence. And to own that she felt likewise with Hew.

Dick Forrester was different from Hew in his attitude towards women—he found it easy to flatter and to be gallant; to run for a cushion to put behind a girl's back, or a footstool at her feet. He had already reached the pitch of telling Briony that Van was a lucky chap to have such a 'lovely girl' for a secretary. But it was all on the surface. She had no illusions. She realized that underneath, Dick was like Hew. Women didn't really count with him. Both these men had but one absorbing passion. To travel. To cut away from convention, from a life of mechanized pleasure, and to find their thrills in danger in unknown, newly discovered territory—*Nature in the raw.*

She felt that if she had sat up all night with Dick alone in this big lonely house—like Hew—Dick would never deviate from the platonic path; never attempt familiarity, or give her any cause for anxiety. They were friends, brother and sister. It was a new experience, and extraordinarily satisfying to Briony after the emotional storm through which she had recently passed. She even found herself able to tell Dick about Clive. Just a few words. She told him of her engagement and how Clive has passed out of her life, how she had taken this job because she needed to find forgetfulness.

Dick was sympathetic but not too much so. Maybe the chap was like old Van and himself, he suggested, and had found that he did not want to be tied down.

'You're all darlings and I love lovely girls!'

chuckled Dick. 'But some fellows need to hang on to their freedom. They are in love with the world.'

Briony grimaced. Clive hadn't wanted to see the world—only to make money. It was sheer ambition, and thirst for power which had shattered *their* romance. She said so. Dick didn't approve. He was the least mercenary of men. His father had left him a bit. He enjoyed good living when he was in England. He had enjoyed buying his Bentley. But he would have been just as happy without it.

'*Travels with a Donkey* and all that,' he grinned at Briony.

No, he had no use for a man who broke his engagement a week before his wedding just because he wanted money and position. He wrote Clive off. She must forget *him,* Dick said, and find someone worthier. Whereupon Briony said that she didn't want to find anybody else. She was going to devote herself now to her job.

'Oh, somebody will make you change your mind one day,' said Dick Forrester with his rich laugh, 'but you take my advice, Briony, and choose a chap who puts money last—never first. The mercenary ones are no use to any woman. They're mean in spirit as well as with the cash. And chaps like myself and Van are no use either—as husbands, don'cher know. We're too restless! A girl needs someone domesticated who wants to settle down.'

'Well, I'm not at all keen to settle down to married life nowadays, I want to work, and I'm terribly interested in this book that Hew is writing,' said Briony, feeling quite proud of her ability to make such a statement and be sincere about it.

'I look forward to seeing the book. I can't write a line myself; never was any good at it, although I can talk about my travels until the cows come home. I envy old Van his literary gift. No excuse for *me* to engage beautiful secretaries to come and cheer me in a lakeside retreat!'

'I'm sure I don't cheer Hew up much. He's very independent, you know,' smiled Briony.

Dick, puffing at the cheroot which he had lit after dinner, launched into further tales about his friend and their expeditions. Yes, old Van *was* independent. But a staunch friend. No man ever had a better. Always ready to give his shirt for somebody else worse off than himself. That brusque bitter side of him ... that was due to his unfortunate past. Did Briony know about Van's personal affairs? Briony said that she didn't. So Dick closed up. He was obviously not prepared to gossip any further.

Briony went to bed that night more than ever intrigued by the personalities of the two men—her employer and his friend. It would be something else to tell Aunt Caroline about, although the old dear would not take too kindly to the idea that her niece was staying in a house with two stalwart wanderers.

Hew did not come back that night, nor the next day. But Dick Forrester stayed on at Monks Farm. And Briony thoroughly enjoyed the hours she spent with him. He was an entertaining companion. He insisted on driving her round the lakes. He, on his part, told her that she was a delightful guide, and made him feel quite ashamed that he had so neglected his own country and had never seen this magnificent part of the world before. He was fully determined to climb Scafell before he went back to the south.

But that same evening the fine weather broke up. The temperature dropped and a cold wet evening set in. A furious storm of rain deluging the farm, blotting out the lake and those wonderful screes; turning what had been a gentle, golden landscape into something sinister and formidable.

'Now you see what our Lakes can be like!' said Briony.

But Dick Forrester thought it all splendid. He stood at the window looking down at the stormy scene with appreciation. It was however, too cold for him. His blood had grown thin after continual travel in the Far East. He shivered and groaned.

Mrs Berry lit a wood fire to warm him. A great condescension for her. But she eyed Briony with a touch of her old asperity as she said:

'I don't know what the master will say coming back to find me burning fuel in the middle of the summer.'

'Do you think he'll be back tonight, Mrs Berry?' asked Dick.

'It's time he was,' she said, with a meaning look from him to Briony. Dick grinned.

'Don't you feel safe in the house with me, Mrs Berry? Well, perhaps you *had* better lock your door tonight. You never know—with a wild man of the woods.'

Briony smothered a laugh. Mrs Berry looked shocked, but was obviously delighted, and went off cackling to herself.

Later that evening the sound of a car mingled with the sigh of wind and spatter of rain against the panes.

Briony sprang up.

'I believe that's Hew. Yes—I am sure it is. Nobody else would be coming down the hill at this hour—'

She was right. Hew Vanner walked into the house, pulling off a dripping mackintosh. An unfamiliar Hew in his dark London suit. He looked tired and rather irritable. But at the sight of the fair man in the lumber jacket and grey flannels, smoking a cheroot, Hew's whole face lit up. He became transformed. Briony felt that he looked right past her without so much as a nod of greeting. His whole attention was concentrated on his friend.

'Blow me down if it isn't old Dick! Why,

you son-of-a-gun! What the devil are you doing here?'

The two men gripped hands. Briony, watching, thought how incredibly changed Hew Vanner was with that thrilled, pleased expression. All traces of bitterness gone. Just now and again, whilst dictating something that reminded him of a particularly exciting moment in his travels, he looked like that, but not often, she thought.

Dick explained his presence and how long he had been there.

'I knew you wouldn't mind. We've got such a lot to talk about. I couldn't leave without seeing you.'

'My dear old fellow, I am delighted. Let's have a drink—'

He rushed to the corner cupboard to find whisky and two glasses. Dick followed him with affectionate gaze.

'You're looking a bit peaky, Van. Time you got back to the wide open spaces. Doesn't appear to suit you, playing the author, my lad.'

Hew flung back his head with that quick nervous gesture, which Briony had grown to recognize. There was nothing wrong with him, he said, only a couple of days in London with bank managers, solicitors, etc., was more than enough. London was hellish. Noisy, full of appalling crowds. He couldn't stand it. He was thankful to be back in Wasdale, even on a night like this.

'Well, I've been charmingly entertained by your secretary,' announced Dick, 'you're to be congratulated.'

Now Hew became aware of Briony and rather guiltily murmured 'Good evening' to her and asked her how she was.

Her red lips curved a trifle ironically.

'Very well, thanks,' she said, and added that she would go to bed and leave the two men to their drinks.

After she had gone, Dick flung himself into a chair and grinned at his friend.

'Charming girl.'

'She is a very good typist.'

'You materialist!' laughed Dick. 'I said she was *charming.*'

'Yes, I suppose so. Actually I find her sympathetic to work with.'

'And apart from work?' Dick's eyes twinkled at him.

Hew looked a bit embarrassed.

'Now you know me, Dick, I am not interested in females.'

'Well, she's a particularly attractive female.'

Hew rubbed the back of his head. He didn't really want to talk about his secretary's attractions. But he had to admit that while he was in London he had thought about Briony once or twice. Thought how pleasant it would be to find her here when he got back, as well as old Berry. Then he had dismissed her from his mind.

'Now, Dick, I want to hear everything that

you have done since we last met,' he said.

'That would fill a volume.'

'Well, get on with it.'

'Well, you know I went out to Malaya ...' began Dick.

Briony wakened in the early hours of the morning to hear doors shutting, and decided sleepily, that the two men must have stayed talking far into the dawn. Already the first faint light was creeping in through the windows and she could hear the pipe of birds.

She wondered whether Dick Forrester had come here for the express purpose of inducing Hew Vanner to join him on a new expedition. If so, that would mean the end of her job. Hew Vanner would pass out of her life as suddenly and dramatically as he had entered it.

She found it hard to go to sleep again, considering that possibility, and was astonished to find that the more she considered it the more unattractive it appeared.

When she had first come here she had felt all this to be unreal and not very pleasing. The lonely farmhouse on the hillside—the saturnine Hew Vanner—the hostile old nurse. She had hungered for Clive, for the past happy if ordinary existence she had once led with her parents in Reigate.

But now it was Clive, and even Mummy and Daddy, and the home she used to live in, which seemed a dream. *This* was reality.

Her life here. Her work with Hew. She was fast becoming part and parcel of it. She knew quite definitely that she did not want it to end.

NINE

That next morning the storm had died down, but it was still grey and dull with a faint mist hanging over the lake, and Scafell half obscured by clouds.

Briony knew that Dick had intended to go on a climbing expedition but the weather was not propitious; one needed a really fine sunny day for climbing. Hew seemed disinclined to get down to any dictation in spite of having just had two days away from his book.

It was so rarely that his friend Dick was with him. He wanted to make the most of it; to go out and about with him.

After breakfast, in the study, Hew dictated a few letters and then called Dick in.

'I'd rather like Briony to make some notes on this new scheme of yours. The one we discussed last night.'

Dick, lighting a pipe, grinned at Briony. By jingo, she looked sweet, he thought, in her tailored grey skirt and blue short-sleeved 'woolly'. Fresh as a flower. Such nimble fingers, too. He had heard her typing, keeping up with old Van's gruelling pace. Hew added:

'I am being roped in for a new expedition, or I think I am, Briony. Dick wants me to go to South America with him at the end of the summer.'

'Well, we've got the chance of an expedition down the Amazon,' said Dick. 'I've been there once already, and it's immense. I know Van would not want to miss it. And there's one branch I am particularly interested in. I've met a chap called Gonzola de Sampaio—he's a descendant of the famous explorer. I met up with him in Singapore and he's planning an expedition down the Napo. It's just Van's and my cup of tea.'

Briony looked from one man to the other. Her large bright eyes grew thoughtful and even envious.

'How wonderful to be able to see all these strange places.'

'Wonderful until you get eaten by tigers, poisoned by snakes, and plagued by mosquitoes,' chuckled Dick.

Hew added:

'I don't really think I can afford to go, Dick.'

'It isn't going to cost you anything. You know Gonzola is as rich as Croesus. He wants to finance the whole expedition, but he needs our company, and in particular he wants to pick your brains, Van, and then for you to write a book about it all when you get back.'

Hew chewed his lips. He was looking better this morning, Briony thought. More rested and with that alert expression in his eyes which she liked to see there. She could tell that he was tempted by his friend's suggestion. There was a restlessness in Hew Vanner that nothing could subdue.

She sat quiet, listening and watching, her notebook ready. At any moment Hew would turn and expect her to take down his dictation without fault. She was used to him now. The two men sat on the edge of the desk examining a large map.

Dick traced a course with the point of his pencil.

'There's the Napo. You see it rises on the flanks of the three volcanoes.'

Hew looked over his shoulder at Briony.

'Just take a note of this. Three volcanoes ...'

He spelt them. *'The Antisana. The Sinchol-agua. The Cotopaxi.'*

Briony began to jot it down. She had to concentrate. They were using words and names she had never heard in her life before. It all sounded wildly exciting and incredibly far away. Gorges on the Equator. Canyons, swamps, lagoons. Jungle-tangled islands.

The Napo was not going to be an easy river to navigate, Dick explained. Its upper waters could be ascended as far as Santa Rosa and on its Coca branch they could penetrate as far up as its middle course. There it would jam between two mountain walls in a deep canyon along which it dashed over high falls and dangerous reefs.

To Briony it all sounded too difficult, but she could see the glint in Hew's eyes and the flush running up under his tan. It was the danger he liked to court.

'It sounds terrific,' he said, 'absolutely first class, Dick.'

'It will be. And with Gonzola's money and knowledge of the language, we can't go wrong. He suggests that we start from here ...'

Dick began to trace another course. Briony was kept busy making notes. The new expedition was talked over and planned until lunch time.

'You're going to come, aren't you, Van?' Dick asked Hew at the end of that session.

Hew gave a short laugh.

'I must admit I am tempted.'

'I knew you would be,' said Dick delightedly.

'But now I have bought this house and settled old Berry in it—'

'All the better,' interrupted Dick, 'they'll be here waiting for you when you get back, and perhaps our beautiful secretary, too, ready to write the history of the Napo.'

Hew glanced toward Briony who met his gaze and then looked quickly away. A slight colour arose in her cheeks. She realized that she hadn't counted to these two men the whole morning except as a recording machine.

'I'm quite certain I shan't be here,' she said coldly.

'And I'm quite sure that old Van won't find anybody else who could do this job so well,' observed Dick, smiling at her over the rim of his glasses.

Hew cleared his throat. He felt faintly embarrassed.

'I'm sure I shan't,' he muttered, and he meant it. He thawed so far as to add: 'I shall hope to keep in touch with you, Briony.'

She did not answer. She had a sudden sinking feeling that the end of Dick Forrester's visit to Monks Farm might very easily mean the end of her short career as Hew's secretary. Dick in his most jocular mood said:

'She is not the sort of girl you'll find waiting around, old boy. She's much too beautiful. The toils of matrimony will close round her and—'

'Don't be silly,' interrupted Briony, and quite red in the face closed her typewriter and marched out of the study.

Hew glanced a trifle uneasily at the door through which the slim figure had just vanished.

'She seemed upset by your remark.'

'I was only pulling her leg. We're quite good friends. I spent the day motoring with her yesterday. She is a very delightful girl.'

Hew frowned again. It was not the first

time Dick had extolled the virtues of his secretary. But she *had* been upset by that allusion to 'matrimonial toil', he felt sure. He was suddenly aware that he knew nothing about Briony's personal affairs, beyond the fact that he had always had a shrewd suspicion of an unfortunate love affair. How well Dick Forrester seemed to have got on with her! But old Dick was more at ease with girls than he himself.

During lunch he noted that Briony talked almost exclusively to Dick. And he even began to envy his friend's faculty for paying pretty compliments and making light cheerful conversation. No doubt a young girl like Briony found him, Hew Vanner, a bad-tempered bore.

It was suggested by Dick that the three of them should take a drive that afternoon, but Briony refused.

'You two go off alone, please.'

'But we'd like her with us, wouldn't we, Van?' said Dick.

Hew looked at Briony. She was covered with confusion. She made haste to say:

'No, really, it's much better for you two men to go off by yourselves.'

Hew then astonished himself and Briony by saying that he insisted upon her accompanying them.

She gave in—her heart beating quickly with pleasure and ran upstairs to put on some slacks, a shirt, and a pair of thick shoes. As she rummaged in her drawer for a scarf, she found that she was really excited. What fun to be included in this afternoon outing with two great explorers. And Hew had not been forced to second Dick's invitation. He could have left her at home to get on with some typing.

A small snapshot fell out of her drawer and she picked it up. Her heart suddenly contracted at the sight of it. She had not known it was there. A snapshot of Clive. An old one, taken in the garden at home. He was smiling in that winning way he used to have. But suddenly it was as though that handsome, smiling face brought her a sensation of scorn—even of disgust. How puny he was beside those two, waiting for her downstairs. Puny not merely in physique, but in mentality, in character.

She tore the snapshot into pieces and ran down the stairs.

And she had an extraordinary feeling of lightness, as though released from a burden; the burden or her old infatuation for Clive.

TEN

It was a glorious afternoon for Briony. They set out directly after lunch. She sat on the broad seat in the front of the lovely racing car between the two men.

'Our little sardine,' Dick laughingly called her. She was extraordinarily happy although now and again she was reminded of days during her engagement to Clive when he used to drive her from Reigate down to Brighton and up on the Downs. She could remember how his hand used to hold hers tightly and what silly gay things they used to say to each other. What intimate heart-stirring little things, one to the other, always beginning and ending with the words: 'I love you.'

That was romance. Romance had gone from her life. Hew, as always, remained rather sternly quiet except when he saw some particular landmark which he pointed out to his friend. It was Dick who kept up a running flow of chatter and joked away the sternness, but nothing of romance in it for Briony, and she didn't want it. She thoroughly enjoyed the spirit of friendship, and she was thoroughly flattered by the thought that the two great travellers and friends had brought her with them. The Bentley went like a bird and Dick was a good and careful driver.

As ever in the Lake District the weather changed with astonishing rapidity. Rain was falling as they reached the Castle Inn, not far from Keswick. There were grey clouds swirling from peak to peak on Skiddaw.

By the time they had moved on through the beautiful Vale of Bassenthwaite, the clouds had cleared and the sun had come out again.

They went to so many places that Briony was made to feel that she had really never seen the Lakes properly before. Windermere, Kendal, Derwentwater—and along one of the loveliest roads she knew. Through glorious woods between Keswick and Watendlath, then came the glory of Derwentwater. Tea—Cumberland ham and new-laid eggs, home-made bread—in a famous oak-beamed cottage, about which so much had been written by Hugh Walpole. Briony had read his books. She talked excitedly about the *Herries Chronicles*. Hew gave her a brief dry smile and said:

'Sorry, I never read novels.'

'You *wouldn't!*' she thought.

Why should he? Love stories were not at all likely to interest Hew Vanner.

But he had plenty to say about the little squirrels or birds—about trees, bushes and flowers. He seemed to be able to put a name to the tiniest, rarest plant.

During tea, which Briony poured out, it was Dick who looked appreciatively at the slim pretty girl. Prettier than ever, he thought, now her face was flushed from the sun, and her radiant curls blown by the wind about her neck.

'I think we're a couple of lucky chaps to have such a charming hostess, Van,' he observed.

Hew having finished a hearty tea, lit his pipe and glanced through the smoke at Briony. Until his friend pointed it out, he had not thought about Briony, but now he, too, noticed how absolutely charming she looked today. He did not as a rule care for women in slacks and yet they suited Briony's boyish slenderness, and so did the cotton shirt showing bare rounded arms and sun-kissed throat. A trifle embarrassed, he glanced away from her and said:

'Very lucky. Well, I must say it's been a nice lazy workless day, hasn't it, Briony?'

'Oh, I think it's been heavenly!' she exclaimed.

'But it's none of it new to you round here,' said Dick.

'Oh, but it *is*—I've seen plenty of places today I haven't been to before. You've just whirled us around! And I've never seen it through such eyes—I mean—you both *see* things, whereas other motorists pass by without seeing. Do you see what I mean?' she finished with a laugh and an apology for her poorly expressed speech.

Dick nodded.

'I see exactly what you mean. The average man and woman is apt to travel blindly.'

'I shall be able to air all my new knowledge to my aunt who lives in Seascale!' she laughed.

'Is she as charming as her niece?' asked Dick.

Hew cocked an eyebrow at his friend.

'I really never realized before what a gift you have for saying the right thing, Dick.'

Briony's cheeks flamed and she giggled a little.

'Well, Aunt Caroline is no longer young, and she wears awful hats, but she is a darling and she has a terrific knowledge of antiques. She runs a Treasure Shop, you know, in Seascale.'

'Let's drive to Seascale on the way home and meet Aunt Caroline,' suggested Dick, but here Hew intervened. It was getting on for half past five and they were a long way from Wasdale, he said. He had a telephone call coming through from London. He had forgotten all about it until this moment. He must be back by seven o'clock to receive it.

But even he—disinterested as he was in the emotions and reactions of human beings—could not fail to note the disappointment in Briony's eyes. He added gruffly:

'Ask your aunt to come over and lunch at Monks Farm next week. I've been thinking she might like a few hours alone among *my* treasures and I am always glad to show them to somebody with knowledge and appreciation. She only glanced at them last time, then rushed away.'

'Thanks—that's very nice of you,' said Briony.

They drove back—over pack-horse bridges, down steep hills, across moorland thick with green bracken, past tumbling, frothing waterfalls and placid pools. Through pine woods that filled the air with pungent perfume and finally back to the splendid sombre isolation of Wast Water. A very contented Briony, arms folded, snug in her seat between the two big men, humming under her breath as they descended the hill.

While she washed and dressed for supper that night, she felt lighter hearted than since the day before Clive so cruelly jilted her.

She decided to take Hew at his word and to phone to Aunt Caro and make an appointment for her to come and lunch at Monks Farm. Aunt Caro must really get to know Hew and see what a clever and nice person he was.

Hew's telephone call came through and during the evening meal he announced that he had been asked to give a talk on the flora and fauna of the Transvaal at the Travellers' Union dinner which was to take place in a London hotel in August.

'You know I'm no good at lecturing,' he added to Dick, 'I can scribble but I I *cannot* talk. But it's right down your street, my dear chap, and I've told them that you will do it for me. They were delighted.'

Dick's blue eyes twinkled at him, and he clucked with his tongue.

'Tch! Tch! Who gave you permission, Van?

Without even consulting me.'

'Well, you'll do it, won't you?' said Hew in his most persuasive voice.

Dick turned to Briony. She looked a treat, he thought, with her glorious warmth of skin and glistening hair. She was all feminine tonight in a floral dirndl skirt and Hungarian blouse. The snowy whiteness of it made her sunburned neck and shoulders golden brown in contrast.

'What do you think? Shall we refuse and make the old boy speak to the masses, stutter and all?'

Briony laughed.

'I think it would be cruel if he hates it so. I know I should die of fright if I had to make a speech.'

'Ah, but you'd look so nice, you wouldn't need to speak, but just let 'em stare at you.'

'There he goes again!' groaned Hew. 'If there was ever a man who kissed the Blarney stone—but you had an Irish mother, hadn't you, Dick?'

Dick made a gesture of protest.

'Come, come! You're not suggesting that I flatter your little secretary with my tongue in my cheek? Wouldn't *you* like to see her standing up on a platform wearing that pretty outfit she has got on tonight? All ready for a gipsy dance!'

Briony went hot and then a trifle hotter as Hew's gaze drifted in her direction.

'Oh I wish you wouldn't, Dick!' she muttered.

Hew, too, wished Dick 'wouldn't'. He was a devil for putting you in an awkward position. He seemed to have fallen hook, line and sinker for Briony. It was funny, but only Dick's continual and flattering allusions to Briony had forced Hew to begin thinking of her as a man thinks about a girl. And he had to confess that his thoughts were not unpleasant. In fact he was beginning to be rather agreeably and conceitedly satisfied that he, personally, had found this little secretary. Not often you got one as attractive as she was efficient.

What years and years it was since he had turned his thoughts to women, and looked at any of them from a personal angle, he reflected. There had been nothing like that—nobody—since *the* one. And ever since that grim tragedy he had stamped his foot on the mere memory of love because it hurt so violently. The hurt had diminished with years and with so much travel. Time dulls the sharpest grief. And because he was not a sentimentalist and could not bear to show emotion, Hew had locked away every photograph that he had ever had of Anne, locked them away with her letters and presents. Better to wipe it right out sternly and absolutely, as *she* had been wiped out, in that horrible night in 1945.

He pulled himself up sharply now. Why

should Briony's presence recall his poor lost love? And yet she did. He had not admitted it until tonight. But it was something in the slender build and 'very young' freshness of Briony Moore which were reminiscent of Anne. Only that. For Anne had been as dark as Briony was fair, with a pale skin that never flushed and large grave brown eyes.

He did not want to be reminded of her and her untimely end. He had rarely given the past a thought until tonight. It was all so long ago. To hell with Dick coming here and putting ideas into his mind. He did not wish to have Briony presented to him in any aspect other than that of a paid employee.

Briony's bright eyes were watching him and that, for some strange reason, made him feel angry. He did not want to be watched, to be made conscious of her feminine charms. He suddenly returned to the old role of the harsh domineering man whom Briony had first met. Gone was the friendly companion of this afternoon.

'Well, do what you want but let me know in time, Dick,' he snapped the words. 'I've got to let them know.'

Somehow Briony sensed that he was annoyed with *her* and she immediately became interested in pouring out the coffee which old Mrs Berry had just brought in.

Dick was not in the least perturbed by what he called 'old Van's moods'. He was used to them. Poor chap, Van had a cause for being moody. It was Dick who had been the one to take him abroad and seen him through that period of black despair and grief, after the V2 had completed its murderous work on poor little Anne Graham. Dick knew that she was the only girl old Van had ever cared a hoot about, and that Van had hoped to marry her.

'I'll make your speech for you,' Dick said soothingly, 'but I'm not going to do it unless our Briony comes, too.'

'Oh, no, *please*—' began Briony.

Hew, without looking at her, scowled and stirred his coffee.

'Is it necessary?' he interrupted. 'It's a long, tedious journey, you know.'

Dick, winked at Briony over his head.

'Not in the Bentley and if I make speeches I want them recorded. I'm having my secretary. That's what a sec's for!'

Hew cleared his throat.

'Well, if they will allow her—'

'Wives and sweethearts always welcome,' broke in the incorrigible Dick with his rich laugh, 'and afterwards you can retire to your club with the *Encyclopaedia Britannica,* old pal, and Briony and I will sneak off on our own and do a supper-dance. I bet you dance like a dream, don't you, Briony?'

Briony began to feel in a decidedly invidious

position. She liked Dick Forrester—he was a darling. There was something so wholesome and humorous about him. He made her laugh. And dancing in London would be a treat. She had so few chances. Oh dear! The last time had been with Clive. They had taken his old father out with them to celebrate Clive's birthday and afterwards danced to Carroll Gibbons's band at the Savoy. Clive was a wonderful dancer and at his best as a host on an occasion like that. She remembered how attractive she had thought him; and one particular moment when they had been playing an old favourite and he had murmured the words against her hair:

'I've got you under my skin!...'

And those last significant lines:

'Use your mentality,
Wake up to reality!'

Well, she had woken up all right to the grimmest possible reality. She rose suddenly from the table. Both the men looked at her. Her face was turned so that they could not see that she had grown paler and that her lips no longer smiled.

'I couldn't possibly come up to town with you, thanks awfully, Dick,' she said coldly.

'Why not?' snapped Hew, with unusual perverseness.

She turned her head in his direction and was almost near to snapping back at him.

'As you said, I'm sure it is not at all necessary.'

She felt almost resentful. She was so sure that it was just that he didn't want her and wouldn't mind whether she missed a dinner-dance or not. Self-centred brute! But to her surprise he looked her straight in the eyes and said:

'If Dick is going to do my job for me, and particularly wants the speech recorded, and they'll let you attend, I shall expect you to go with us.'

She bit her lip and her heart-beats quickened.

'If those are my orders, yes—of course,' she said in an ice-cold voice and walked to the door, adding: 'I'll say good-night to you both.'

'We'll have that dance,' Dick called after her.

She did not answer. She felt suddenly and unreasonably upset. She felt that Hew was upset, too, for other causes, and that he was just an exacting and inhuman creature—certainly without any human interest in or feeling for *her,* no matter how hard she worked for him.

Her enjoyment of the afternoon faded. Neither did she give another thought to

Dick's invitation. It was of Hew Vanner, her employer, she thought, and about whom she worried. Though if anybody could have asked her why she could not have given an answer. She just did not know, herself.

ELEVEN

Dick Forrester left Monks Farm in high spirits. He liked lecturing and he was quite happy to take Hew's place at the dinner. It was arranged that Briony should also go up to town with them.

Hew went back to work. He and Briony plunged deep into the exciting travel book again and with little time to spare. But she had plenty to write home about and plenty to talk over with Aunt Caroline when she visited Seascale on her next day 'off'.

Aunt Caroline remained slightly anxious for her niece in what she called 'that bachelor household', and still more perturbed when she heard about the new friend, Dick Forrester. Yet *another* bachelor!

It was bad enough Briony living in that isolated farmhouse alone with Hew Vanner. Already there were rumours. They had reached Miss Dukes, the librarian, at the lending library in Seascale. She had a cousin who worked in the hotel at Wasdale.

Gossip was already drifting in its subtle but sure fashion from mouth to mouth. Miss Dukes said little to Aunt Caroline when she went to change her book, beyond the fact that her friend often saw Mr Vanner going into the local for a beer and that everyone thought him 'a queer customer'. Taciturn and unfriendly and there was an air of mystery about him. Miss Dukes was quite surprised, and so was everyone else she said, to hear that little Miss Moore had taken a secretarial post with him. Of course, there was the housekeeper, Mrs Berry, in the farm, *but* ... It was that significant *'but'* which was so suggestive, and which worried Aunt Caroline. Really, although she had a sense of humour and her policy was *live and let live,* this *was* an awkward affair; not the sort of job she would have wished for poor Briony. She had hoped the girl would have been back in Seascale by now looking for younger and brighter companionship. But no! She seemed more than ever settled. Aunt Caro had been holding a lengthy correspondence with her sister Lorna on the subject. Lorna and Geoffrey were not equally worried about their daughter. They, too, were modern—tolerant parents. They did not approve of trying to dominate over their young daughter or control her life. She had chosen this job and it *seemed* in order and she *seemed* so much more cheerful and philosophic about Clive—that was really what they had wanted. So why grumble? Besides, the whole family *knew* Briony. She was sensible and could take care of herself.

But yet another man around the place! Who *was* this Dick Forrester? Aunt Caroline hummed and hawed and tentatively questioned her niece while they had tea together in the garden.

'I haven't the least idea who he is except that he is just a Mr Forrester who is well known as a member of the Travellers' Union, and a famous lecturer,' said Briony airily.

She had described her jaunt in the Bentley—a glowing account of that wonderful tour of the Lakes.

'*Very* nice, dear,' murmured Miss Shaw, and had a horrible vision of her innocent niece crushed between those two mysterious men—*both* wanting to make love to her! *So* lucky Briony was a *good* girl, but it must be a temptation—for *them,* anyhow!

'Don't you think it's time you went down to Reigate to see your parents, dear?' she added to Briony.

But Briony said that although she longed to see Mummy and Daddy again, she could not get away at the moment because Hew was working like a nigger on the book; in fact he dictated so fast now that she was in arrears with the typing. Lots of carbon work and so on—copies to be sent to America. Thrilling! She couldn't describe how much she loved the job.

Aunt Caroline saw that there was no getting

Briony away from Monks Farm.

That night when Briony returned home from Seascale—after she had had supper with Aunt Caroline—she found Hew in the study to which she had been drawn by the sound of a clicking typewriter. She was amused to find him solemnly poking two fingers slowly over the keys, and dragging the roller back so irritably that the bell clanged a protest.

'Hi!' said Briony. 'That's my machine. Mind out!'

He looked up, pipe between his teeth and brows knit.

'I thought it was *my* machine,' he snapped.

She giggled.

'*Our* machine! But as I've got to use it, I don't want amateurs putting it out of gear.'

Now a slow smile broke the severity of Hew's face. Briony never failed to notice what charm there was in that face when Hew smiled. He got up and threw his pipe on the desk.

'You win! I can't type for toffee.'

'What were you trying to do, anyhow, if I may ask?'

He scratched his head.

'Oh, get some of this stuff copied. I've been going such a rate and you're such a long way behind. That's not a reproach to you, of course. I've just not given you the time for transcription.'

Briony took off the short coat she was wearing over her cotton frock and unwound the scarf from her head. She looked very pretty in the soft lamplight. She was really a *pet,* he decided, with a stirring of his blood. He had never known her difficult or exacting like other women and—thank the lord—never deliberately coquettish. She seemed to be a finely balanced young woman, with a genius for platonic friendship.

'I'm not in the least tired,' she said. 'I've been lying in Aunt Caro's garden sun-bathing. Then I went down and had a swim and now I feel I could jump over the moon, and, by the way, there is a very beautiful moon tonight.'

'Are you suggesting I should jump over it?'

She laughed. It was delightful finding Hew in this mood. She seated herself at the typewriter and adroitly slipped in three sheets of paper with carbon.

'What are you doing?' he asked.

'An hour's typing—perhaps more.'

Said Hew firmly:

'Absolutely not. Much too late and this is your day off.'

'Don't bully me,' said Briony, 'I like typing at night.'

He argued, but in vain. She turned a deaf ear. Now he looked at the straight, graceful figure and watched the incredible speed with which the slim, sun-browned fingers moved over those keys, and again he felt his heart stir with strange affection for her. She was a game little thing as well as a nice one. What a lot of compliments old Dick had paid her! He had seemed quite taken with Briony. Well, what man wouldn't be? Heavens! That flaming golden red of her hair—what a colour! Glorious!

A little ashamed of his feelings, Hew sat down at his desk and began to correct the chapter that he had dictated yesterday.

Nothing would stop Briony from typing for two solid hours but at half past eleven he resorted to physical force. He took both her wrists in one hand and held her tightly while he pulled the cover over the typewriter.

'You go to bed, young woman! No Union would permit overtime at his nocturnal hour.'

She laughed and stretched.

'Well, I *do* feel a bit tired now.'

'I should think so! You must have done at least five thousand words by the look of it. Terrific! Thanks a lot.'

'Good night,' she said.

'Good night, Briony. And don't get up too early if you feel exhausted.'

'I shall be at my typewriter at the usual time, so don't use that as an excuse to oversleep *yourself,'* she said, laughing again, as she walked out of the room.

She was absolutely thunderstruck about twenty minutes later when she heard his voice in the passage outside her room. A rather sheepish voice which said:

'You'll find a cup of tea on the mat outside

your door. Typing's thirsty work, I'm sure. Good night.'

She opened her door and found the little tray. Cup and saucer were odd. The tea was too strong and so black that she fluttered her eyelashes at it. And it was horribly sweet. But it was wet and warm and she drank it gratefully, giggling a little to herself. Really, how unexpected of Hew! Making tea for her!—Obviously he had never done such a thing before. He did not know how to make good tea. Or was it that they drank that kind in the 'bush'? She could just see him and Dick Forrester sipping some such liquid out of a tin can, over a camp fire, with hyenas howling around them (or tiger with eyes like headlamps in the dark!).

She thought a lot about the two travellers, and in particular about Hew, while she threatened her digestion by drinking the powerful tea. And the more she thought, the more she liked him. She was beginning to find out that he had a heart; a streak of great kindness. Any display of weakness reduced him to a stammering schoolboy—that big, clever, courageous fellow. Most unusual! But one had to like him.

During the week that followed, these two—author and secretary—came to know and like each other much better. It rained every day but neither of them noticed that. They were so busy. But one or two evenings when it was dry and a full moon silvered the beautiful wild lake, they went out walking together after supper. Hew paid her one or two compliments awkwardly. She was a good walker—like a boy—tireless, and it was a treat to go out with her, he said. He was sure she could outwalk any girl. And he liked her spirit of contentment, he said. He couldn't bear people who were always grousing.

'I am a bad-tempered fellow so I don't like others to emulate my example,' he said one evening with a laugh, as they climbed the hill back to the farmhouse.

'I haven't found you bad tempered,' said Briony, 'except when you have been provoked, now and again.'

'I can remember being very unpleasant to you when you first came.'

'I dare say I asked for it,' she said generously.

She was amazed because he was actually apologizing for his gruffness. And for the first time since she arrived at Monks Farm, she no longer felt afraid of offending him, or being flung out of the place at a moment's notice. He had silently but definitely offered her the hand of friendship since Dick Forrester left.

Hew Vanner, himself, was staggered to find how much he had grown to rely on this young girl, not only for work but for companionship. He enjoyed their walks—and their talks. Deep down within him he had envied Dick Forrester his facile manner with women. Wished he could have that kind of camaraderie with Briony. Perhaps he had been more than envious, even a little *jealous* of the way Dick had appropriated her.

They climbed the hill arm in arm. It was the first time he had ever taken her arm like this. She felt an extraordinary vibration right through her—the strongest and strangest thrill of delight—a sensation of security, too—of strength. *His* strength.

When they reached the door of the farm, he turned her round and bade her look down at the glistening lake, then at the dark purple of the mountain etched sharply against the moon-silvered sky. A sky studded with a million stars.

'I've never seen it more beautiful,' he said, 'have you?'

'Never,' she said.

It sprang to his mind suddenly that he should have added the words, 'nor you'. For there was an almost unearthly loveliness about Briony, with her flaming hair subdued to silver in that brilliant moonlight, the stars drowning in her eyes. For the first time in many long years the man was stirred to passion—to a wild leaping of the blood which urged him to draw this moon-nymph into his arms. Her face was upturned to his with a half-shy, half-provocative smile. What would she do if he kissed her? He hardly dared to think, except that he was sure that wide soft mouth of hers would be extraordinarily sweet to kiss. Then Briony's face seemed to dissolve in a mist of painful recollections. He seemed to see that *other* face—pale and tragic—the features of his lost Anne. No, *no,* he told himself fiercely. He could never love another woman; never go through that hell again. He was mad even to contemplate kissing Briony. What was the matter with him? Had this glorious summer's night and a pretty friendly girl bewitched him?

He turned from Briony and spoke with a harshness he was far from feeling:

'You cut along to bed—I'm going to have a final pipe. I want to do some research.'

Briony's own inexplicable thrill vanished. Somehow the way he looked at her and spoke to her now made her feel ashamed of herself—even resentful. Just when she thought he was so nice.

'Good night,' she said with an abruptness to match his own, 'thanks for the walk.'

And so passed a crucial moment in both their lives.

He worked her almost to a standstill during the next forty-eight hours, and was extraordinarily irritable as well. He reduced her to a state of nerves. Nothing that she did was right, and she had to re-type thousands of words to please him. She was at a loss to understand his sudden change of attitude. It was so illogical, when he had apologized for being a bear and seemed anxious to make amends. She began to wish Dick Forrester would come back so that there could be a little more gaiety and relaxation in the house.

She did not suggest sitting with Hew in the study or going out for walks with him as usual once their work was over. She gave him no chance to suggest it either. She felt quite hurt. She either went into the kitchen to chat to old Mrs Berry (who was much more friendly these days and had grown used to her presence in the house), or went to bed.

They worked all Saturday that week-end. At four o'clock Hew stopped.

'I think I shall scrap everything I have dictated today,' he said in a growling voice.

Briony flushed and pursed her lips. Really he had been impossible lately and he was tiring her out.

'That would seem a pity,' she said.

He rang three times, then snapped:

'What goes on? Where the dickens *is* Berry? Is the bell broken?'

'I'll go and see,' said Briony coldly, 'the bell is in order. I heard it ring.'

He looked after the charming figure. He realized that he had been most unpleasant to his young secretary lately and he thought badly of himself for it. And yet—it wouldn't do to let himself go 'soft in the brain about a pretty girl,' he thought darkly, especially one who was living under his own roof. Nothing doing! It wasn't done. Old Dick could be flirtatious and get away with it, but *he* just wasn't built that way. Possibly he took life too seriously. But the leopard couldn't change his spots. And he never had been one to give a light kiss and forget it. He would not 'start anything' with Briony Moore.

He wondered what had happened to Berry, and why tea hadn't come up. He looked briefly through the pages Briony had typed today and disliked what he had written. Utterly dissatisfied with his work—with himself—with his loveless, restless existence—he suddenly and savagely tore his manuscript into pieces.

TWELVE

Briony walked into the kitchen feeling—for her—in a poor humour. She had had about enough of Mr Hew Vanner for today, she decided, and neither his brain-power nor his glamour as an explorer nor his occasional flashes of charm could make up for the way in which he treated her. She had worn herself out working for him and her only reward was his snarling temper.

'Men think they can get away with anything!' said Miss Briony Moore aloud, with a toss of her red-gold head.

She paused as she walked into the kitchen. Mrs Berry was crouching in her wicker chair by the window, looking like a sick monkey, nursing a bandaged hand.

'Oh,' exclaimed Briony, 'goodness! You've had an accident, Berry.'

She had dropped the 'Mrs' some time ago. She had got so accustomed to hearing Hew shout 'Berry' all over the house, and the old woman was no longer ill-disposed towards her, although, to be sure, she did as little for Briony as she could and still muttered about 'extra work' and 'these seketaries'. But Briony had become tolerant of her particular humours and could understand them. The old nurse was in her seventies. She suffered from rheumatism and a back strained in her youth, but she did more in a day than any woman half her age.

Mrs Berry grunted at the girl.

'Scalded meself. Drat the thing! It was the old kettle. I knocked it over. Must be getting old.'

Briony drew near her, much distressed. She could never bear to see anybody in pain.

'Oh, dear, how hideous for you! Nothing can be more painful than a scald. What have you done for it?'

Mrs Berry sniffed and avoided the girl's sympathetic gaze.

'Put a bit of butter on and tied it up.'

'Absolutely wrong!'

'What's wrong?' snapped Mrs Berry and cast one of her old angry glances at the young secretary. She wasn't going to be told her place by a young chit, even if she could type fast and appeared to be all she should be. In actual fact, Mrs Berry had developed a sneaking admiration for Briony. Her primary feelings of jealous loathing had gradually faded. She had been forced to admit that this was a *nice* young lady. Did her share of the work without murmur and never 'told on her', where others might have complained. And always pleasant to *her*. She had to admit, that too.

Briony was telling her the modern method of treating burns and scalds.

'What you want, Berry, is a nice soothing saline compress, and I shall put it on for you right now.'

'You go back to your typewriter,' began the old woman. 'I was only waiting to get me breath and then I'll come along with the tea.'

'You'll do nothing of the sort. *I'll* get the tea. I'll take Mr Hew his cup and then I'll be back to see you.'

Mrs Berry grunted but relaxed in her chair with a feeling of secret relief. It was her right hand, and giving her 'gyp'. She sat silent and watched out of the corners of her eyes while Briony moved around preparing the tea-tray. Efficient, all right. No nonsense about her, and a pretty picture, too, with her flushed face and her bright hair and her graceful young figure. It was quite nice to have something young about the house. Emma Berry was becoming a very old lonely bitter woman. The one great love of her life had been Master Hew. It had been grand getting him back under her care, but she knew it was only a temporary thing and that he would soon be gone again, on one of his wanderings. The long years of looking after Mr Berry hadn't been very happy ones for her. She'd only married him because she was lonely and on the shelf. Then she had found out that the only thing that mattered to William Berry was the bottle. She had had years of humiliation trying to keep the neighbours from knowing that William drank. It had really been a relief when he had lurched one night out of the pub and got himself run over. She had wanted a child passionately, too, and even that had been denied her. She had felt miserable and thwarted. *This* girl might have been a daughter of hers, she thought—no—a grand-daughter. She was losing herself in daydreams while she nursed the injured hand. Briony took the tea-tray into the study and then returned and threw Mrs Berry a mischievous smile.

'Our lord and master isn't too pleased that I am not going on typing. But I'm *not.* I am going to do your hand up and then have a cup of tea with you, Berry.'

The old woman was delighted but she snapped:

'Mercy on us—you can't!'

'I shall, too! I am not going to be slave-driven. I am a modern girl,' said Briony with a giggle, and added: 'You know, Berry, you and your precious Master Hew must think you are living in the dark ages when people hurled orders at their menials. I don't mind occasional tantrums, but I'm not going to be stormed at for nothing. For two pins I'd pack up and go back to Seascale tonight.'

This was where she might have expected the old nurse to say: 'Good riddance.' She was quite surprised when Berry gave her a shocked and disapproving look and said:

'Don't you dare walk out on my Master Hew. He needs you for his book.'

Briony raised an eyebrow. She had mixed a bowl of saline, taken a chair beside Mrs Berry, and started to unbandage the injured hand. This was where Mummy's training came in, she reflected. Mummy was a great authority on first-aid treatment, having been a V.A.D. during the war.

'I thought you'd be glad to get rid of me, Berry,' she said.

'Ouch, you're hurting me, *mind out!*'

'Sorry, ducks, I'll be as gentle as I can,' said Briony, full of pity as she exposed the burn.

'And don't you call me "ducks",' muttered Mrs Berry with a sniff.

Briony laughed.

'Aren't you a "ducks"?'

'No, I'm not, and you know it.'

Briony continued to tease and Mrs Berry to snap. But by the time the poor hand was finally treated and put in a sling—Briony had fetched one of her own scarves to make it—Mrs Berry had thawed out completely. She told Briony where to find the special shortcake she had made yesterday, and they sat together over their tea, chatting like two old cronies.

Briony had never known the old nurse so friendly—so forthcoming. She forgot Hew's bad temper and began to enjoy the relaxation of this hour in the lovely kitchen with its bright copper pans, and white scrubbed table, and red-tiled floor. It was one of the best and brightest rooms in the house, and beautifully warm. That was because of the new, shining stove which Hew had put in when he bought the place.

Now Mrs Berry was asking her why Master Hew was in such a bad mood.

'That's what annoys me, Berry,' said the girl. 'He seems to get annoyed about nothing. He picks on the first person at hand, and I suppose it is the poor secretary. But was he *always* like that?'

She had finished her tea and started to polish some silver which Mrs Berry had collected on the table just before she had scalded her hand. Briony was cleaning it well, which further enhanced her in the old woman's eyes. Mrs Berry became confidential.

Master Hew had certainly not always been 'like that'. He used to be the 'loveliest boy', she said. She had a photo upstairs, she'd like to show Miss Briony. A picture he was, with his thick dark curls and bright eyes and sturdy little figure. He'd always been strong and brave. He used to play at 'explorers'. Lived in a world of his own. Poor lonely child. What had he to help him grow up into a happy man? Precious little. No mother, and that devil of a stepmother, and a foolish gone-to-seed father. Little wonder Master Hew lost his natural gaiety and became morose.

'Little wonder,' Briony echoed and now began to feel more kindly disposed towards her employer again. She, herself, had had such a divinely happy childhood with Mummy and Daddy. She could pity lonely, neglected children. And she could see how old Berry must have worshipped Hew and what it had meant to her when she was turned out by the horrid stepmother.

'What a boy my Hew was,' old Berry sighed, watching while the girl burnished one piece of silver after another, 'what a one for bringing home strange plants and animals. Filled his room with curios, he did! He had a soft heart, too, and grieved when any of the animals died. He used to come to me with his eyes full of tears and say: "Nanny" (that's what he called me then), "Nanny, why do such beautiful warm creatures have to die? Why is Nature so cruel? What is the meaning of it all?" But I couldn't tell him. And I was his only friend. He used to go off by himself on long walks in the country and get into trouble because he got back late. His father never understood him. It was a tragedy his mother died, because she was a proper lovely lady. From the Highlands. Beautiful and good. I'll show you a picture of her, too.'

And old Berry insisted on going to her room and bringing back the photographs. Briony found herself strangely interested. She stopped polishing and looked long and curiously at the grave, lovely face of Margaret Vanner—the Scottish girl who had brought Hew into the world. Briony could see now from whom Hew had inherited his fine features. Mrs Vanner looked as though she might have been a trifle 'fey'—hers was a truly Celtic face. They were full of temperament and feeling, the Highlanders. What a lot the boy must have suffered when his father brought that common painted little second wife into the home. How he must have hated her!

'Tell me more, Berry,' said Briony.

There was nothing old Berry liked more than to talk about her Master Hew. He had wanted to go into the Navy, she said, but it was not to be. He could not satisfy his passion for world travel *that way*. The Don had wanted him to get a degree and eventually become a scholar and follow in his own staid footsteps.

Then the Don had died, and stepmother disappeared and Hew—was hurled into the World War.

'I was the only one to see him off to it,' Mrs Berry sighed.

And the only one to write to him while he was abroad. The only one to feel a mother's anguish when she knew that Hew—then in the Commandos—was sent on one dangerous expedition after another. Burma, Chindits, and finally the landing in France. He had been in it all. Twice he was wounded but by the grace of God only superficially. A few weeks in hospital and back to what he considered the greatest war of all times. The war to end wars.

'And let's hope it does,' added the old nurse darkly.

'I couldn't agree more!' said Briony.

Another sigh from the old woman who was sorting snapshots in a box and handing them from time to time to the girl. Briony examined them. It was odd and satisfying learning to know Hew like this, through the eyes of one who must surely know him better than anyone in the world, since she had been everything to him from babyhood. How she loved her photos! Hew, as a schoolboy looking embarrassed. Hew, serious-eyed—distinguished even as a stripling—at Oxford. Hew, in uniform taken out East. Briony could appreciate the strong bond that there was between the man and his old devoted nurse. She began to understand a little better, why he was given to outbreaks of temper, and so much bitterness. He must at one time have been the loneliest boy in the world. And then when old Berry told her about the one girl in his life, and that dire tragedy, she was shocked almost to speechlessness. Her own romantic young heart was touched to the quick by the story of Anne Graham—the beautiful girl blown to pieces in that dreadful raid.

'Oh poor, *poor* Hew!' Briony cried with a catch in her voice. 'How perfectly *awful* for him, just when he thought he had found a wife.'

'Ay!' said Mrs Berry, nodding. 'There's been a dark fate against my boy from his birth, and *I* have seen how he has suffered.'

'Did you ever meet Miss Graham? Did you approve?'

'Ay. She was a beautiful young lady with a sweet nature. I had tea with them both a month before the V2 fell.'

A bell clanged noisily through the kitchen. It clanged again. Mrs Berry pursed her lips and started to get up.

'That'll be the master.'

'I expect it will be for me. He probably thinks that I have sat in here nattering long enough. I'll go,' said Briony. 'You stay "put" and don't dare use that hand. I'm going to cook the dinner tonight. No arguments, Berry, you can give me all the directions and I'll carry them out.'

'Well, it's very good of you and I'm sure I don't know how I'd have managed without you,' said Mrs Berry.

With these words of tremendous concession ringing in her ears, Briony left the old nurse and went to answer Hew's call.

He was sitting on the edge of his desk gnawing at a thumb-nail and frowning at the manuscript he held. He flung Briony a critical glance as she entered the study.

'I suppose you think you've finished work for today?' he said.

Briony, whose mind was teeming with all that the old nurse had told her, felt more than usually generous and inclined to humour this man. It was extraordinary, she thought, how those photographs and the detailed account of his boyhood had made him seem so familiar to her. He was now someone whom she knew very well. Someone for whom she might feel compassion as well as admiration.

'I'll do a bit more work,' she said, 'if that's what you want.'

He knew he had been unpardonably churlish and he regretted it. He gave her the faintest smile. (She knew that lift of his lip—the first faint indication that Hew was 'melting'.)

'I don't really think that I ought to make you do any more. It's nearly six,' he said.

'I can take it,' said Briony.

'Well, just a page or two—something I've thought of.'

'Okay,' said Briony.

He glanced at her dubiously.

'You've very gay all of a sudden,' he observed.

'I thought I was always the soul of brightness,' she said.

'Humph, I hadn't noticed it.'

'Ah, but then you never notice anything,' said Briony. Then grew hot and pink and added: 'Sorry. A girl mustn't speak to her employer like that.'

His brows drew together. He stared at her nonplussed. What had got into her? He'd never known her to be so flippant. What a provocative little devil! A shaft of late sunlight filtered through the window and became tangled in her glorious hair. Swiftly he looked away from it and back at his manuscript. He didn't want to be disturbed by the beauty of this girl or her fresh charm. He would not let her destroy his peace—dig too deep under the surface of his emotions. It wasn't that she was deliberately doing so; he was sure of that. She probably hated him and looked on him as a disagreeable tyrant, but she was a darling, the way she put up with him.

'How's old Berry's hand?' he asked gruffly.

'Better. But she won't be able to use it for a few days. I'm going to cook the dinner.'

He stared.

'*You.* She won't let you.'

Briony rolled some paper into the machine.

'Oh, yes, she will. Berry and I are now the best of friends.'

Hew rubbed the back of his head with one hand.

'My goodness me! The world will come to an end if Berry allows another woman to step into her shoes in *her* kitchen.'

Briony flung him a withering look.

'How do you expect her to manage with one hand in a sling?'

'Very good of you to have done it up for her,' muttered Hew.

'Well, she can't use it, and that's that. And she's quite willing to let me work under her directions.'

'I'll hand it to you if you have really conquered my Berry!'

'She's jolly nice once you get to know her,' said Briony.

Now Hew's severe granite face broke into a real smile.

'She must think you're "jolly nice", too,' he said, 'and quite rightly. I think it's very sporting of you to be so kind. She was pretty unpleasant to you when you first came.'

This unexpected praise brought the colour into Briony's cheeks. She felt too embarrassed to look at him. She took refuge in further flippancy.

'Folks in Monks Farm seem to like being unpleasant.'

'Touché,' said Hew. 'Sorry, Briony. We do behave badly to you, and the only person who knows how to say "thank you" really

nicely for all that you do, is old Dick. And he doesn't live here. I shall have to ask him to come and stay and make the balance.'

Suddenly Briony felt unaccountably irritated.

'Do you find it so difficult to say "thank you", yourself?'

'Perhaps I do,' Hew admitted.

'Oh, well—let's get on with the work,' said Briony, and added with a sniff: 'And please don't worry about my feelings. I don't really take the slightest notice of you or Berry.'

'I'm sure you don't. Why should you? A bright young thing like you coming into this dismal old house, with its dismal occupants.'

Briony was staggered by such humility. She was also touched. But it had the effect of making her self-conscious and, in a way, she did not want this proud dominant man to 'climb down' because of her. So she astonished both Hew and herself by flushing bright scarlet and snapping his head off. Yes, it was *she* this time who was being temperamental.

'Oh, for goodness sake let's get on with the work and stop blathering!' she exclaimed.

Meekly, Hew began to concentrate on his book and dictate. But the expression in his eyes when he raised them and looked at Briony's straight young back and bright lovely head, was extraordinarily tender.

THIRTEEN

One morning towards the beginning of August, Hew came down to breakfast somewhat later than usual. He had slept badly after having had one of his worst nightmares. And those nightmares of Hew's were concerned with some of the truly appalling experiences which he had undergone during the war years. They were getting less now and the memories dimmer, but they recurred when he was overtired. Last night he had sat up till the early hours—long after his young secretary had gone to bed—revising a particularly difficult chapter in his book.

He paused in the hall to sort the mail and heard two voices in the study.

Briony's fresh one said:

'Now don't lecture me, Berry. I think it looks very nice and it's going to stay there.'

Then Berry's voice—surprisingly soft and gentle:

'You *are* a caution, Miss, I never thought of doing such a thing for *him*. He isn't one for that sort of thing. But I admit it looks nice.'

Hew's brows contracted, what on earth was the *'it'* to which they kept referring? He was beginning to feel that these two females were conspiring against him. But he had had to hand it to young Briony that she had broken through his old nurse's defences. That was all to the good. It meant peace in the household. Berry, herself, had commented on the excellence of Briony's cooking during those days when she had scalded her hand.

'It's a rare thing to find a young lady who can make such good pastry,' she had said.

Hew had agreed. He had enjoyed Briony's cooking and he had begun to discover quite a lot of things that were 'rare' in this girl whom he had taken on as his secretary. Now in the long summer evenings, she was even to be seen doing a bit of gardening; trying to make something out of the wilderness. She was never idle. And they had resumed their habit of walking together by the lake and taking an occasional visit in his car to old bookshops in the neighbouring towns.

He was slowly but surely beginning to get used to her feminine companionship and to the little touches that only a woman could bring into the house. Small material comforts which the old nurse did not think of. Berry's kingdom was the kitchen and the washing and the ironing. But Briony took an interest in the rest of the house. With his permission she had altered the drawing-room considerably. Found some beautiful material which had belonged to his own mother and had been kept locked in a moth-proof trunk—heavy silky stuff—which she made into curtains. She had rearranged rugs and cushions. Kept the room bright with fresh-cut flowers. He had never thought of entering it before but now found himself often wandering there, finding the cool fragrant feminine *salon* refreshing and a unique experience for the hardened bachelor.

What was the *'it'*? He must see. Letters in hand, he wandered into the study.

The old nurse bade him 'Good morning' and hurried to the kitchen to put on the coffee. Briony looked bashful. And now he followed her gaze and saw that she had placed a huge silver bowl of red roses on his desk. She must just have picked them for they still had the morning dew pearling on their velvet petals. He blinked at them.

'For me? Good lord! I think you ought to put them in your own room, my dear child.'

'What?' she challenged. 'Don't you like roses?'

'Of course, but on my dusty old desk—'

'It isn't dusty. I've just dusted it.'

He bent and inhaled the fragrance of the flowers. He hardly cared to show how touched he was by this personal attention. Gruffly he said:

'Nice child! You are always doing something agreeable. You know—I think you must be a very happy person, Briony.'

'Why?'

He looked down at her thoughtfully. She was as fresh and fragrant as one of the roses, he thought. The day promised to be hot and she wore what he presumed these young women called 'a sun suit', with two straps over bare tanned shoulders. She looked delicious in it. He felt a brotherly affection for her and wanted suddenly to hug her. Then with an unaccounted leaping of the pulses, he knew that it was no brotherly affection that he felt. But the altogether dangerous and heady passion of a man who might easily fall in love. That he should even *think* so far horrified him. But as she repeated the question: 'Why?', he stammered an answer:

'Because—well—old Berry herself was only saying the other day you are like a sunbeam in the house.'

She grimaced and laughed.

'How horrible! I don't want to be a sunbeam. It sounds too *too* sweet!'

That was the sort of jargon he did not quite understand. He supposed he took life too seriously. Never, even at this girl's age, had he been so blithe of heart. He added:

'What she meant and what I meant is—you give a lot of happiness out to those around you. That must come from inside *you.*'

For a moment she did not answer. She had picked those roses and placed them on his desk with some trepidation, in case the gesture annoyed him. You never knew with Hew. The fact that he seemed pleased about it and was paying her a compliment increased the tempo of her heart, but she did not answer him because she was thinking how queer it was that *he* should think her happy and say that she gave happiness to others. How could that be? When she had come here in June, it had been with a broken heart and a life shattered by Clive's cruelty. All love—all hope of love—had been taken from her. When she had folded and put away the things in her trousseau she had felt that she was folding up a great big piece of her life; that the lid had closed down on it for ever.

How was it that now she felt such new happiness? Yet it was so—she had revived much of her zest for life, and the fount of her tears had dried up since she had started her job in this queer old house in Wasdale. There were times when she forgot that Clive ever existed. But she thought of him now. She thought of him and remembered the anguish of love—the anguish and the breath-taking ecstasy. There was still that strange look of Clive about Hew Vanner. Just at times, when there was softness in his gaze, he became Clive to her again. Retaining always his own strong individuality. But for the most part he was such a man as Clive Dormer could never hope to be.

Her silence—a queer shyness which had overtaken her—suddenly made itself felt by Hew. It troubled him. He gave her an almost anxious look.

'You *are* happy at Monks Farm, aren't you, Briony?'

'Yes, of course.' She jerked out the words, her face carnation pink under the golden tan. He found his gaze wandering to slender polished shoulders and the beauty of rounded arms and dimpled elbows. Heavens! he thought. Did she realize what an effect she had upon a man? *Upon him?*

'Breakfast time!' he suddenly said in a loud and masterful voice. 'Come along, young woman.'

She followed him, conscious of her swiftly beating heart. In that moment, deep in her consciousness, she thought:

'If Clive appeared here and now and took me in his arms as he used to and begged me to love him again, I wouldn't. *I couldn't.* I've fallen out of love with him.'

But she had not fallen out of love *with love.* There was no real accounting for the fact that she had grown so absolutely content in Hew Vanner's house, despite the solitude, the long hours of hard work and the complete lack of gaiety.

Her people could not understand it. Aunt Caroline could not understand and kept making dark allusions to the 'unsuitability of the job'. Mummy kept writing and asking her when she was going home. But she didn't want to go. She had no intention of going. *She couldn't bear to go.* And why? She wasn't prepared to answer that question. She sat in stony silence at the breakfast table, with Hew who had buried himself in *The Times* and never gave her another look.

Just before he got up from the table she reminded him that this was the day that Aunt Caroline had been invited to lunch, to see his treasures.

'Oh yes,' he said vaguely, 'I remember. Well, you and Berry fix the meal between you and later on I'll try to interest Miss—er—Shaw in my collection.'

Which he did in no uncertain way. He was in a good mood and showed up at his best as host. Briony felt quite proud of him as though *she* personally was responsible. He had beautiful manners when he wanted to produce them and a nice taste in wines and Aunt Caroline appreciated good wine. He had also taken the trouble to change, before she came, into his best grey flannel suit and a clean white shirt. And he brushed his hair (which made Briony giggle). If only Aunt Caroline knew what that mane of hair looked like when he was working! She grinned to herself as she glanced at the well-groomed master of the house. She was very much 'odd man out' while he and Aunt Caroline discussed his travels. He seemed pleased because Aunt Caroline was a good *raconteur* and had visited both India and China in her extreme youth and knew what she was talking about.

Afterwards, they had a high old time examining boxes and boxes of exquisite ivories from Peking. China from Nanking.

Carved teak and ebony from Burma. Oriental rugs. Queer coins. Relics of all kinds from Far Eastern civilizations. Innumerable photographs and paintings. Aunt Caroline, hat off, spectacles on, sat gloating; using now and again, a magnifying spy glass that she had brought with her.

Once she raised an awed face to her host and exclaimed.

'I wonder if you realize the value of some of these things which you call "your junk", Mr Vanner.'

'Perhaps I don't,' he smiled. 'It's been an enlightening afternoon for me. You know much more about the stuff than I do. Perhaps you would like to take a car load away some time for your antique shop.'

'I'd adore to,' said Aunt Caroline, delighted. 'They're priceless.'

At his special request she stayed on to tea. Briony was enchanted because she could see for herself that Hew had quite 'fallen' for her darling aunt.

She had never known him to be so nice, but she might not have felt so pleased could she have delved into her aunt's mind. Miss Shaw, although impressed by Mr Vanner's knowledge and perfectly certain that he was every inch a *gentleman,* and quite a personality, was filled with grave misgivings. She had come here with them, and they increased during her visit to Monks Farm. She kept thinking about the Vicar's wife, who knew somebody who *knew somebody else* in Wasdale. And all the 'somebodies' were talking. Hateful gossip! Aunt Caroline despised it. But one had to be sensible and bow to convention in this world and it was *not* within the convention for a young and pretty girl to be living in a house with such a young and attractive man. The very fact that Hew Vanner did not show his difficult side (Bri was always saying how grumpy and cross he was), and that he was being revealed to Aunt Caroline as a charming fellow, made the whole thing worse. Bri might fall in love with him. That silly old nurse was no chaperone. Aunt Caroline could not help feeling that Bri was in mortal danger (though of what she hardly knew). But nothing escaped her notice. The happiness that radiated from Briony. *Why should she be so happy?* She was supposed to be recovering from an unhappy love-affair. She ought to be hating this job and this lonely old house. And why did Mr Vanner follow Briony round with his gaze? Once or twice Aunt Caroline fancied she intercepted a look between them. A *decided* look, when Mr Vanner openly remarked on the difference Briony had made to his house. All these floral decorations—they were open proofs of Briony's interests in Mr Vanner's establishment. It was all very suspicious and Aunt Caroline did not like it.

She broke her resolutions not to interfere in her niece's life. She forgot to be sensible and intelligent, and she tackled Briony when they were next alone. On Briony's next visit to Seascale.

'Really, darling, you just *cannot* stay at Monks Farm. It's not decent. Mr Vanner is in love with you. Not that I'm surprised. You're very very pretty and he may be a confirmed bachelor (if there is such a thing) but he's only human and—'

'*Aunty!* please!' Briony cut in. She had sprung to her feet and she was looking quite white and shocked.

Miss Shaw bit her lip and began to polish her spectacles.

'Well, my dear, it was obvious to me when I was there. He never stopped looking at you.'

'It's absolutely absurd! I've never heard anything so ridiculous. I don't mean to be rude, Aunt Caroline, but honestly it is absolute *rubbish.*'

'You may think so, my dear, I know better.'

Briony's heart thumped.

'But he could not possibly be in love with me. He isn't in love with *anybody.* He isn't that sort.'

'How do you know?'

Briony gulped. She was trembling. She did not know why her aunt's statement should have upset her so much.

'I just do know. I work with him every day. I know his mind—'

'Now you're talking rubbish, dear. One never knows what lies in a man's mind.

Mr Vanner may not even realize yet that he is in love with you—but he is, and he will suddenly become aware of it. Then there will be trouble.'

Briony stared at her aunt speechlessly. Aunt Caroline had put something into *her* mind which had not been there before. She felt aghast. And furious with Aunt Caroline. It couldn't be true—it just *couldn't.* If Hew were in love with anybody or anything, it was with the memory of Anne Graham. He was awfully nice to her, Briony, at times. He could be charming. But only in the most platonic way. He regarded her as a secretary—*a child.* He often addressed her as 'my dear child'. But *in love* with her—no! Aunt Caroline was mad to suggest such a thing. Briony began to protest stoutly—to tell Aunt Caroline what she thought.

'Besides, even if he were, it wouldn't cut any ice with me—I'm not in love with him, so I am *not* in any danger, as you suggest.'

Aunt Caroline glanced at her niece—at that hot indignant young face.

'Methinks she doth protest too much ...' Aunt Caroline tried to remember exactly what Shakespeare had said. She was so bad at quotations. She became more than ever suspicious. After Briony had gone home she decided that it was high time her sister Lorna came up here and took Briony away.

The girl had been badly hurt by Clive. What can be more vulnerable than a tender woman's heart, bruised and hurt by unhappy love? She was so liable to feel another love on the rebound and that was the most potent and dangerous of all. Hew Vanner was an admirable fellow in many ways but there was far too much gossip going on about him in the Lake District—he was far too mysterious to be safe. It just would not do for the child to continue living under his roof, with nobody but that old woman to safeguard her.

Miss Shaw did not want to interfere or do anything drastic but she felt that her sister ought to know what *might* happen between Briony and that man—before it actually happened; before it was too late. For Hew Vanner could never be any good to Briony. He was a wanderer. *Probably an adventurer.* Anyhow, he was absolutely the wrong man for Lorna's little girl.

Aunt Caroline said no more to her niece. She was going to wait for the cheap-rate time—then telephone to Briony's home in Reigate.

FOURTEEN

'I'll have another three minutes,' said Miss Shaw clearly and firmly to the operator who had just informed her that she had already had six, to Reigate. Never in her life had she done anything so extravagant even in the cheap-rate hours. But she considered that this occasion demanded it. Her young niece was in jeopardy. She must make it quite clear to Lorna that she should trump up some excuse to get her away. That was why she had put this call through to Reigate after Briony left Seascale.

Briony's mother sounded less perturbed than Aunt Caroline, if a little surprised.

'I really feel, my dear Caroline, that Bri can take care of herself and knows what she is doing. Geoff and I don't believe in interfering—'

'Neither do I!' broke in Miss Shaw, 'and I wouldn't mind if it was just that Bri had found a nice young man to take Clive's place. I would consider it the best thing that could happen. It was what we wanted. But this man—I won't mention names over the wires—is *most* peculiar. And there is Briony often alone with those *two* men—'

'But surely the second one doesn't live at Monks Farm, too?' interrupted Mrs Moore.

'No. But he stays there.'

'Well, there's safety in numbers,' said Mrs Moore with a touch of humour.

Miss Shaw grew angry.

'I don't think you're being very sensible, Lorna. I tell you that it's not advisable to let a pretty young girl like Briony stay in that house with *him*. He has a bad reputation.'

This was not strictly true but Aunt Caroline

in order to get her own way was being unscrupulous—all out of her genuine concern for her niece, of course. But like so many women who wish to gain a point, she was not averse to exaggerating a story.

Before that three minutes was up, she had cast an all too lurid light upon the explorer to whom Briony was secretary, and had wiped old Mrs Berry out as a useless chaperone. She ended, indeed, by disturbing Briony's mother. After all, Briony was all that they had. Clive Dormer had broken her heart and they certainly did *not* want her to fall in love with an undesirable man and so court a second disaster. Hew Vanner sounded a trifle 'odd' to say the least of it. Perhaps he already had a wife living somewhere, apart from him. One read such awful things in the papers. Who was to know? Lorna had never really wanted Briony to take that job. Besides, she missed her girl. She would have so much preferred her to settle in a post nearer home. Lorna ended by soothing her sister's fears.

'Now don't fly off the handle, my dear Caro, I'll talk to Geoff and we'll think what is best to do. It's all very trying because Bri's letters have been so happy lately and we had hoped that she was getting over the Clive business.'

'Yes. And pray who is *helping* her to get over it?' asked Miss Shaw with sinister emphasis. Then she added:

'Why don't you come up north for a bit

and stay with me and see Bri? Or stay at the hotel at Wasdale near Monks Farm? There has been more rain than usual this summer but I think we are in for a dry spell and ...'

Here the call ended, Miss Shaw was not prepared to have another three minutes even for Briony. Lorna just had time to tell her that Geoff could not get away at the moment. He was doing an important job connected with the Festival of Britain. But they would try and induce Briony to come home if only for a week-end—and see for themselves what she was like. They would get her back, somehow, Lorna would think of a way.

With this, Miss Shaw felt easier. In Wasdale that same evening Briony returned to Monks Farm with mixed feelings.

Before going off to Seascale for her usual weekly outing, she had felt light-hearted—pleased with life—her job and the niche she had made for herself at Monks Farm.

Now everything seemed mysteriously and indefinably changed. She had laughed at Aunt Caroline's 'nonsense' about Hew falling in love with her. She knew it to be untrue and absurd. She had scoffed at the accusation that she was in love with *him*.

But all the way back to the farm, her aunt's words kept recurring and troubling her. Usually, as she made the journey from Seascale to Wast Water, Briony gave herself up to purely aesthetic pleasure in the wonderful scenery. But this evening she saw nothing. She remained wrapped in troubled thought. And the more she tried to repudiate her aunt's suggestions and laugh at them, the more uneasy she became.

The idea had been put into her head. Subtly but potently it worked upon her imagination. She knew perfectly well that she had learned to like, to admire and to have implicit trust in Hew Vanner, which was saying a lot. At times, of course, he was fiendish—put all her nerves on edge—drove her to distraction because he was so difficult and sometimes so overbearing. But those other times ... when he was charming and paused a moment to break through the clouds in which he seemed to surround himself and become human and friendly ... were they not very wonderful? And supposing he stopped being the man whose whole interest lay in exploring—in voyages of discovery? Supposing what Aunt Caroline imagined became a truth ... and he began to look at *her,* as an ordinary man looked at an ordinary woman? As Briony was *used* to being looked at. With a thoroughly normal male admiration for a pretty girl? What would she think about it? What effect would it have upon her? He was so utterly different from Clive. Older and a more powerful character. There was something almost frighteningly harsh about Hew at times. How could one possibly imagine him melting sufficiently to behave like a love-sick boy; to come down from his high intellectual altitude to an ordinary romantic level?

She still tried to laugh scornfully at the mere idea. It wasn't possible. Hew Vanner would never fall in love with *her*. Any heart that he ever had, lay buried with poor little Anne Graham. Nevertheless, Briony remained conscious of that indefinable change in her own feelings. For she *could* imagine a situation arising in which she was stirred to more than platonic friendship for *him*. She *could* imagine a woman—herself—falling frantically in love with Hew. Not in the happy carefree *young* way that she had loved Clive. Oh, that Briony had gone for ever—so ignorant of the world—so very mundane—blissfully in love with a fascinating boy who seemed equally in love with her. They had been engaged. They were to have been married. And she had thought the world ended when he walked out on her.

But it hadn't ended. Life had only just begun. The laughing, careless girl had become a more serious and knowledgeable Briony who felt herself capable of more profound emotion. *Frighteningly* capable.

And once having admitted to herself that there might be something in what her aunt had said, there was no turning back. The notion worked like a drug, insidiously, until her whole being became absorbed by it. She could not look at him without remembering what had been suggested. She was afraid not of him but of herself. She must not let this thing happen. She would only be hurt again and perhaps far more badly. For she was certain that this man who had come so suddenly and strangely into her life would depart from it with equal suddenness. She would be crazy to allow herself to care for him *that* way. And if, indeed, the dangerous seed that Aunt Caroline had planted in her mind should blossom into reality—better to kill it on the spot. She must not allow such madness to develop. Hew Vanner would never be any good to her or any woman. He was wedded to his work.

But Briony felt more than a little perturbed when she faced Hew that same evening. It was dreadful, she reflected, her cheeks hot, that her aunt's remarks could have such effect. That she, Briony, could no longer look into Hew Vanner's eyes with the same frank unconcern and coolness. She felt her lashes flutter as he glanced in her direction. Her heart gave a meaningless extra beat.

'Had a good day?' her asked quite genially.

They had met in the hall when she walked into the house. He was looking his untidiest, hair ruffled, shirt open at the neck, pipe in the corner of his mouth. He carried a large box.

'I've got a lot of papers packed in here that I want to sort,' he told her. 'Some notes and photographs that I need for tomorrow's dictation. I should have done it this afternoon but a boring old archaeologist who had been given my name and address called on me and stayed and blathered and wasted my whole day.'

Then he walked into the study with his usual lack of ceremony. Briony followed. Balancing on the edge of her desk, she watched a moment while Hew rummaged in the box of papers. Now and again he pulled out a photograph and tossed it to her.

'I shall use these,' he said.

She looked at them, biting her lips. Her heart-beats had calmed down. She could almost laugh at the way she had allowed herself to get worked up. Here they were back to normal. As for him looking at her with any romantic inclination—Aunt Caroline could not be more wrong. Briony Moore was nothing to Hew Vanner but a good typist. He was not really interested in what she had done today at Seascale. Why should he be? With his usual absorption in himself and his work, he now began to draw her into it—at nine o'clock at night—as though she had never been out.

This went on for about half an hour. Then suddenly Hew put down his pipe and pushed back his chair.

'I didn't really mean to get started and I'm sure it is time you were in bed,' he said.

She slid off the desk and picked up her scarf and gloves.

'I think I'll go and make myself a cuppa.'

He looked at his wrist watch.

'Oh—I thought it was later. It's only half past nine. What's it like out?'

'Perfect. The light has just faded. It should be wonderful soon—full moon tonight.'

'Are you tired?'

'Why?' Her heart was starting to beat fast again. He was focusing his attention upon her. That little smile lifted the corner of his mouth. That sudden look of *Clive.* It *was* disturbing. She really felt much safer and happier when he was the brusque hard taskmaster with whom she could have a tussle.

He walked to the window and looked out.

'Yes—it's a pretty fine evening. I have been stuffed up in the house all day and I wouldn't mind a walk. How about coming?'

Now she found herself stammering.

'Wouldn't you rather go alone—you can get farther?'

'No, I'd like you to join me. I don't mean a long trek, my dear girl. Just a turn—down to the water's edge.'

She wanted to go. She wanted to refuse. She did not know what she wanted. But inevitably she was pleased with his invitation. It was like that, with Hew. His friendly overtures were so few and far between—one could not help being flattered by them.

After her conversation with Aunt Caroline, she knew that she ought to say 'No', and go up to her room. This was the sort of thing which would horrify Aunt Caroline—her taking a lonely walk by the lake in the moonlight with Hew!

'Just a moment—I'll get my other coat. It's a bit cooler now,' she said and turned and ran out of the room.

She came down again wearing a short red jacket in which he had seen her before. He liked it. Red suited her. He was surprised to find what a lot of things he noticed about this girl now. She was a familiar figure in this house. And she was fast becoming a necessary part of his life. He had missed her while she was at Seascale today. And it was not the first time that he had become conscious of a blank when she was out of the house. Of course, he didn't notice it when he was working, but when he stopped work—like this—he found himself definitely requiring her presence. As for their evening walk—that had become a ritual; something to look forward to. She was a charming companion. Old Dick was quite right—he had been lucky to find Briony Moore.

He mentioned Dick's name as they walked down the hill.

'I had a letter from old Dick this morning. You know this business—this speech he is making for me—the dinner is all fixed for the three of us. We're both going to town, aren't we?'

'I think you ordered me to accompany you,

sir,' said Briony demurely.

He gave her a quick smile.

'Now, now. It's not as bad as that. I can't *really* order you about.'

'But you do.'

He gave a sudden sigh.

'Ah me! What an unattractive chap I must be! I have none of old Dick's graces. He'd be a pleasant fellow to work for. Poor Briony, I'm afraid you've had a tough time at Monks Farm.'

Before she could restrain herself, she said: 'I'd rather work for you than for Dick Forrester.'

Hew found himself extraordinarily intrigued by this remark.

'Now why?'

'Oh, I like Dick immensely—he's great fun—but I couldn't stand his flippancy all the time,' said Briony.

'Flippancy? You mean the way he pays you compliments?'

'Rather too many of them.'

Hew's eyes opened wide. He didn't know much about women, but he thought they could do with any amount of praise. What a funny little thing Briony was! He rather liked the fact that she did not wish to be flattered.

'Well, well,' he said, 'what you say is a bit of a reflection on me, actually. I never praise you at all.'

Now she gave him a quick upward look

and dug her hands firmly into her pockets as they walked along. It was, as she had prophesied, fast becoming a glorious night. The moon had risen. The sky was cloudless and a deep purple blue. The stars were coming out in their millions. The mountains looked mysterious and beautiful against that luminous sky. And Wast Water was a sheet of purest silver. The only sound came from the throat of some night bird frightened by their approach, winging into the shadows of the trees.

Briony decided to ignore what Hew had said. She plunged into another subject.

'Isn't this more beautiful than any of your jungles? Doesn't it compare favourably with any of the great lakes or rivers of the continents you have explored?'

'I admit I have learned to love this part of the world,' he said, 'it is soft and gentle. But it doesn't always appeal to me.'

'No—you don't really like softness or gentleness—you like things to be fast and harsh and frightening.'

'My dear child, what a sweeping statement. How do you know what I like?'

'I can only judge from what I have learned from my association with you.'

He raised his brow and thought a moment before he spoke again and then he said:

'As a matter of fact you're wrong. I may like the odd grand canyon, and mighty river, and inaccessible mountain peak—what you might call formidable country. But I like *people* to be gentle. I have no use for human cruelty.'

'Nature is cruel—Nature in the raw—isn't it?'

'Very often.'

'Well, you're crazy about Nature.'

Now he flung her an almost humorous look.

'What are you trying to prove—that I am a monster?'

She gave a laugh which held a tinge of nervousness.

'Not at all. But I think you enjoy being *thought* a monster.'

'My dear, funny little Briony. I rarely worry what people think about me. You ought to know that. But if I'm so hard and lacking in the soft sentimental side which old Dick produces now and again, perhaps it is the result of my unfortunate boyhood, and a still more unfortunate episode in my life during the war.'

She knew that he was alluding to Anne. With swift sympathy, she said:

'I understand. And really I don't think you are all that hard. And, anyhow, we've got right away from our original discussion. I meant it when I said that I would rather work for you than Dick Forrester.'

He felt suddenly and ridiculously pleased.

'Well, thanks, Briony. And I think you've been absolutely grand,' he said. 'I can never thank you enough for the way in which you have worked for and with me. If my book is a success I shall owe a great deal to your intelligent and industrious assistance.'

It was her turn to feel pleased but she gave a little giggle.

'You do sound pompous!'

'There you are! Even when I pay a compliment, it is in the wrong way,' he grinned. 'I wonder you put up with me. But you won't have much more, so cheer up.'

Now she turned and gave him a quick look of dismay.

'Why do you say that?'

'Well, another month, perhaps more—perhaps less—we shall be through with the book.'

'Does that mean I'll get the sack, then?'

'Don't put it that way. Just that I shan't have any more work for you and I shall probably be going off to the Amazon with Dick.'

'Oh,' said Briony in a small voice.

They were standing now by the water's edge. The lake shimmering before them. They were absolutely alone in the splendid desolation of this loneliest of the lakes. Briony felt as though a cold wind blew chill upon her. As though all the radiance went suddenly out of the stars.

In that moment she knew definitely that she could not bear her life with this man to end. And so terrifying and overwhelming was that revelation of her feeling towards him, that it flung her into a state of panic. *She must not feel this way.* She had been saying so to herself the whole evening. She had been trying to forget Aunt Caroline's absurd accusation and here it was smiting her in the very face.

Hew threw the end of the cigarette which he had been smoking into the water. He slid an arm casually through the girl's. He was surprised to feel that the slight graceful figure was shaking.

'Are you cold?' he asked with concern. 'Even on these summer nights by the lake, you know, there is always a treacherous little chill in the winds.'

'I'm not cold,' she said.

He thought that he had never seen her look more charming. Her head was classic and beautiful; her curls silver in the drenching moonlight. But his observant gaze noted the trembling of her lips and he could not fail to see that something was wrong.

'What is wrong, my dear?' he asked.

'Nothing, nothing at all.'

'Do you want to turn back now?'

'Yes.' She whispered the word.

He felt an inexplicable disturbance of his own heart and soul. His senses were alive, too, to her beauty—her soft femininity. It was an intoxicating night. With some cynicism he told himself that Dick or any other man might have made the best of a sentimental hour with a lovely girl on the shores of this glorious lonely lake. What held him back? Was he so feelingless these days—so hidebound by his life's work and travel that he could no longer be stirred by such a night—and by such a girl as Briony? Had all emotion dried up inside him for ever ... because of Anne?

It seemed to him that suddenly the ghost of Anne crept through the shadows and joined them there by the silver water, looked at them both and crept away again. What had she come to say? To beg him to go on being true to her memory ... or to put all thought of her aside and take to himself another love? *Briony.*

This sudden idea so shattered Hew that for a moment he could neither move nor speak. It was as though he were held in a thrall. But he had a sudden desperate longing to break through the granite crust and become the young, tender-hearted Hew who had loved Anne Graham—who had wanted a wife and children—the precious intimacy of love instead of the lone hard trail of the explorer.

For an instant he lost his head. With a rough brisk movement he drew Briony into his arms.

'You are cold. You are trembling, my dear. Why?'

He stammered the words. And she in his arms, felt such immense astonishment, such a suffocating rapture that she had to lean her full weight against him in order to keep herself from falling.

'Oh, don't,' she said in a terrified voice. *'Don't,* Hew.'

'What are you afraid of? Dear little Briony—you are so very sweet—I would never hurt you. You were made to be loved, *darling—'*

The endearment broke through his lips with difficulty as though torn from him. A word he had not used through all the long bitter years during which he had mourned for Anne. But now that it was said, it was as though a bomb exploded at their feet. Passion mounted in Hew's head like wine as he felt the soft fragrance of Briony in his arms. A strand of her hair drifted against his cheek. He buried his face in that red-gold hair and breathed a little harder.

'Briony ... look at me ... let me kiss you, Briony.'

But for her this was far too perilous. It was as though the stars and moon together had shattered into a million atoms and she was caught up into one dizzy crazy kaleidoscope. She felt that if he so much as touched her mouth with his she would lose all sanity—all reason. For the briefest moment she clung to him, close, close, so close that she could feel the thudding of his heart against her breast. The moment was hers for the taking. Whatever happened in the future she knew that now it was she who might control the destiny of this strange fascinating man. He was not only Hew in this hour. *He was*

Clive. Her past love—her future love. All the loves of the ages rolled into one. It was a victorious, exhilarating moment. But young though she was she could still be sufficiently controlled and far-seeing to call a 'halt'; not allow this thing to happen. For Aunt Charlotte was right—oh, so right! She was in love with him, passionately and madly, and far more seriously than she had ever been in love with Clive. But he did not love her. This would not last with him. He was only surrendering to the weakness of the moment. A kiss—an embrace—and then back to work. Nothing to him—he was a man! But for her it meant another end of another world. A fresh tragedy and this time one from which she would never recover. For as she stood there in his arms she knew that no woman could love or once be loved by Hew Vanner and then forget.

She felt his hand on her hair, his fingers tracing the contour of her face. She heard that new vibrant note in his voice, urgent with desire.

'Kiss me, Briony—'

But she tore herself out of his arms and without uttering a word, began to run away from him. He called after her:

'Briony, wait.'

She did not answer and did not wait. She ran as though she were pursued by all the demons of a darker region. It was herself from which she was flying, not him. Of that she was well aware. Her eyes flooded with tears and her breath came in great sobbing gasps as she climbed up the hill. She ran blindly. Once she looked over her shoulder but she saw nothing. He had not followed. Naturally. She knew her Hew. Nothing would have induced him to pursue her. No doubt he was so humiliated by the way in which she had accepted 'his sentimental moment' that he would never take her for another walk. Perhaps he would not even want to work with her any more.

Oh, Aunt Caroline, you put it into my head and I hate you for it. I hate you. It must have been there all the time—this surging, terrific emotion of love for him. It must have been waiting like a volcano to flame into action. But I didn't know it. I was happy and at peace. Now I shall never know peace any more and I shall never be able to be friends with Hew again.

FIFTEEN

Briony found it difficult, after she got back to the house that night, to get herself into the right mood for sleep. It was an alarming and more than disturbing thing for her to realize how intensely she felt about Hew. And she kept wondering, in a positive fever, how he would behave when he saw her next. The fact that he had drawn her into his arms and called her 'darling' did not mislead her. Briony had never been vain. And it never entered her head that Hew Vanner would look twice at her seriously. She told herself with wry humour that all he had done was to prove himself human. The great Hew could, after all, be carried away by the glamour of moonlight and a girl. But, thank goodness, he hadn't kissed her. At least she hadn't given herself away too badly. But if she had felt his lips on hers, *that* would have been different! She knew that she could not have helped responding.

What could she do now? How could she go on living at Monks Farm, knowing herself to be in love with her employer? How could she bear it? Perhaps he wouldn't want her to stay. But *yes,* she argued to herself. It was most important that he should finish this book. Typists of her speed and precision were not to be picked up easily in a district like this. He couldn't do without her. Rather proudly she decided upon this. Up and down her bedroom she walked, smoking one cigarette after another, until the small half packet which she had left, was empty. Then she thought she heard the front door slam. Her heart gave a tremendous jolt. Hew had come home. Oh, goodness, she thought, he would be in an awful mood! He had probably done the 'strong silent man act' and gone for a long walk and come back fuming at his own weakness.

Suddenly, wildly, Briony began to laugh. But it was hysterical laughter that threatened to end in tears. She controlled it, hastily dabbed powder on her nose, combed through her hair and decided to go downstairs and face the lord and master of Monks Farm. She just *couldn't* sleep until she had seen him. She would never close her eyes. In her impulsive way she felt that she *must* re-establish a correct relationship between herself and Hew before this night ended.

'But I won't forgive you, Aunt Caroline. You put it into my head. You have wrecked my peace.'

Here was where she must act a part, whatever she felt. If only to recover her own pride and sense of lost dignity. And she must help the poor man to recover his.

She ran down the stairs. Afterwards, when she thought about it, she almost laughed at the way she was shaking from head to foot. She wasn't going to let Hew know it. He was in the study. He had poured himself out a mug of beer and sat on the edge of the desk, drinking it slowly. He looked grim, she thought, absolutely grim. How he must hate himself for having asked a girl to kiss him and have her run away as though she had seen a spook!

He went positively scarlet when he saw her, gave her a quick half-scared look and then stared into his beer mug.

'Oh, hallo,' he said in a rather foolish voice.

'Hallo,' said Briony, and felt the sweat break out on her forehead and the palms of her hands. What she really wanted to do was to rush forward and throw herself into his arms, run her fingers through his thick untidy mane of hair, press her cheek against his and whisper:

'I want you to kiss me—I want it more than anything else in the world. You big, blundering idiot, I love you. I worship the ground you walk on. What I felt about Clive was just luke-warm compared with this. It is like a raging torrent drowning me—'

Instead of which she said:

'I say, I'm sorry I rushed away like that.'

And that, of course, was a foolish opening gambit but she just couldn't think of anything else.

Then Hew, who had lost his colour, gave her a cold and somewhat hostile glance and said:

'My dear girl, don't apologize. The apology is due from me to you. I am afraid I behaved like a damn fool. Quite unlike myself. One worse than old Dick ...' he ended with a quite mirthless laugh.

Briony echoed the laugh, feeling as though she were walking on hot bricks—all her nerves quivering.

'My dear Hew, my own behaviour was far worse. You must have thought I was an imbecile. But I assure you it wasn't that I was *scared* of you or—or—anything like that—just, well—I can't explain—but it was so unexpected, it rather shook me. I was once engaged to be married, you know, and you look a bit like, like—the man. I just felt suddenly quite loopy and I tore up the hill—'

The silly words came tumbling out. Like a schoolgirl, she thought; stammering incoherently.

He seemed relieved by her attitude.

'I quite understand,' he said stiffly, 'it was really very idiotic of me and most unorthodox. After all—I am your employer. I do apologize. Please forget it.'

'Oh, I will, I will!' exclaimed Briony wildly. 'I shan't give it another thought.'

Oh, Briony, what a lie? You'll never stop thinking about it. But he's doing exactly what you knew he'd do—regretting it. And you've saved your face, my girl, so carry on.

How could she know she completely misunderstood him? Or how, in his ignorance of women and their ways, he equally misinterpreted her behaviour of tonight? If he had been a Clive Dormer he would have seized her in his arms now this moment and taken that kiss perforce and learned how much she loved him. But he fully believed she had run away because she had been alarmed and even disgusted by his attempted embrace. He had half expected to come back and find her packing. It was a colossal relief to him to find her—in quite a cheerful mood—behaving as though nothing abnormal had happened; taking it all in her stride. He had walked for an hour after she had run away, fighting his inclination to run after her. To behave like a love-sick schoolboy, begging her to be kind; to look upon him with favour.

Fool! *Fool!* he had thought with bitterness. As if a young and beautiful girl could ever look at a grim, dull devil like himself! Besides, he must have offended her susceptibilities. He knew that she had had an unhappy love affair. He ought to have respected her feelings. She was probably still in love with the other fellow. It was generous of her to be so nice about it.

But what of himself? What in heaven's name had led *him* to lose his head down there by the lake? Was it merely a moment of madness—the result of the intoxicating beauty of the summer's night with all the majesty of Scafell towering before them; the utter loneliness and *stillness* down there? And the way *she* had looked ... so very lovely; so desirable.

Or had he really tumbled headlong into love with Briony Moore? If so, then all the more reason why he should control himself, tear this passion out of his heart and mind before it went farther. He was not a marrying man. The only woman he had ever wanted to marry was Anne. He was going to South America with Dick. He had no earthly right to make love to Briony. Even if she had melted in his arms and kissed him he wouldn't have had the right. It would have been even worse.

Yet as he had walked home, brooding over it all, he had felt horribly depressed. And what could that depression mean except that he had a deep underlying longing to turn that moment's madness into something real and long lasting. Into a serious affair? She had been so very sweet in his arms. He had not been able to stop remembering the rich, red curve of her mouth. He had wanted to kiss it. *He wanted it still.*

He turned his back on her.

'Our little stroll seems to have been somewhat disastrous,' he said abruptly. 'I apologize again. It won't recur.'

Briony forced herself to maintain her attitude of nonchalance. She even giggled.

'One never knows what a glamorous night will do.'

His hands clenched. In sudden fury with himself—not with her—he said:

'Oh well, get off to bed—it's late. I want to do some serious work in the morning.'

Her lashes drooped. She thought:

'The same old Hew! How right I was to keep my sense of proportion.'

With a cool 'Good night' she walked out of the study. She found it hard to get to sleep and she knew that Hew stayed up working until the early hours, for she heard his own door shut and saw by her clock that it was past two.

She woke in the morning to hear the telephone bell ringing, and Mrs Berry knocking on her door, calling her:

'Miss Briony—miss, *please,* there's a telegram come over the wires for you, miss. Will you come down and take it?'

Briony, drowsy, and not feeling her best this morning, after such a disturbed night, hastily threw on a dressing-gown and ran down to the telephone. The telegram which was repeated to her, was both puzzling and worrying to Briony. It said:

Want you come home immediately explain when here.

It was signed *Daddy.*

SIXTEEN

A wire so mystifying and ambiguous was bound to throw Briony into a panic. Her immediate reaction to it was: *Mummy must be ill.*

And at once she had a heart-stirring recollection of her pretty, delightful and still young mother who had always been so good to her. Spoiled her from babyhood. Given her that gorgeous trousseau when she was going to marry Clive. Stood by her and helped her through the shattering days after Clive walked out, and been so tender and understanding when Briony left home. Whereas other mothers might have been offended and tried to make their daughters stay with them. Mrs Moore had never been possessive or selfish.

Of course, it mightn't be that Mummy was ill but she *must* find out, Briony reflected. Daddy's wire told her nothing. She would pay Hew and get a telephone call through to Reigate.

Within five minutes Briony learned why Daddy had wired instead of phoning from her home. The old Reigate number was out of order. Briony rang off.

There was only one thing to be done now. She must go straight home. She would catch the early morning express to London. If Daddy had seen fit to wire for her there must be some very good reason.

And what about Hew and her job? She felt awful about *that.*

What Hew felt when she told him the news was indescribable. The moment he walked into the dining-room and saw her, his heart sank. She wore a suit and looked very much as though she was about to take a journey. She was talking to Mrs Berry, who hurriedly left the dining-room when Hew entered it.

For one awful moment Hew thought that Briony had thought twice about remaining with him after last night, but her first words dispelled that fear.

'I've got to to go home at once. My father has sent for me. I am most terribly sorry to let you down. Mummy must be ill. But I'll let you know, and come back as soon as I possibly can.'

Hew did not speak for a moment. He was tired and cross, anyhow. He had been looking forward to losing himself and his personal grievances in a hard day's work. Dismayed, he realized that this meant no work, either today or tomorrow, nor perhaps even the next day. He realized he was about to be thoroughly unpleasant and unsympathetic, but he could not control himself. He almost snarled at Briony. Probably because he was so terrified of losing her. He had grown used to the sight of his young secretary in cotton frocks or slacks, looking about seventeen. This was a very different Briony. A young woman wearing a well-fitting navy gaberdine suit, with touches of crisp white at throat and wrists and a saucy little white boater on the red-gold curls. Ravishing, in fact. Why, good lord! he reminded himself glumly, she *was* once to have been married. She *was* mature. And with more make-up than she usually wore, and that red tempting mouth, she looked both glamorous and sophisticated this morning. He both loved and hated her, with damnable perversity.

'You can't go!' the words came through his

clenched teeth. 'You can't possibly leave me at a moment's notice like this. I told you we had just reached the most important part in my book. It is all in my mind and ready for this morning's dictation. You can't do this to me.'

Briony reddened. At first she felt remorseful.

'Oh, I know it's awful, and I am *terribly* sorry, Hew, but—'

'It isn't a matter of life and death, is it?' he interrupted. 'Nothing else could justify you flying down to London like this.'

'I don't know what is wrong. My father has wired for me.'

'Very inconsiderate of him. Doesn't he know that you are in a job?'

Briony resented this.

'My dear Hew! Daddy wouldn't have wired for me if it hadn't been something urgent.'

His brilliant moody eyes raked the attractive figure. Its very attraction seemed to infuriate him still further.

'Well, if it *isn't* desperately urgent, you ought at least to wait and find out more details. Then we could get in another day or two's work.'

Briony now began to feel as angry with him as he was with her. With crimson cheeks and tightly compressed lips she returned his scrutiny.

'You are quite impossible! Don't you ever think of anybody but yourself?'

'Aren't you thinking of *your*self, young woman?' he snapped.

Afterwards he was slightly ashamed of such childishness. He had seldom felt more unreasonably annoyed—to say nothing of dismayed. His gaze drifted to the suitcase, which stood by the door. So she had packed and really meant to go. The thought of losing her was intolerable. But much more intolerable was the knowledge that he *felt* it to be so—and his own helplessness.

'I won't have it!' he shouted. 'Get off that absurd-looking hat and be sensible. I—'

'I'll do nothing of the sort,' she interrupted. 'I've never met anybody so lacking in human feeling—'

She choked over the words. She had an altogether disturbing memory of a far more human Hew who had so recently taken her in his arms, buried his face against her hair and implored her to kiss him. She heard his furious voice again.

'Typical of a woman! Let's a chap down when she's most needed. You know damn well that I'm working against time to finish this book before I go away. You know it, yet you calmly pack your bag and walk out and leave me high and dry.'

Now Briony raised her voice.

'And you don't care whether my mother is ill or not—you brute!'

'Who said your mother was ill? You're presupposing it!'

'Daddy wouldn't have wired for me if it hadn't been something serious.'

'Well, find out. Ring them up.'

'You idiot. I've already done so and the line is out of order,' stormed Briony, and choked again, aghast at herself for speaking thus to the great Hew Vanner. But if he could be unreasonable and angry, so could she.

He looked quite white. Those brilliant eyes of his were dark with passion. Yes, his rage was quite passionate. And yet she wasn't at all afraid of him. She could stand up to him any time, she told herself, and felt strangely thrilled by the knowledge.

Then he said in a low voice:

'If you leave—you needn't come back.'

Her heart gave a great jerk.

'Very well, I assure you I shan't in the least want to do so.'

'Tell me what I owe you and I'll send you a cheque,' he said and found himself shaking.

She flashed back:

'Don't bother. I haven't given you notice so you needn't pay me.'

'I *will* pay you,' he shouted, 'and don't try and put me in the wrong. You're the one who is walking out.'

She did not answer. She was positively appalled by the turn events had taken. She could not trust herself to speak to him, otherwise she knew she would throw herself into his arms and beg him never to look at her or speak to her so angrily again.

'I've telephoned for a car from the garage,' she said when at length she did find her tongue. 'It will be here any moment. I'm sorry if I have upset you so badly. Good-bye.'

He did not answer. He was filled with an appalling sense of despair. He was also confident, in this moment, that he loved this girl. Yet he could not admit it. Could not break through the iron bars that years of suffering and loneliness had forged around his heart and soul. It was better for her to go. He turned and walked out of the dining-room leaving his breakfast untasted. Briony, trembling from head to foot, walked into the kitchen. Mrs Berry took a saucepan of milk off the fire and turned to her. Her wrinkled, witch-like face was extraordinarily anxious—even tender.

'You've been having a row with Master Hew. I heard you both. It's fairly upset me. And I'm very upset you're going. But you must come back, Miss Briony.'

'I shan't. I haven't time to pack my trunk, but I'll get my aunt to come and do so and send it on to me.'

'Oh, miss, you can't do that. You can't leave *him* in the middle of his book when you know what it means.'

'Your Master Hew is thoroughly spoilt and selfish. He does not think about *me*. My poor mother may be dying, for all he knows.'

'Now, Miss Briony, if he really thought she

was dying, he would be kindness itself and you know it.'

Briony bit furiously at her quivering lower lip.

'Well, he's *had* it as far as I am concerned. I don't want his sympathy.'

The old nurse came close to her and laid a hand on her shoulder.

'Look, me dear, forgive the impertinence, but I know Master Hew so well. After you've gone he'll be wild with himself for not being nicer to you. He only lost his temper because he saw you were going. It's because he likes you so much,' the old nurse added cunningly. She did not want her beloved master to lose his efficient secretary. And she personally did not want the girl to go. She had grown sincerely attached to her.

But nothing that she could say or do held Briony back. Probably she *was* being rather too impetuous—racing home in answer to this wire without waiting for further details. But it was the way in which Hew had received the news that annoyed her. The station taxi came, and Briony stepped into it. For a moment, as they moved away from Monks Farm, she had an awful feeling that she was turning her back on happiness. For she *had* been happy lately working for Hew and living in the lovely old house full of treasures. No more long sessions on the typewriter listening to Hew's stirring adventures. No more strolls down to that heavenly lake—or drives in Dick Forrester's

Bentley. No going to the dinner to hear Dick's speech, either. No party, afterwards.

What had she done? Wasn't she mad to be leaving it all for ever, just because they had both lost their tempers?

The irony of it was that she was about to depart on the most perfect morning of this summer so far. Cloudless sky, no wind, the lake, down there, looking like blue silk. Everything so fresh and green. Scafell Pike rising majestically into the infinite blueness. The sun beating down on the walled-in garden, the grey stone of the farmhouse.

Then, suddenly, Briony saw Hew running after the taxi. Her heart leaped to her throat. She banged on the window and told the man to stop. Hew reached the car. She opened the door. He stood there, panting. He was red and the perspiration ran down his cheeks. He looked at her with an expression of deep embarrassment.

'I say—look here—I didn't want you to go without me saying—' he stammered like a schoolboy, and stopped as though at a loss for words. Briony's heart went out to him in a great rush of tenderness.

'Saying what?' she asked breathlessly.

'That I hope you'll find your mother is all right. I behaved monstrously just now. I do apologize.'

Silence. Briony's face grew red and then white. She realized what it had cost him to run after her and make this apology. She was glad that he had come, and yet ... she was bitterly disappointed. If only he had come to beg her to stay with him—to tell her that he could not bear to let her go—not because of the work, but because he needed her, *her*—she would have been the happiest girl in the world.

But she took her cue from him.

'Thanks awfully,' she said, 'it was very nice of you to bother. I'll ... I'll come back if you like. We'll finish the book as soon as I've found out what's wrong at home. That is if you would like me to.'

She would never know what those words meant to Hew. He felt as though he had been reprieved. A strange load was lifted from his shoulders. He actually put out a hand and gripped one of hers.

'You're a dear—thank *you,*' he said. 'I must say I want my secretary back again!'

His secretary! Inwardly Briony fumed and fretted. That was all she was to Hew—as usual. Her flash of tenderness passed. She banged the car door.

'Good-bye, I must go, or I'll lose my train. I'll let you know when I can get back—that is if you will be good enough to hold the job open,' she said with a formality she was far from feeling.

The taxi moved off. Hew stared at the cloud of dust the wheels raised. When it was out of sight, he turned and walked slowly back to the house. His old nurse met him in the hall and eyed him anxiously.

'A real nuisance for you, Master Hew, just when you are so full of your work,' she began.

He did not answer her. She knew what *that* meant. She knew all his moods. He was going to miss that girl and no mistake.

Hew shut himself in his study. He supposed if he forced himself, he could manage to do some writing in longhand. But he hated it. It was slow and laborious after the easy dictation.

He looked at Briony's empty chair. Painfully empty this morning. Her typewriter was still covered. Her desk had a forlorn air. His heart began to sink very low indeed. It wasn't possible, surely, he told himself, that losing her could mean so much to him. Yet he felt absolutely bereft by her sudden departure. And it wasn't only because of the book. It was because of *her*. He would miss that charming young figure, the hours of writing with her. Their meals together. Her youth and her gay laughter. All the grace and fun and brightness she had brought into his home.

He kept wondering whether that story of the wire had been trumped up and whether she had gone because he really had offended her last night. Yet no—that couldn't be true. She had had the wire, all right. He had heard the early telephone call, up in his bedroom. Possibly one of her parents *was* ill.

He tried to shut out the memory of his

secretary. He must be mad, he told himself savagely, to let such a thing get him down. A man with important work to do and fresh adventure waiting for him—a man who led a life in which a girl like Briony Moore could play no part.

He picked up his pen and began to go through the notes he had made in the early hours of this morning. He thought of Briony at the station now getting into the train. Damn the girl! Why had he ever taken her on and allowed her to upset the even tenor of his existence? She had said that she would come back. But he wasn't sure he'd take her. He wasn't at all sure that he wouldn't write and tell her that it was best that she should stay at home, once she got there.

He did no work this morning. Fuming helplessly he gave it up, tore up some of the pages on which he had scribbled, and flung the pieces in the direction of Briony's deserted chair. Mrs Berry came in with a cup of coffee. He drank it, but when she started to talk about Briony, he made an excuse to get away from her, and took himself for a walk into the village to buy some tobacco.

He wasn't going down to the lake. No—*not there*—to be reminded of last night and his infernal weakness.

He returned to Monks Farm.

He did not do a stroke of work. He could not. Briony's face was continually before him. Her departure had thrown his work—to say nothing of himself—completely out of gear.

Briony meanwhile found the long journey down to London singularly trying. Not only was she worried about the mysterious summons from home but about the man she had left behind her. She really did feel guilty about the work. She had quite decided that she would get back as soon as she could. Even if she never saw Hew again afterwards, she must help him finish his job.

Late that evening, her station taxi drew up outside the old home in Reigate. She had really only been away a short time, but it felt like years. The half-tiled, red-brick house was so familiar and yet had grown strange; looked curiously small and modern compared with the age-old rambling stone farmhouse up in Wast Water. And Reigate seemed enormous—a city—bustling with people and activity after the splendid desolation and loneliness of the lakes.

She had left this house an unhappy heart-broken young girl—romantic in the extreme—curiously undeveloped mentally—and emotionally.

She felt as though she had changed into a much more experienced Briony. As though her association with Hew Vanner had helped her to 'grow up'. One thing at least it had done, she told herself, it had cured her of her heart-break for *Clive.* There was no place in her heart for him now—not even a tender memory. She rather despised him. He had never really loved her. And she had not loved him. She felt that she had had a merciful escape, and she might have married him and been utterly miserable. Now that she knew Hew and had grown to love him—now that she knew what a tremendous thing love could be—the whole affair with Clive seemed insignificant.

Then she was in her father's arms, and they were hugging each other.

'My word!' exclaimed Mr Moore, holding her away from him and looking at her tanned face and sparkling eyes, 'you look splendid, darling. It's a treat to see you.'

She took off her hat and shook back the beautiful red-gold hair with a gesture he remembered.

'Oh, Daddy, I've been so worried. You didn't say a thing in the wire and I couldn't get through when I phoned you.'

'No, it was a dashed nuisance. *I* tried to get *you* but they were working on our line, and we are only just back in order.'

'Is Mummy very ill?'

Mr Moore coughed and avoided his daughter's gaze. Now that he had got her all the way down from Wasdale Head, he felt a little guilty. Lorna was in bed with an exceedingly bad cold, and a temperature only one point above normal. Nobody could call her 'very ill'. Certainly there had been no necessity to send for Briony. But after Caroline's warning, they had decided that the best thing for them to do was to get the child home and see for themselves what was 'cooking', as Lorna put it. Probably Aunt Caroline had exaggerated. She was a bit of an old maid—straitlaced for these modern times. They trusted their daughter implicitly, but they had felt that it would be good to see how the land lay; to see *her*.

Lorna had insisted on that wire being sent, and exaggerated the cold into an 'illness' which required a daughter's tender care. It couldn't do any harm. Bri's own letters all suggested that she had been working at high pressure. It was time she had a rest.

Mr Moore answered Briony's anxious questioning with reserve, took her upstairs and left her alone with her mother, in a man's cowardly fashion. Let Lorna get on with it! This business about the man Bri was working for—probably a lot of nonsense—but Lorna would soon find out. *He* wasn't worried. He had never seen the child so fit. It was a relief when he remembered the thin tragic-eyed girl who left this house, soon after her broken engagement.

Up in her mother's room, Briony sat beside the bed, held Mrs Moore's hand and felt a trifle bewildered. Mummy didn't look at all ill. She was sitting up in bed in a fetching bed-jacket. And on a table lay a tray which suggested that she had just eaten a hearty meal.

'What's it all about?' Briony asked. 'Why

the desperate wire? You're not *really* ill, darling?'

Mrs Moore coughed. She, too, felt guilty. But she, like her husband, was delighted to see such a changed Briony. The girl had put on weight. She looked beautiful and quite radiant. Obviously the Lake District and her job suited her.

But why the subtle radiance?

Immediately the mother was suspicious; and bitten with curiosity. But she asked no questions during the first half-hour. She knew her Briony. The girl had always confided in her and she would soon tell her mother all there was to know about Hew Vanner. But it wouldn't do to shoot questions at her or she would shut up like a clam. So Mrs Moore talked for a bit about herself.

'I think I have got a bad chill. I've had terrible headaches and I knew you wouldn't mind looking after me for a few days. Daddy does his best, but you know he's useless in the house! He spends his whole time in the garden. And our Mrs Mellin is away. Her child has measles. There is just *no one* to do anything for me. Was it awful of us getting you all the way down here, darling?'

That was quite enough to soften Briony's heart and make her feel that she had not come in vain. She adored her pretty mother. She bent and kissed her and said:

'No, of course not, I'm glad I've come. *Of course* I'll look after you, Mums. Just for a few days, anyhow. And then I ought to get back to Monks Farm, because I'm on the most important job.'

Mrs Moore sat quiet. Ah! Now she would hear more.

'Get me a cigarette and have one yourself, darling,' she murmured. 'You had food on the train, didn't you? It's so lovely to see you. Now we can settle down to a nice long talk.'

SEVENTEEN

One week later, Hew Vanner sat at his desk laboriously writing on a sheet of foolscap. At last he thrust it away from him with a scowl. What an infernal time it took, writing when one was used to dictating. He had done less this week than he usually did in one day with Briony.

Lord! How he had missed the girl.

He had not thought it possible to miss anybody so much—except, of course, poor little Anne, after she died.

Even old Berry had mentioned how quiet the place seemed without Miss Briony. It wasn't only that Hew missed her help in his work, either. He found it a dull household without her. His meals were lonely. His walks still more so. And once or twice when he passed that spot in which they had stood together on that fateful evening, he found himself remembering with a wild thrill, what intoxication it had been—holding her in his arms.

Damn it! He would fall in love with Briony if he wasn't careful. Fatal to a man's work and peace of mind.

When was she coming back? Hew lit a pipe and picked up a letter which he had received from her this morning. A short, rather formal little note. He had heard from her telling him of her safe arrival and apologizing for interrupting his job. He had not replied. This one said:

I thought I would be able to get back before but although my mother has nothing seriously wrong she seems to need me. She has such terrible headaches and our daily woman is still away. I simply cannot leave her to get all her own meals when she isn't fit. But our woman has promised to come back on Monday and then I'll rush back to Monks Farm.

It was signed *Yours, Briony.*

He had read it several times. Why? There was nothing in it. What was he trying to *put* in it? How had he expected her to write? Something affectionate? Good lord, he must be getting soft, he told himself cynically. He, himself, was incapable of writing anybody an affectionate letter. He envied people who could express themselves emotionally on paper. He could write reams about a tiger hunt or a trek through the jungle. But not one sentimental word. Yet he might quite easily have written:

I want you back more than I've wanted anything for years. I can't go on without you.

He pushed his chair away from the desk and stood up, grimacing. Yes, he was getting damned soft. The sooner he sailed away from England, and back to the wide open spaces with old Dick, the better.

Berry knocked on the door.

'Please, Master Hew, I'm sorry to interrupt, but a gentleman has called to see Miss Briony.'

'Well, tell him she isn't here, you old noodle.'

'Master Hew, he says now he wants to see you. He says it's important.'

Hew flung his pen on the blotter. Work seemed at a standstill, anyhow. Who was this 'gentleman'?

In a few moments he knew. A slimly built, good-looking young man walked into the study. A man nothing like as powerfully built as himself and yet with a curious resemblance which even Hew could not fail to see. His heart jerked. This must be the man of whom Briony had spoken. *The man she had been going to marry.*

Then the visitor said: 'May I introduce myself? My name is Dormer—Clive Dormer.'

'Ah, yes,' said Hew, and held out a hand.

The two men looked at each other warily. Hew's first opinion of Clive had been one of astonishment over the resemblance to himself. His second was unpleasant. He knew at once that he was not going to like Dormer. He mistrusted the type. Smartly tailored; rather too smooth. Attractive to women, no doubt. What Hew termed a 'dancing man'. The sort one saw on the London dance floors, in night clubs in the great cities of the world. Seldom in the 'wide open spaces'.

Clive said:

'I thought I would find Briony here but your housekeeper tells me that she has gone down to town.'

'Yes, she went home because her father wired for her. I believe her mother is ill.'

Clive pulled out a cigarette case.

'Have one of mine and take a chair,' said Hew passing him a packet of cigarettes.

Clive sat down. Hew lit a match for him, then began to pack his pipe. Clive glanced round the study.

'This looks like hard work.'

'Yes, I'm in the middle of a book on the Transvaal.'

'And Briony has been helping you?'

'Yes, she is my secretary,' said Hew rather coldly.

'Perhaps you are wondering why I asked

to see you as she isn't here,' said Clive. 'And maybe my presence is best explained by the fact that Briony and I were to have been married a month or two ago.'

Hew felt the muscles of his cheeks stiffen. His eyes narrowed. In just such a way they narrowed when, in some lone spot, he encountered an animal which had suddenly become dangerous.

'Oh yes?' he said.

Clive regarded his cigarette end speculatively. 'I don't know whether Briony told you about our engagement,' he added.

'Miss Moore came here as my secretary. I am a very busy man and we have not had much time to discuss personal affairs. But I understood that she was to have been married. I also understood that you broke the engagement.'

This was by way of being a challenge and Clive seized it.

'Is that what she said?'

'I repeat—we did not have much time to gossip,' said Hew in his coldest voice.

Clive raised an eyebrow. He felt himself to be slightly at an unfair disadvantage with Hew Vanner. What an uncouth chap! Far from polite. Physically a rough and bigger edition of himself. Yes, Clive too, saw the likeness and was mildly amused. Little Briony must have been reminded of him quite often, he thought.

Clive Dormer had come here this morning

to make a final and desperate effort to recapture the heart of his former fiancée. After their unsatisfactory meeting in Seascale, his journey to Nigeria had been further postponed. But he had tried to put Briony out of his mind and consider the affair to be a closed book. But he had been unable to do so. Briony was unforgettable. He cursed himself without ceasing, for ever having walked out on her. He had lost something rare and beautiful. No other girl he met came up to her, either in looks or courage or character. He wanted her back. He wanted to make her believe that her happiness lay with him. She had once loved him desperately and he was vain enough to believe that she would forgive him and love him again.

He had also tried to see Miss Shaw at Seascale and failed. But he had soon discovered where Briony was working. One could find out that sort of thing in a small place like Seascale. Hanging round the local pubs, he had also heard stories of the hermit-like explorer in whose house Briony lived. Mysterious—but youngish, and not unattractive—they said. Nobody in the old farmhouse but himself and an ancient housekeeper. It had made Clive a bit uneasy. What sort of chap *was* Hew Vanner? Briony had no right to be living there with him and an old servant.

He still felt uneasy now that he was actually in the house and talking to Briony's employer.

What was going on? Was Vanner attracted by Briony? Did Briony like him? Clive being such a conceited man soon reached the conclusion that Vanner was far too rough and brusque to interest a sensitive girl like Briony. He, Clive, was the sort she liked. But he could see that Hew had something against him. Of course, everybody criticized the way he had jilted Bri. He couldn't blame them. He had behaved like a fool. He should have married her and trusted to luck that he would still get his job.

'Look here, Vanner,' Clive began. 'I don't know how much Briony *has* told you but I feel it only fair to myself to give you a few facts.'

'There isn't the slightest need—' began Hew.

'But I think there is,' broke in Clive. 'Briony hasn't been quite just to me, and I've been pretty hard hit, I tell you. You know I've only just found out her hiding place'—he waved an arm round the room—'no one would tell me before. It's all very well. But I care tremendously for Briony. Everything I've done and planned has been for her. I can't tell you what it has meant to me to have her vanish out of my life like this.'

'None of this concerns me,' said Hew shortly.

'Doesn't it?' Clive put his tongue in his cheek. 'Well, you see, I've heard that Briony has been making your place a sort of hide-out and that you've been aiding and abetting her.'

Silence for a moment. Hew had drawn in his breath sharply. When he next spoke it was in a voice of ice.

'A—hide-out—' he repeated slowly. 'What exactly do you infer?'

'I don't mean to be unpleasant,' said Clive, 'and I'm sure that you don't quite realize that you have been coming between me and my future wife?'

Now Hew changed colour.

'How can Briony be your future wife. You broke the engagement.'

'*She* says I broke it. I say *she* did. Or perhaps at the time it was mutual. I suggested that we should postpone our wedding until we see eye to eye, and she went off like that ...' Clive snapped his fingers in the air. 'When we met in Seascale later on she admitted that she had been too impulsive. But she's stubborn, is Briony. She wouldn't quite make it up with me. But she still loves me. I know that. All I want is a fair chance with her. And I won't get it while she is here—with you. After all—if you were engaged to a lovely girl like Briony, and she dashed off and hid herself in some bachelor's household—how would you view it?'

Those words were like a lighted match to an explosive. The explosive being in Hew's mind. He had listened to what Clive Dormer had to say with a variety of emotions. Jealousy was predominant. He had found out that he was furiously jealous of Clive and his pretentions to being Briony's lover. His mere statement that Briony still loved him had made Hew recoil as though from a sharp blow.

He didn't really know the full story about Briony and her former fiancé. He only knew that she had been on the very verge of getting married to this man. *Was* it her fault? Was she just a difficult young woman who wanted her own way and played fast and loose with a man's feelings? Was she just a shallow flirt instead of the serious-minded girl of his imagination? That night when she had run away from him—had *that* been mere coquetry, for instance? Had she expected him to follow?

He did not know. But, suddenly, furiously, he said:

'I don't know why you are telling me all this, Dormer, but I had better make it quite clear to you that I am *not* interested.'

Clive stood up.

'I wonder,' he said softly. 'I wonder if Briony isn't at this very moment—shall we say—upstairs or in the garden? Is she *really* down south? Aren't you helping to keep her from me? If so, you are doing me a great wrong. And her, too. Briony belongs to me. I am going to marry her. I've got the ring and I've got the licence. And she wants to marry me. She would do so tomorrow if a lot of mischief hadn't been made. You are trying to make it worse, and people are talking. Do you see?'

Then Hew's dangerous temper flared up. He laid his pipe down on the desk. He came within a few inches of Clive, who stepped back, suddenly realizing that this was a very much bigger and better man than himself.

'Get out of here,' said Hew through his teeth. 'Get out and stay out ... I don't want to see you again and I'm not interested in your future wife and, if it satisfies you, she need not come back here. She won't. I'll see to that. Now *get out.*'

Clive cleared his throat and moistened his lips a trifle nervously.

He felt that he had done himself a bit of good in forcing this interview. Rightly he concluded that Briony really was down south with her people. So he could follow her there, where he would have a better chance with her in their old haunts, he reflected. But wrongfully he decided that he need not look upon Hew Vanner as a rival. Briony would never look at him.

He picked up his hat and walked out of the room without so much as a 'Good-bye'.

After he had gone, old Berry returned to her kitchen. Unashamedly she had been listening to this dispute outside the study door. She had chuckled to herself gleefully. Master Hew was throwing out the young man, and well done! She hadn't liked the look of him or the way he had demanded to see Miss Briony. And if that was the young gentleman Miss Briony had been going to marry, she was well out of it. He would never be any good to *her.* But one thing was quite certain. Master Hew was 'dead nuts' about Miss Briony. That's why he had 'gone up in the air', Berry knew. And in Berry's opinion, she was *just* the girl for him. The old nurse was going to pray hard that they would eventually come together—bless their hearts.

Hew sat down at his desk and stared for a moment blindly at his papers. He was shaking with rage. With more than that—with the knowledge (which seemed to him disastrous) that he loved Briony. There could be no other reason why Clive Dormer could have upset him so badly. He had loathed the sight of Clive. He hated the mere idea that Briony might still love Clive, and still meant, as Clive insinuated, to marry him.

Why had she come here in the first place, pretending to be heart-broken and deserted, if the fellow was still so much in love with her? She must have been holding out on Clive. Perhaps she was by no means as innocent and badly done by as she made herself out to be. The whole thing was confusing to Hew, but the one piercing fact stood out: that he loved Briony and that already he was disillusioned. Already this deep new love threatened to destroy him. He was not going to have it said by Clive Dormer or anybody else that he was helping Briony to 'hide' in Monks Farm. He was not going to let his home be used for that purpose. And he was damned if he would allow his name and Briony's to be coupled and discussed, with a lot of low-down insinuations, in the district.

Furiously he began to write a letter to Briony.

He was enclosing a cheque, he said, for salary in lieu of notice. He would ask her aunt to remove her belongings. He couldn't hold the job open. He meant to get another typist at once. And so on. Then he read what he had written. Slowly, deliberately, he tore letter and cheque in half. He shouted:

'Berry! Berry! Come here!'

The old nurse came running in.

'Yes, Master Hew.'

'Pack a bag for me, Berry,' he said, 'and ring up for a taxi. I'm going to take the mid-day train down to London.'

EIGHTEEN

Briony sat with her Cousin Elizabeth under the chestnut tree which shaded them from the warm August sun. It was wonderful, thought Briony, that the fine spell had lasted for her visit home. Mummy was better and lying in a deck-chair just outside the house under a striped umbrella. Briony had just had an exciting half-hour with Liz who was showing her all the latest snapshots of her fiancé and telling her the plans for her wedding.

Liz and her squadron leader—Derek Forbes—were to be married in a fortnight's time.

'I do think it's rotten that you can't get down to be bridesmaid,' Liz complained.

'Well, I can't—it's impossible—if Mummy goes on being well, I shall be going back to the Lakes and staying there for at least another month.'

'You seem awfully keen on your job,' said Liz with a mischievous glance at her cousin.

Briony, glancing for the second time through a small album of snapshots, all of the good-looking Derek with whom Liz seemed so much in love, maintained a discreet silence. Just how 'keen' she was on that job, she was not prepared to confess to Liz or anyone else. The whole thing was useless, anyhow. She had not lied when she had told her mother that there was 'nothing' between herself and Hew Vanner. There was nothing and never could be. But she loved him. In her most secret heart. These few days while she had been away from Monks Farm seemed like weary years. In fact it had been a most nerve-racking time for Briony. It was good to be in the old home, of course, and down south it was much warmer than in Cumberland. She had managed to put in an hour or two of real hard sun-bathing on the lawn in the good old way, and play tennis with some of her old friends in the district. It had been quite fun and not all nursing Mummy or cooking. But, oh, how she hungered for a word from Hew who had not bothered to answer either of her letters. She kept wondering what was happening at Monks Farm and whether he missed her even a little bit—other than as a good typist! She even longed to see Berry again. In fact her heart was up there, by Wast Water, and it could not be denied.

Sometimes she had found herself lying awake re-living that moment down by the lake when she had been held so close in Hew's arms. And she had thought: 'Why didn't I let him kiss me—why did I run away or worry about the future? Why didn't I live just for the moment?'

It might have been such a wonderful moment. And he might never, never again wish to kiss her.

'I must get back, Liz,' she repeated firmly. 'Hew is desperate to finish his book and I promised I would help him.'

'Do tell me what he is like. Aunt Lorna says he sounds a bit odd.'

'Not at all—just like his name—Hew—*rough -hewn,*' said Briony dreamily. 'He is quite handsome and has a fine brain and he's very kind under his gruff exterior. His old nurse just worships him. He had a rotten time as a boy and then ...'

She launched into the story of Hew's love for Anne Graham and its tragic conclusion.

This immediately drew an expression of sympathy from the tender-hearted Elizabeth.

'Oh!' she breathed. 'If it had been *my Derek* ... how awful to learn that the person you loved had been blown to smithereens. How lucky we were to have missed the war. At least, to have been so young while it was going on.'

'I agree. And let's hope we don't have another. Hew says things are jolly bad all over the world.'

Suddenly Liz said:

'Have you ever heard of Clive again? Peter refuses to see him. He tried once or twice.'

Briony coloured.

'Not since that lunch we had at Seascale. I can't tell you how grim it was. You know he wanted to get me back.'

'He had a nerve,' said Liz hotly, 'considering the way he behaved!'

'Oh, he tried to make out that what he did was all for my sake. And that he could not have got this big job as a married man and he wanted to have it all to offer me.'

'Well, it may be true but it didn't justify him postponing the wedding at the last moment. Anyway, *you* should have had the final say. I think he was more in love with the thought of money and power than with you.'

Briony half closed her eyes and looked

through her lashes at the familiar garden of her childhood—the tiny star-white clematis rioting over the front of the house, almost concealing the hanging tiles. The round bed full of Mummy's favourite roses and border of violas. The herbaceous border with the tall delphiniums which were Daddy's delight. The little rock garden, the ornamental pool full of goldfish. Vividly she remembered the day when she had sat under this very tree looking at this same scene, with Liz and Penelope who were to have been her bridesmaids; how the postman had brought another present—*and* that letter from Clive. Even now the remembered pain made her feel a bit sick. Then she gave a short laugh.

'Well, thank goodness I couldn't care less nowadays whether he loves me or not,' she said.

Then she saw Mummy waving to her wildly. Mrs Mellin, their famous 'daily', was standing beside her.

Briony put down the photograph album and ran across the lawn.

Mrs Moore looked flushed and anxious.

'Bri, darling, this is dreadful—'

'What's dreadful?'

'Well, whatever do you think. Mrs Mellin says that Clive is here.'

'Clive who?' began Briony stupidly, and then clapped a hand to her mouth. 'Oh, heavens!'

'Don't see him!' exclaimed Mrs Moore

dramatically. 'I shouldn't give him the satisfaction. How dare he come?'

'Well, if you don't want to see him, Miss Briony, I'll tell him to go away,' said Mrs Mellin obligingly, wiping her forehead on the sleeve of her overall.

After she had gone, mother and daughter stared at each other speechlessly. Before they had time to recover themselves, Mrs Mellin returned pushing wisps of hair back from her perspiring face.

'Well, my word, he's a cool customer. Sat down in the drawing-room he has, and says he isn't budging, till Miss Briony sees him.'

'Then he can wait until Mr Moore comes home and throws him out,' began Mrs Moore.

But Briony, who had grown rather pale, broke in:

'I don't think we need make such a drama of it. I don't know why he's come but I'll go and find out. I'll soon get rid of him.'

She walked into the drawing-room, which was cool and rather dim. The curtains had been drawn to keep the strong sun off the green Chinese carpet which was Mummy's pride and joy.

Clive stood up.

It seemed to Briony in that moment that time slipped back. It was Clive looking as she had seen him many times in this very room, wearing a grey flannel suit, reddish tie and silk handkerchief to match. Dark hair sleekly brushed. He really was very good looking. She was not surprised that he had once made her young heart flutter. She was only a few months older and yet felt quite changed deep down within herself. She looked at him with the cool critical experienced eyes of a woman and wondered why she had ever loved him.

And today she did not even think that he looked like Hew. (Her big, strong, rough-haired impatient Hew whom she adored.)

'I don't suppose you're pleased to see me,' began Clive, 'but I'm really very thankful to see you again, Briony. And if you don't mind me saying so you are looking absolutely wonderful.'

His flattery left her unmoved. She had altered, Clive Dormer reflected, in some indefinable and fascinating way. The enthusiastic, bubbling-over-with-spirits girl had become so cool and serious. There was an expression in her eyes which somewhat disturbed him. It was utterly hostile. He said:

'Briony, I had to come. I had to see you. I have been through hell since you sent me away after our meeting in Seascale.'

'Hell?' she repeated dryly. 'Surely not. That is reserved for girls who have to pack up wedding presents and send them back and tell their friends they have been jilted.'

He went red.

'Oh come, I know I behaved badly, but you needn't rub it in.'

'I have no wish to discuss it. It bores me,' said Briony in a languid voice. 'I would just like to know why you have bothered to come, Clive. I thought I made it quite clear in Seascale that I didn't want to see you again.'

He came closer to her. How exquisitely the sun had tanned her skin, he thought. And how right his father had been the other night when he had told him that there were no two girls like Briony in the world. He had money in his pockets these days and prospects, but the thing he had done to Briony had started to fester in him and it was poisoning his whole life. He wanted her back. God, how he wanted her back!'

'Please,' he said in a low pleading voice, 'give me another chance, Briony. Don't be too bitter. *Please.*'

She went scarlet. This sort of approach embarrassed her, without rousing a single thrill of pleasure.

'I told you in Seascale that things between us could never be reopened. I repeat it now. You have wasted your time!'

'Why won't you give me a chance? You can't have forgotten how much you used to—'

She interrupted:

'Please don't go on, Clive. I *have* forgotten *everything*. I'm not in the least in love with you any more.'

'Are you sure?'

She looked frankly and directly into his eyes. Hew's eyes with a difference—just all the difference. They might be the same shape and colour, but the expression ... *nothing* similar. She said:

'I am quite sure. I repeat, you are wasting your time.'

'Briony, I beg you to reconsider the whole thing,' he said stubbornly. 'I'm mad about you. I always was. You put the completely wrong construction on my behaviour. I've already admitted that I handled it tactlessly and afterwards, when I thought it over, I was ashamed of myself for causing you so much pain. I was a fool. But not a knave. I did not dream that you would chuck me altogether. I hoped that you would agree to a longer engagement and that—'

Again Briony stopped him. 'You really are wasting breath. We've had all this out once. I wish you would go away, Clive.'

He went pale with anger.

'I suppose you aren't imagining yourself in love with another man, by any chance? With *Hew Vanner,* for instance?'

Her eyes sparkled with an anger to match his.

'Don't dare mention his name. What do you know about him? Nothing!'

Clive gave an unpleasant smile.

'But I do, my dear. Much more than you think.'

'You haven't even met him.'

'Ah! But I have. I had a long talk with the great Mr Vanner in his study about this time yesterday,' said Clive looking at his wrist watch.

She gasped.

'You were at Monks Farm *yesterday?*'

'I was.'

Now Briony went quite white. Her pupils dilated.

'What right had you to go there?'

'My dear girl, it's a free country. I just called to see you and as you weren't there, I had a few words with Mr Vanner.'

She was suddenly bitten with curiosity.

'What did you have to say to him? What did *he* say?'

Clive seated himself on the arm of a chair. He went on smiling at her, hands in his pockets.

'You'd be surprised.'

'What did you say to him?' she repeated furiously. 'I hope you didn't tell him anything about me.'

'I told him about our engagement and how misunderstood I am.'

Briony felt suddenly a little sick and frightened. She could not bear to think Clive had been discussing her intimately with Hew.

'You had no right to drag our private affairs up before him.'

'I assure you he was much interested.'

'What did you *say?*' she repeated, exasperated.

'I told him the truth,' went on Clive. 'That I still loved you and that I hoped to win you back. I also said that I thought that in your heart you still loved me.'

Briony changed from scarlet to dead-white. Her heart beat so fast with anger that she could hardly breathe. She burst out:

'How *dared* you? You had no right to say such a thing. It isn't even true.'

Clive shrugged his shoulders.

'I hoped to make it true. But I must admit that you are not giving me a very pleasant reception.'

She began to walk up and down the drawing-room with quick nervous steps. Her eyes glared at him.

'You had no right to say such a thing to him or anybody else. I don't love you. I don't. And I don't think I ever did.'

'Oh yes, you did, Briony!'

'Well, you killed it. It's stone dead. And I shall tell Hew so.'

'You seem a little, shall we say, *het up* about Mr Vanner and what he thinks.'

'If I am, that's my affair.'

Now Clive's gaze narrowed. He stood up and drew nearer to her.

'Take my advice, little Briony, and lay off your Mr Vanner. Nothing doing. He's writing to you—at least, so he told me—to ask you not to go back to Monks Farm—he does not want to be involved. There is a lot of gossip about you being there and it has reached his ears. Save yourself the humiliation of being given the sack and just don't go back.'

For a moment—dead silence.

Briony stood quite still. She breathed so fast that she thought she was going to choke. She was appalled by what Clive had just said. Then she gasped:

'I don't believe it.'

'Ring him up and ask him, if you want to be snubbed. But I dare say you'll get a letter from him in the morning. He said he just did not want to have you back and that I could tell you so.'

'Then you've made mischief. You've said something that's made him change his mind, because he *did* want me to carry on with my job.'

'Women are not the only creatures who are allowed to change their minds,' drawled Clive. He was now past caring what he said or how he behaved. He had made a last attempt to get Briony back and failed. And when Clive couldn't get a thing he wanted, he could be nasty. He knew Briony. He could see that she was upset. And he was quite sure that she was attracted by—if not in love with—Vanner. Well—if he could put a spanner in that wheel—he was going to.

He heard her voice—rather hysterically—telling him to get out of the house. He picked up his hat and gloves and a folded newspaper and bowed to her with mock gallantry.

'Okay, my dear. This, as they say in films

and books, is the end! You're a darned little idiot. We might have been very happy together. But as a final warning—don't go back to Monks Farm because your reception won't be too good.'

She made no answer. There seemed nothing else to say. When the door closed on Clive, she realized that it was the last time they would ever meet. He had gone out of her life finally and taken with him even her nicest memories of the love which had once existed between them. To her, he was now the lowest thing on earth.

She heard her mother's voice anxiously calling her. She felt herself trembling. Her anger had subsided and in its place crept a horrid sensation of fear. She was afraid that Clive really had done or said something to make Hew reverse his decision to have her back at Monks Farm. Of course, she could deny it all. She would. But that would not stop Hew from sacking her. The mere thought that she might never see him again, or get back to Wast Water, filled her with acute dismay.

Her mother kept on calling her. She opened the door and called back, trying to steady her voice.

'It's okay, Mummy, Clive's gone. Just ask Liz to chat to you for a moment. There's something I want to do.'

Then she walked into the hall and picked up the telephone receiver. She couldn't care less whether it was cheap rates or not. She would pay Daddy. She *must* speak to Hew.

The few seconds in which she waited for that call to get through to Wasdale Head seemed terrifyingly long. Her heart thumped and hurt her. The sweat broke out on her forehead. She hadn't the least idea of what she was going to say but she did know that she must contact him. Clive was such a liar. He might have fabricated the whole story. Or he might really have seen Hew and made mischief She must find out. Then she heard Berry's cracked old voice.

'Yes? 'Oo's calling?'

'Berry—it's me—it's Miss Briony. I want to speak to Mr Vanner.'

''Oo is it?' repeated Berry, obviously not having heard.

Briony almost screamed. She knew Berry was a bit deaf.

'Miss Briony. Bri-o-ny. Don't you know me? Miss Briony. The secretary!' she ended desperately.

At last the old nurse seemed to understand. 'Oh, it's you, Miss. Well, Master Hew isn't here.'

'How long will he be? I must speak to him urgently.'

'He's gone to London, Miss.'

'To London,' echoed Briony in dismay.

'Yes, Miss. He's just this moment left for London in Mr Forrester's car. Mr Forrester arrived yesterday. They should be in London late tonight.'

'Has he gone down on business?'

'I don't know, Miss. He was a bit queer. But he said he'd be back in a day or two.'

Briony's heart sank. And it sank still further when Mrs Berry added that there had been a visit from 'a young gentleman named Mr Dormer' which had upset Master Hew. And soon after that Mr Forrester turned up.

And Berry did not know where Hew had gone or where she could contact him.

A six-minute call brought Briony no satisfaction. It was a very wretched girl who walked back to the garden to her mother and cousin. Clive had, after all, seen Hew. Heaven knows what he had said but it must have upset Hew to send him south so suddenly. *Did he, by any chance, mean to come and see her?* That would be too much to hope for. No, he had probably seized the chance of a lift in Dick's car to come down to town and engage a new secretary.

Two big tears suddenly oozed through Briony's lashes. She felt thoroughly upset. And the whole thing was worse because she did not know what had happened; what Hew thought about her. But she did feel abominably cut off from him. Maybe she would never be able to establish contact with him again. That would be *the end.* Worse—much worse—than losing Clive. Even though she and Clive had once got so near to a wedding; and Hew did not love her. But she loved him and that was all that seemed to matter. Just to be allowed to love him and to go on seeing him and working for him.

She almost disliked her cousin, Liz, who sat there looking so smug and happy, chatting about her forthcoming marriage. Gloomily Briony seated herself by the side of her mother.

'Oh, Bri, what *did* Clive say?' began Mrs Moore, and then paused. She knew her daughter so well. She was slightly alarmed by the complete change in the girl's appearance. She looked as though she had received a shock. She had lost all her colour, and her hands were shaking.

'Darling, is everything all right? Clive hasn't upset you?'

'Not in the least,' said Briony. And then, terrified that she was going to burst into tears, she dashed away up to her room. Mrs Moore and her niece nodded.

'I believe she's still in love with Clive,' whispered Liz, 'poor old Bri.'

Mrs Moore frowned in a puzzled way.

'Well, he certainly seems to have upset her. I don't understand it. I've got it firmly fixed in my mind that she has fallen in love with this mysterious man she works for.'

Upstairs, the object of their discussion lay face downwards on her bed, weeping bitterly.

NINETEEN

About an hour later the Moore family were seated at lunch. Liz had gone home. Briony had pulled herself together, bathed her eyes and dished up the meal with Mrs Moore's help. She still looked very pale, Lorna thought, but as she offered no explanation of her sudden change of spirit—for she had been quite gay earlier this morning—the mother asked no questions. Briony would probably tell her later.

'When do you want to get back to Wasdale, dear,' she began in a cheerful voice, 'because I'm quite well enough to be left now?'

Briony cut in rather sharply.

'As a matter of fact there is no particular hurry. Hew's away on business.'

'Oh, is he?' said Mrs Moore. And wondered how Briony had found this out. Did she get letters from him that she didn't mention? Her mother was still secretly concerned about Briony and her explorer.

The telephone bell rang.

Mr Moore looked up from his plate.

'Bound to be for you, my dear,' he addressed Briony.

With heightened colour she went out into the hall. Her heart had jolted. Of course, it was absurd of her to hope that this might be *Hew.* She would probably never hear his rich exciting voice again. But her wild hope that it might be him was furthered when the operator told her to hold the line for a call from Millom.

Millom! That was near the Lakes. Hew sometimes went in there to search for reference books, or buy some things that he wanted.

Breathlessly she waited. And she found herself praying like an infatuated schoolgirl.

'Please God let it be Hew. Let him say that I can go back!'

But it was not Hew. Her spirits went right down to zero again. It was a strange voice. And it said:

'Is that Miss Briony Moore?'

'Yes, who is it?'

'Hold the line. A Mr Forrester wishes to speak to you.'

Briony's volatile spirits, soared again. Dick ... that at least meant some kind of contact with Hew. Dick might have news for her.

He did. But it was news of a grave kind which Briony had never anticipated. It drove every vestige of colour from her already pale young face.

'Hallo, Briony. It's me—Dick. I am afraid there's been an accident, Briony. I felt I had to tell you at once. It's pretty grim. And I'm to blame. I was driving the car.'

Briony gasped:

'What sort of accident? Where? Is Hew hurt?'

'I'm afraid so.'

'Oh, my God!' Briony choked. 'In what way? Tell me all ... what happened, Dick?'

He told her in a voice hardly recognizable as Dick's usually cheery laughing one. He sounded badly shaken, although he himself had escaped with cuts and bruises. They had been making a detour to Millom as he had some business to do there—going perhaps a bit faster than he should have done at the time, but it wouldn't have mattered, he said, if an enormous lorry, also going at some speed, hadn't come into the main road from a side turning without warning. It hit the Bentley on the off-side. Swung her round and she turned over. It was poor old Hew who got the worst of it.

'I'll never forgive myself,' groaned Dick, 'it's the most damned awful thing to have happened.'

Briony's hand shook so that she could hardly hold the receiver to her ear. She closed her eyes as though to shut out the terrifying vision of the lorry crashing into Dick's beautiful car ... broadside on ... just where *he* was sitting ... oh, heavens!

Somehow or other she managed to ask Dick for further details. He could only tell her that nobody knew at the moment how extensive Hew's injuries really were. It might be his spine ... he seemed paralysed at the moment, and he had concussion. He was in the best possible hands in hospital in Millom. Dick, himself, had crawled out of the wreck, miraculously unhurt except for those superficial cuts. He had been discharged from hospital and was at the main hotel where he intended to stay until he was quite sure that old Hew was out of danger.

Despair quietened Briony down. She asked: 'Is he *in* danger, then?'

'Well, he's not too good at the moment. Although the doctors seem optimistic. But he looks pretty awful and I don't want to leave him.'

'Shall I come up? Can I do anything to help?'

'No, my dear, not a thing, and you wouldn't be allowed to see him, anyhow.'

'Oh, I'm so sorry for *you*, poor old Dick.'

Dick gave a miserable laugh.

'It's sweet of you, Briony. But you needn't worry about me. It's Hew I'm worried about. I'll never forgive myself for this day's work. You know he and I have been on many a trek together and I little thought I'd be responsible for smashing him up.'

Briony shuddered. It was more than she could bear to think of Hew as 'smashed up'; lying unconscious and bandaged in a hospital bed. Hew, who had been so enormously strong and vital.

'Please tell me how he goes on,' she said in a choked voice. 'Please ring me later tonight.

Please. I'm so dreadfully upset.'

'I knew you would be. And I'll phone you later, of course.'

Knowing what he must be feeling, she tried to add a few words of comfort.

'I know how guilty you must feel, but it was the lorry's fault—not yours. Please don't blame yourself, Dick dear. And let us pray God he will be all right.'

When she returned to the family lunch, her father and mother both looked at her with concern. The mother's was immediate. The father's gradually dawned. He was slower to perceive.

Briony looked so ill that Mrs Moore stood up, laid down her table napkin and approached her.

'Darling, have you had bad news?'

'Yes, very.'

'What's wrong?' came from her father.

Briony sat down in her place slowly, as though dazed. She said:

'Hew has been in a frightful car smash and he's seriously injured. He was on his way down south.'

Her parents eyed each other. Mrs Moore bit her lip. She had received so many letters from Monks Farm giving her details about Briony's employer and her work, that she felt she knew him and this came as quite a shock to her.

'Oh dear, how awful!'

And she felt that that was putting it mildly.

It was awful in more ways than one. For she could quite well see that her sympathies need not only be with the injured man but with her young daughter. The child's eyes had taken on that same look of blind anguish they had held when her wedding had been cancelled.

So it was as she had feared! Briony was in love with her employer.

With her usual tact, Mrs Moore tried to put the whole thing on an impersonal basis. She uttered a few well-chosen words to express her distress, then said quietly:

'This means you won't be going back to Wast Water, I suppose?'

Briony blinked at her mother. She felt horribly sick. She kept thinking of Hew ... smashed up ... paralysed ... that was what poor Dick had said. He must have received a spinal injury. Oh, dear heaven, but she suffered for him! *She loved him.*

She tried to answer her mother, conscious that she was giving herself away.

'No—I don't suppose I—will be wanted now. I don't know when ... he will finish this book ... *if ever.*'

Then she put the tip of her fingers against her mouth as though in reproach for those last two words. He wasn't going to die. He *mustn't die.* Suddenly she said in a choked voice:

'If you don't mind, Mummy, I think I'll go into the kitchen and help Mrs Mellin wash up.'

'Mrs Mellin has gone, dear.'

'Oh yes, of course,' said Briony vaguely. 'I can manage ...'

She walked out of the dining-room as though she walked in her sleep. Lorna Moore pursed her lips and nodded at her husband.

'There you are, Geoff. Another calamity. Poor little Bri! She does choose 'em!'

'What do you mean, dear?'

'Don't be tiresome, darling, you must see for yourself that she is in love with this man.'

'Sticking to that theory?'

'But isn't it obvious?'

'She certainly seemed upset. But anybody would be to hear that their employer had just been critically injured in a car smash.'

Mrs Moore sighed.

'Oh, Geoff, you're so unromantic.'

He tweaked his ear.

'Well, if you can find romance in a car smash—'

'I am not *talking* about the car smash, dear. I am talking about the way Briony took the news.'

Geoffrey shook his head. Women seemed to see things men didn't, he thought. Lorna was always putting a sinister construction on something that was being said or done. The nuisance was, he told himself wryly, that nine times out of ten she was right. As he lit his pipe, he said:

'Ah well! I dare say she knows what she is

about. And if the chap is lying on his back in hospital I don't think you need worry about Bri.'

Lorna Moore went a trifle pink in the face.

'Really, darling, you can be frightfully dense. This is just the sort of thing to push her over the edge, so to speak.'

'The edge of *what?*'

'Oh, Geoff darling, go and buy yourself a row of houses and keep quiet,' exclaimed Mrs Moore, and went in search of her daughter.

But Briony was not to be found. She had not after all even abandoned herself to the washing up. Neither was she in the garden. This, Lorna took to be a poor sign. Briony must be in such a state of mind that she had thought a walk essential. Lorna remembered when Bri was a little girl, after getting in some kind of a scrape, she used to want to go for along walk to 'think things out'.

When Briony returned from that walk, she did not mention Hew Vanner and she had slightly more colour, so her mother discreetly refrained from questioning her. But she was still anxious because she felt Briony's calm to be rather unnatural.

It was as though she were waiting for something ... news, perhaps, of the injured man?

And that was precisely what Briony *was* waiting for. With her whole heart and mind concentrated on Hew. And a desperate feeling of anxiety driving all other thoughts from her mind. When at last the call came through—just before the evening meal, she rushed to the telephone with her cheeks on fire and her heart racing.

As she lifted the receiver, she prayed:

'Please God let him be better. Please God don't let Dick say that he is dead.'

It was not the promised call from Dick, but, in fact, old Berry telephoning her from Monks Farm.

With a great deal of snuffling and weeping, and scarcely audible, Hew's old nurse moaned about the accident.

She had had the shock of her life when Mr Forrester told her the news, she said. And there was nothing for it but she must see her darling and make sure that he was still alive. She who had been like mother as well as nurse to him all his life. So she'd broken in on her savings and hired the car from the Crown and Feathers and driven to Millom, to the hospital.

'Oh, Berry, how was he?' Briony was silently crying with the old nurse, the tears rolling down her cheeks. She kept wiping them away with the back of her hand like a boy, ashamed of such an exhibition.

The old nurse said that Master Hew had looked like a mummy, swathed in bandages, except for his head which had mercifully been untouched. White as the sheets over him, he was, and barely conscious, although God was merciful and he was alive and *going* to live, they said.

'Thank God!' exclaimed Briony.

Berry echoed this, but added mournfully:

'Oh, but my heart aches for him, Miss Briony. The terrible news they gave me! It's his spine. He may never walk again, my dear Master Hew—never. Imagine it.'

Briony shut her eyes tight.

'Oh, *God!*' she said under her breath.

'They don't know yet, of course. It may be days before they get to the full extent of the trouble.'

'Did he recognize you, Berry?'

'Yes, bless him. He had only just opened his eyes for the first time. He called me by my name. And he said: "Stay with me, Nanny" ... and that just about broke me down. He hasn't called me "Nanny" for thirty years! But he said something else. About *you,* Miss Briony.'

Briony's heart seemed to stop beating.

'What about me?'

'He called your name, Miss. Then he said: "Briony. I want you. Come to me."'

For a moment the earth and the sun, and the moon and the stars all seemed to stand still for Briony. Down lunged her heart and up went her pulse rate. Her whole body flamed.

'Oh, Berry!' she said in a suffocating voice. 'Is it true—does he really want me? Say that again.'

The cold voice of an operator intercepted: 'Your time is up, caller. Will you have another three minutes?' Then the line went dead. In an agony of excitement, of misery and anxiety and all the emotions rolled into one, Briony banged the instrument, trying madly to get back to Berry. The operator spoke again (which nearly drove her crazy):

'Number, please.'

Then she knew that Berry had rung off. And there was so much more that Briony wanted to know. *Much* more. About Hew and the wonderful, dazzling fact that he had asked her to go to him.

TWENTY

It was pouring with rain and very much colder on the evening that Briony walked into the hotel in Millom and asked to speak to Mr Forrester. He was in that particular place which Dick frequented when he was alone and in a poor humour. The bar. With a mug of ale in his hand he was glancing at an evening paper when Briony walked into the bar preceded by a porter.

The paper almost dropped from Dick's hand. He had spoken to Briony the night before but she had said nothing about coming up. They had had only a brief talk about

Hew's condition.

Dick's sea-blue eyes lit up.

'Well, this *is* a pleasant surprise!' he exclaimed.

With a faint smile she walked up to him and held out her hand. He thought that she looked tired and more serious than he had ever seen her. She was shocked by the change in him. He was a sad edition of the old cheery Dick. His left hand bandaged, sticking plaster over his eyebrow and a swollen lip. He looked thoroughly dejected.

'Hallo, Dick, I had to come,' she said. 'Old Berry said that Hew has asked to see me.'

'Well, I'm dashed glad to see you but—' He paused, as he wrung her hand. He had been about to say that he did not know that Hew had sent for Briony. And, in fact, neither of them knew that the scheming old nurse had done a bit of embroidering on that particular theme. When she had sat beside him, Hew had muttered Briony's name once, but he had certainly not asked her to come to him.

But here she was and with all her heart aching and longing to be with him. The one thing that had kept her from despair was the knowledge that he had sent for her; therefore she must mean something to him other than that 'recording machine'.

Dick said:

'Well, I'm sure you would be a sight for any sore eyes, but I did not think they were allowing poor old Hew to see anybody just at the moment.'

Briony flushed. 'But if he asks for me—' she began.

Now it struck Dick straight between the eyes that this girl was in love with his old friend and fellow traveller. Good lord, he thought, here was a poser! Old Hew was not a marrying man. Incredible to think that he could have inspired young Briony with such devotion. Much as Dick admired his friend, he looked upon him entirely as a *man's* man. The knowledge depressed Dick from his own point of view, for he himself was well on the way to being in love with Briony. The one thing he had been looking forward to most was his dinner and dance with her in London next week ... well, that would have to be cancelled now. At least, Briony's and Hew's share in it, although he, Dick, must still fulfil the engagement and give the lecture.

Briony was begging him to take her to the hospital at once. He did not know what to say to her. He felt very puzzled about the whole affair and not at all sure they would admit her to the ward at this time of night. Then he said:

'Look here, Briony, you had better stay here the night. I suppose you meant to anyhow, didn't you?'

Yes, she had thought she would stay one night at the hotel. She was ringing Aunt Caroline and telling her that she would be going back to Seascale tomorrow to stay until she knew Hew was out of danger. She could at least get over here during the day if and when Hew needed to see her.

She had also tried to convince herself that Hew would soon be better and that they could go back to Monks Farm and finish the book together.

'We'll have a drink and let's think things out,' suggested Dick.

She did not want a drink. She did not want a rest. Nothing would satisfy her but to go straight to the hospital. Dick, despite his own disappointment—for he fully realized that he meant nothing to this girl but a casual friend—was ever gallant. He wanted to bring a smile back to Briony's beautiful young face and he would do so at any price, he told himself. But he warned her that she might not be allowed to see Hew.

Hew was better. But he had had an exhausting day with the radiologist. They were X-raying his spine. He was fully conscious now and had had some food. He was recovering slowly but surely from the initial shock.

'He has the constitution of an ox, so I don't think we need worry overmuch,' said Dick, who was trying to be optimistic. Although he felt that he, Dick, would never recover from the knowledge that it was in *his* car, driven by *him*—that Hew had met with this accident.

Tomorrow, he told Briony, Hew was being moved into a private ward. He so hated the public casualty ward to which he had been taken.

'You know Hew—how much he likes to be alone and fortunately they have got a private room coming vacant tomorrow. You'll stand a better chance of being allowed to see him there.'

Briony agreed but could not settle down until she had been up to the hospital. Dick took her along. He was well known to them now. And with his usual charm and ability to 'bluff' he saw the sister in charge of the ward and managed to persuade her to allow Briony one moment, if no longer, with Mr Vanner.

She had prepared herself for a shock but it none the less made her heart sink to the very depths when she first looked upon Hew. There were screens around him. The big frame seemed rigid and frighteningly still under the blankets in the narrow bed. As Dick had said, Hew's head had been miraculously spared but his colour was bad. His fine eyes were sunken. Otherwise it was a curiously young-looking Hew with the dark rough hair falling across his brow. He moved his head continually, restlessly. His hands were as strong looking and brown as ever. The long fingers curved and uncurved—twisting a fold of sheet.

When he saw her, Hew looked both startled and amazed. The nurse left them alone,

Briony moved to his side, dropped on one knee and put one of her hands over his.

'Hew,' she said in a choked voice.

That was all she could find to say. There welled up in her such a tremendous surge of longing to fold her arms round the ominously still figure and press her cheek against his. The stubble was growing on his chin. His cheeks were waxen. She hardly knew how to restrain herself. She had to control herself with silence—with a pressure of the hand.

In the man, also, was the necessity for supreme self-control. He had not expected to see Briony. He did not want to see her. It upset him. He had been fighting the demons of despair ever since they brought him here and he feared that he was semi-paralysed and might never walk again. For any man—even the laziest and most effeminate—that must be a grim fate. But for Hew Vanner, the traveller, the man of action—to whom health, strength and virility meant everything—it was a profound, a terrible tragedy.

For twenty-four hours he had been barely conscious—lost in a shadow-world of darkness, interwoven with strange sinister dreams. From these he had awakened to the knowledge that he was in a hospital, unable to move. Again and again he had asked nurses and doctors what had happened to him. He demanded that the radiologist should tell him—fretting and fuming whilst they X-rayed his spine. Their reticence, their refusal to answer definitely drove him crazy.

'We don't know yet—we can't tell—'

Those were the sort of evasive replies they gave him. He hated them all. He wanted *facts.* He had never been a coward. He could find courage to face up to the worst news.

He had spoken to Dick. Poor old Dick who was so shattered by the accident. He had spoken to old Berry. Neither of them could tell him a thing.

For hours he had lain here, racked with suspense, and helpless. And during those hours he had thought a great deal about Briony Moore. He had been going down to London to Reigate to see her when Dick's car collided with that damned lorry. After the scene with Clive he had accepted the fact that he loved Briony. He was not prepared to believe Clive's account of the broken engagement. He must see her and ask for the truth. Had he been going to tell her that he loved her? Had he been going to say that he could not have her back at Monks Farm *because* he loved her? Or propose marriage to her—like a lunatic? He hardly knew. All was confusion in his mind. One thing only was paramount. The knowledge that he could never now ask her to marry him. He might have overcome previous obstacles; forsaken his bachelorhood and the old shibboleths for her love and companionship. But now—a hopeless wreck—he had nothing whatsoever to offer a woman, and he was not going to distress Briony by letting her know how near he had been to asking her to marry him. How much he had missed her, hungered for her and how deeply he desired to take her in his arms again. The dark welter of doubts and miseries in his brain drove back the present desire to hold out a hand and pull her down to him until those fresh lovely lips of hers touched his mouth. ('It would be,' he thought, 'like cool spring water against the lips of a man dying of thirst.') It was fine to see her again. He thought he had lost her for ever.

But he growled at her in the old way:

'What are you doing here? Don't kneel by my bed and cry, for heaven's sake.'

She did not know whether to disobey him and to laugh or weep. She had, perhaps, expected a more affectionate greeting. But it was good to see him alive—to know that he had not lost his spirit. She would have hated to find him reduced to a moaning wreck. But, of course, as Dick told her, he did not suffer; that was one of the most ominous symptoms—the fact that he felt nothing. *He was paralysed.* The thought made her catch her breath with fear and pity.

She stood up, and withdrew her hand.

'The nurse said I mustn't stay, but I wanted to tell you what a terrible shock your accident was to me, Hew. I came straight up here because—' She had been about to say 'because you asked me to', but the words stuck in her throat. The first great surge of emotion had been beaten back by his chilly reception of her. She even began to tell herself that she must have dreamed that Berry said he had asked to see her.

Hew said:

'Very nice of you to come all this way to see me. Well! Well! Mad child!'

Her face flushed burning red. Her heart-beats quickened.

'Oh, but I—I came specially to ask if I could help you—I thought you might need me—' she broke off covered in confusion.

He lay still a moment, his eyes brooding.

It would have been so easy to be selfish about this. He was quite certain in his own mind that she was fond of him—how fond he wouldn't quite know—and equally certain that she was no longer in love with her former fiancé! And if she had travelled all this way up from Reigate just to offer him her services she *must* have more than an ordinary affection for him. He was deeply moved. He wanted to take advantage of it and to throw himself on her mercy. To tell her that he needed her more than anything on God's earth—more now than before—instead he said:

'I dare say I won't have anything else to do in the future except dictate. You had better keep the old typewriter in practice until I come out of hospital.'

That gave her hope. But she eyed him doubtfully.

'Why do you speak like that? You aren't always going to be chained to your bed. You're going to get better. Well enough to go down the Amazon with Dick as you've planned,' she added with forced brightness.

He twisted his lips.

'No, I have a feeling that I shall never go down the Amazon with Dick. Haven't they told you—it's my spine?'

'Yes, but it may not be a permanent injury. They have wonderful ways of curing one now. All kinds of electrical treatment—physiotherapy, etc—injections that work miracles! You'll see.'

He gave a short laugh.

'You are quite the little consoler, but I'm afraid I shan't believe a word of it until I find that I can stand on my two feet again.'

'Oh, Hew—you mustn't be too depressed—' she began huskily.

'Don't be sympathetic. I can't stand it,' he said under his breath.

Now her eyes glittered with unshed tears. A feeling of deep depression crept over her. So he was not going to allow her to comfort him. Probably that old fool Berry *had* made a mistake and he hadn't wanted her to come up here. She felt humiliated and ashamed. And yet she could not have done otherwise than come—see for herself what she could do for him. She said:

'I'd better go. Sister said I mustn't stay. I'll drop in tomorrow if I may.'

'By all means, if I don't bore you.'

He said the words without even looking at her. He was staring straight in front of him so that she could not see the stark misery in his own eyes. She murmured a few more words of sympathy but they only seemed to make him cross, so she went away.

Out in the hall, Dick looked at her wet lashes and set lips and felt worried.

'He isn't worse, is he?'

'No—better, they say. And very much himself, snapping my head off,' she said with an unhappy laugh.

'Well, that's a good sign,' said Dick.

She laughed again. But she had seldom felt more disappointed—for Hew's sake so much more than her own. Dick insisted upon her dining with him. She let Aunt Caroline know that she would be late back. She felt that it would be only right for her to try and cheer poor Dick a little. They talked entirely about Hew. That was what she wanted. The result of the X-rays had not yet been disclosed, Dick told her. They would know more about Hew's spine tomorrow.

'I'll be over every day from Seascale,' Briony told Dick before she left him. 'And as soon as he's well enough I suppose he'll be taken back to Monks Farm. Hospitals need beds these days and Berry can nurse him so well—more devotedly than any strange nurse.'

'Yes,' said Dick, 'that was what Hew

wanted—to be taken back to his own home the moment they allow him to be moved.'

'And then perhaps he'll need his secretary and I'll be of some use to him,' said Briony in a small voice.

In that moment Dick Forrester longed to take her hand and say:

'Don't eat your heart out for old Hew. He's no use to you. Try and love me because I love you and I'd marry you tomorrow if you would let me, sweet, beautiful Briony.'

But he was far too loyal to Hew to say anything of the sort. With as much cheer as he could muster, he bade her 'Good-night' and told her that he would meet her at the hotel tomorrow.

Briony returned to Seascale, walked into Holly Cottage, feeling dog-tired and, as she put it to herself, at rock-bottom.

When Aunt Caroline met her with outstretched arms she walked into them with a choked little sound and put her face against a shoulder upon which she had so often leaned for comfort in her childhood. Dear Aunt Caro! Ever understanding.

Aunt Caroline said:

'So you love Hew Vanner, my poor darling! I'm so deeply sorry for you, and for him.'

Briony burst into tears.

TWENTY-ONE

It was another three weeks before they allowed Hew to be taken from the hospital back to his home. Three weeks of mental suffering, not only for him but for those who loved him. A condition far worse than any anguish of the body.

For Hew, the impatient and somewhat intolerant man of action—the long hours of lying in bed helpless and hopeless were dark and destructive to his whole inner being. They tried to dope him, to make him sleep well, but he refused drugs. They also found it difficult to make him eat as much as he needed. He grew painfully thin—hollow-cheeked—gaunt—until it seemed that the big frame was all skin and bones.

The first X-ray plates had not made the specialist in charge of his case over-optimistic. There *was* definitely injury to the spine. The nerve centres were affected. He could not move either of his legs. They had had other similar cases. There were, of course, many histories of recovery. Both physicians and nurses repeated such stories to Hew in the endeavour to lift him out of the slough of despond into which he had fallen. But a dense cloud darkened his spirit. He saw no light. He did not believe he could ever be cured. He was convinced that he must remain a hopeless cripple for the remainder of his days, it not bedridden, tied to some sort of spinal carriage. The prospect appalled him.

Poor Dick Forrester—whose own minor cuts and bruises had healed—suffered acutely on his friend's account. He left the cherished Bentley a buckled wreck in the garage to which it had been towed. He did not care that he had lost a new and valuable car. The insurance would cover that. It could be repaired. But they could not repair old Hew. That was what bit into Dick like acid. He knew exactly what his friend must be feeling—how *he,* himself, would have felt in similar circumstances. It seemed a grim ending to their hopes for further adventure and travel together. Certainly it looked as though the trip which they had mapped out in South America would never now materialize.

Dick cancelled most of his own appointments and remained in the Lake District until it seemed futile for him to stay there any longer. There was little he could do except sit by his friend and talk and try—somewhat in vain—to cheer him up. What could one say to a man whose greatest joy in life had been to sail the sea, to walk, to ride, to lead a man's life out of doors; and, if possible, explore wild and unknown territory? In the long run, the two friends fell into gloomy silence. Finally Dick was forced to go south because he had his commitments. For one thing, his only niece was getting married. The daughter of a sister ten years older than Dick. Dick had to give her away in the absence of her father who was in Canada on business, unable to get back in time. So, reluctantly, Dick bade Hew farewell but with the intention of returning to Cumberland at the first possible opportunity. He still felt responsible for the ghastly fate that had overtaken Hew. He must do everything in his power to alleviate the hours which must be so long and desperately trying for Hew.

There was another spot of worry for Dick, too. Centred upon Briony whom he now so dearly loved. Every day, the girl drove over from Seascale to see Hew. These visits were not pleasant for her, so far as Dick could gather. If Hew hadn't been such a sick man, Dick would have been annoyed with him. He snubbed the poor child so mercilessly. She was in love with him. It was written for all the world to see—in her lovely compassionate eyes. Frequently, she came out of the hospital in tears. Not once but many times, she said to Dick:

'Oh, it's so awful! None of the cures seem to help him. He still can't move. He hates it so—poor, *poor* Hew—he hates it so!'

Her tears were for him and not for herself. Yet during the conversations that followed Dick gathered that Hew was a bear to her; and gave her scant gratitude for all her attentions. He forbade her to take him flowers or fruit or spend her money on him which she yearned to do. Dick couldn't understand it. In Hew's place, Dick would have been thankful to have anybody as young and charming as Briony to sit beside him and 'hold his hand'. But—old Hew wasn't the 'hand-holding type'. And whatever he felt about Briony, he seemed determined not to show it. Now and again Dick was suspicious that there *was* more to it than met the eye; that Hew might indeed care much more for Briony than he dared show. He was such an independent type—he would never tie a woman down to him, believing that he was going to be a hopeless cripple.

Once Briony gave away her own feelings to Dick.

'I'd do anything in the world to help Hew. But he seems to resent even my sympathy. It upsets me so. He almost hates me now. He dictates his letters, and once or twice he has tried to get on with the book but failed and told me to get out. Oh, Dick, it hurts me so.'

Yes, Dick knew that she loved Hew. And that hurt *him*. But he said nothing. In his kindly, selfless way he even tried to lessen her burden a little.

'Don't take any notice of old Hew. He doesn't mean it. He thinks a lot of you, I know it.'

But Briony didn't know it and suffered accordingly.

It was quite a relief to be able to discuss it all with her aunt who was kindness itself and extraordinarily understanding these days. Miss Shaw had quite given up either thinking or speaking with suspicion of Hew Vanner. The tragedy of his accident roused all her pity. She was genuinely worried about his spine and every night when her niece returned to Seascale questioned her anxiously about his condition.

On the last day before he left the hospital, Hew saw a new specialist—a visiting surgeon who was considering the possible consequences of an operation. The treatment so far had failed. That was why they were letting him go home. But Maitland-Gibson was more hopeful than the rest of the medical staff. He had taken further X-rays, and he intended to visit Hew at Wasdale Head after he had had a course of injections. Maitland-Gibson wished to see how Hew reacted to these. The injections could be given by the local doctor, and treatment by a visiting masseuse so there was no need for Hew to stay in hospital. The expense of a private room was enormous, and there was need for economy, as Hew grimly declared.

Never would Briony forget the day that he was brought home to Monks Farm. He had told her not once but a dozen times while he was in hospital that he could not afford to go on employing a resident secretary. But in this she had openly defied him. She did not want pay, she said. It was not as though she *needed* it in order to live. She had her father and mother behind her. She was going to finish that book with him, paid or not.

'And I refuse to be chucked out until it is finished,' she had told him at the end of one of their regular disputes.

The sunken brilliant eyes had smouldered at her. For a moment his lips had quivered into a ghost of a smile—almost a look of tenderness. Then he had growled:

'Stubborn little brute! Well, have your own way. But if you type for me, you'll get paid for it. Now leave me alone. You annoy me.'

That had sent her out of his room in the depths. But with a certain exhilaration because he had not flatly refused to allow her to stay at Monks Farm.

Whether they cured him or not, she decided his work must continue. She felt that he needed the distraction *and* the money. Already Part I of the book had gone up to the publishers who were very interested. His other travel book had done well. They were willing to pay him quite a tidy sum in advance of royalties, as soon as he had completed this new one. It was better written and much more exciting than the first, they said. And he had wonderful photographs for the purpose of illustration. They seemed quite certain that Hew Vanner's second book—the agreed title was to be *Bird and Beast*—would be a best-seller.

So, Briony—once more the resident secretary—went back to Monks Farm. Old Berry, who had been lonely and depressed, was overjoyed to see her. Together they prepared the house for its master. It was a sad day for the old nurse, who must watch her beloved boy being lifted on a stretcher out of an ambulance and carried indoors. But he was coming home. That was what mattered.

Briony cautioned her not to be sentimental.

'You're not to shed a single tear, Berry—or fuss over him. He loathes it. Just behave as though everything is quite normal.'

Berry sniffed at this but admitted that Miss Briony was right. Berry did her bit of crying while she made up his bed, which was now in his study. There he would be amongst his favourite books, and could lie, by day, close to the French windows and let the sun shine upon him and watch his beloved birds in the garden. It was merciful that Berry was still capable of nursing him, Briony observed. He would not have liked a stranger in the house.

'I'll help you with the cooking and housework while you look after *him,*' Briony declared.

The old woman gave her a look over the rim of her spectacles.

'I believe you love him as much as I do, Miss.'

Briony flushed.

'Maybe I do. But for heavens' sake don't give me away. He's only got to get that into his head, and he'll boot me straight out.'

Berry went out of the room muttering under her breath, 'We'll see about that.'

She had already tricked Miss Briony into coming back to the Lake District and she had other ideas up her sleeve. The only person in the world she was not jealous of, these days, was Briony Moore. Absorbed by her love for Master Hew, old Berry had decided since the accident that now, more than ever, he needed a wife to look after him; and that wife must be Miss Briony.

So Hew came home.

His feelings were indescribable as they drove him slowly down the hill and he gazed upon the old stone house and familiar garden once more. Old Berry and Briony were waiting by the gate. For a moment Hew's gaze rested in anguish on the slim girl with the sunlight gilding her lovely hair. She wore a pale blue linen dress which he remembered, and which made her look very young. It was wonderful to see her. Yet terrible. He knew how hateful he had been to her, how ungrateful for all her attention while he was in hospital. She would never know how he had longed to be otherwise. But he dared not surrender to his weakness. She was his delight and she was his torment. But he could never, never ask her to marry him now even though he wanted to.

The ambulance attendants finally laid the big paralysed man on his bed. The white vehicle rolled away. Berry, excited and happy to be nursing Master Hew—her baby once more—saw to it that he was comfortable then left him smoking, and drinking a cup of the strong tea which she knew he liked. It was a glorious afternoon. The warm sun poured through the French windows. Hew lifted his gaunt face to it and shut his eyes.

The very warmth of that sun gave him a pang of longing to be out in it. This was *hell.* A black period of life from which he saw no release. Here he must stay supine—looking out at this garden and nothing else unless they carried him into a car or wheeled him out in a spinal carriage. The very thought nauseated him.

Restlessly he opened his eyes again and stared round his study. He looked long and bitterly at a big bison's head which hung on the wall; remembering the day when he had shot the animal; the long trek before he found and cornered it. Then down at the tiger skin on the floor ... and thought about the extreme danger of the moment just before he had put the bullet into the tawny creature's heart. How strong, how splendidly well, he had felt that morning. How magnificently he had been able to walk without growing tired. Hew set his teeth and clenched his hands until the knuckles were strained and white as ivory.

Under his breath, he groaned:

'I wish somebody could shoot me as I shot that poor beast. I wish I had died in that car smash. I don't want to live *like this!*'

Into the room came Briony. She gave him a nervous glance and rather nervously picked up a flower which had fallen from the bowl of roses which she had arranged on his desk. She spoke with forced brightness.

'Aren't these lovely, Hew? The second blooming. The garden has really done quite well.'

'So have I—haven't I?' he sneered.

She flushed.

'Tell me when you'd like to do some work,' she said. 'You can dictate to me any time you like. Even if you can't sleep in the middle of the night I'll come down—'

'For heaven's sake don't make a martyr of yourself for me!' he broke in. 'You oughtn't to be here at all. Why are you so obstinate? Why don't you go home and stay there?'

This was a Hew whom she thought she knew and understood. She was determined to stick it out.

'You know perfectly well that we've got to work on that book.'

'You can tear it up as far as I'm concerned. I'm not interested.'

'Oh yes, you are. And really, Hew, I know you've had a rotten break, but you are behaving childishly.'

She did not know how she brought herself

to utter such words when she wanted to fall down beside his bed and press her lips to his hands—to cover that tortured face with kisses, to tell him that she was suffering abominably for his sake; that it broke her heart to see him like this, instead of perching on the edge of his desk, in the old careless way.

Then to her relief he burst out laughing. It was the first laugh she had heard from him since his accident six weeks ago. He said:

'You're quite right. You're very long-suffering, Briony, my dear, and I am a perfect monster. But I always was, wasn't I?'

She fought back the inclination to cry.

'Not in the least,' she said, marched to the desk and whipped off the typewriter cover. 'Come on, let's get down to some dictation and stop all this nonsense.'

He looked at her back—that straight courageous young figure. He adored her for standing up to him. For *putting up* with him. And he knew that he would have given anything in the world to be as fit as he used to be ... to feel justified in telling her what really lay in his heart. He knew so well that if she had not been here today to welcome him home—nothing on God's earth could have given him the will to carry on. But she was giving it to him; by virtue of the fact that she, herself, was indomitable and so inexpressibly sweet and patient.

She pressed the manuscript into his hands. She made him look through the last chapter.

She found his notes. She tried to be her old flippant self.

'A nice lot you did after I left! About one page. What were you doing after I left? Playing noughts and crosses with Berry?'

Now she caught a twinkle in his eyes.

'Shut up,' he said, 'let me think what I am going to say.'

Her heart leapt. So he *was* going to dictate. He was going to let her help him. Oh, glorious thought!

They worked together for two solid hours. At the end of which Hew threw his papers on the floor and said he couldn't do any more. He was too tired.

She left it at that, and with shining eyes went out to tell Berry the good news.

She had learned to control her emotions, terrified to exhibit any kind of softness before Hew. But when she took her evening walk alone to the lake—reminding her so poignantly of the strolls she had always had with *him*—she abandoned herself to her grief for him and for herself. And the patient and bright little secretary was reduced to the status of a heart-broken girl, consumed with love for a man who would never return it.

That same night while old Berry washed her master and prepared him for the night's rest, she put in a sly word about his secretary.

'Miss Briony's looking very poorly, Master Hew.'

He flung her a look.

'Poorly? That girl? Nonsense—she's the picture of health.'

'Not at all, Master Hew. She's right off her food and she's lost pounds since your accident. I reckon it's because she's very upset about *you,* Master Hew.'

The slow red crept up under Hew's fast-fading tan. He grunted:

'You talk the most indescribable nonsense, Berry.'

'I speak the truth, Master Hew. And sometimes it's best to face up to truth. *You* always used to, when you was a little lad. I always knew where I was with you. But I reckon now neither Miss Briony nor me know where we are.'

'What *are* you drivelling about, you old stupid?'

She combed back his hair, her stiffened fingers unutterably tender.

'Well, Master Hew, you see I know just how Miss Briony feels for you. And the way you snap at her it isn't *natural.* Why, you know quite well how glad you really are to have her with you.'

The man's heart felt suddenly near to bursting. He pushed the old nurse's hand away and turned his face to his pillow.

'Oh, get out, Berry—you don't understand,' the words came thickly, as though wrung from him.

The old woman's eyes filled with tears. She understood only too well. She said no more, but walked out of the room.

'Do you think he's any better?' Briony asked the old woman anxiously as she entered into the kitchen where Briony was making an omelette for Hew's supper.

The old woman set down the basin of water and shook her head.

'He's very low spirited, Miss Briony, and it isn't only because he has lost hope of standing on his legs again.'

'What else could it be?'

'I think it's *you,* Miss Briony.'

The girl's heart gave a terrific lunge and the pupils of her eyes dilated.

'*Me?* How can it be me?'

'I just think it is, that's all. I read into his mind tonight. It's as plain to me as though he said the words. Sure as eggs is eggs, Miss. He snarls at you *because he loves you.* He loves you and he dursn't say so with him being an invalid, and nothing to offer you!'

TWENTY-TWO

Briony did not move or speak for a moment. She looked unbelievingly at the old nurse. Once before dear old Berry had exaggerated—to put it mildly—what Hew had said. With the best motives she had brought Briony up to Millom to see Hew. Under false pretences, Briony no longer could believe all that Berry said. She refused to allow herself to get excited.

'Get away with you, Berry—you're an old romancer,' at length she said with a gulp.

The nurse poured the pan of soapy water into the sink and shot a knowing glance at Briony over her shoulder.

'Oh no. I haven't made *this* up. When I mentioned your name just now, Master Hew said something about me 'not understanding', then he turned his face to the pillow. What can that mean but that he's fretting about you but won't bring himself to say so.'

Briony stayed silent for another moment. Then she walked speechlessly out of the kitchen. If Berry were right ... oh, heavens! If only it was true, that Hew was fretting for her. That he was just a little bit in love with her, behind that façade of cold disapproval.

She walked out into the front garden. Mechanically she stooped to snip off a dead rose. The little garden was her handywork. She had worked at it in her spare time ever since she came to Monks Farm. She had longed to see the roses. Now she wished passionately that it was spring again—that Hew was as he used to be—strong and well.

The sun had just gone in. There were threatening clouds behind Scafell Pike. The lake lay half in sunshine, half in shadow. A ripple disturbed the metallic sheen of the water. Briony sighed. She knew these signs.

A storm was blowing up. The morning had been altogether too bright and dazzling and, too hot. There was thunder in the air. She mustn't think any more about Hew. And she wouldn't take any notice of the silly things Berry said. She was growing old and foolish.

Hew was fretting for her. No—it couldn't be true.

A little later, when Briony brought herself to open, gently, the door of the study which was now the invalid's bedroom, she saw that Hew had fallen asleep. One hand rested under his cheek. He looked pale and sad and exhausted. Possibly the ride from the hospital, and dictating this afternoon had sapped his already depleted store of energy.

'Oh, my darling,' she said under her breath, 'I can't bear to see you like this. You must get better. What wouldn't I give to be able to work a miracle so that you could walk again!'

The storm hung around Wast Water for the rest of the evening and broke in the small hours of morning.

Briony woke to hear the crash of thunder and torrential rain, sluicing against her window panes.

A good old Lake District storm, she thought as she turned over. Then she woke herself right up. Berry would be too deaf to hear, and supposing Hew had been disturbed and wanted a drink; or anything?

Briony was up and out of bed. She pulled on a pair of slacks and a jersey, and ran downstairs, rubbing the sleep out of her eyes and smoothing back her tumbled hair as she went.

She saw a light under the study door. She knocked.

Hew answered:

'Come in!'

She found him fully awake, with the lamp burning beside his bed, and a book in his hand.

He gave her a curious glance—not at all hostile or angry. And he spoke more gently than she had heard him speak to her for some time.

'What are you doing up at this hour, my dear, it's two o'clock?'

'The thunder woke me. I wondered if it had disturbed you and if you wanted anything,' she said shyly.

He put down the book. His eyes were extraordinarily sad in that moment.

'Only the use of my legs, Briony. Only to be able to walk again,' he said.

That almost broke her heart. But she gave him a swift confident smile as she advanced nearer the bed.

'Dear Hew, don't despair—I'm quite sure you *will* walk again.'

He gave a short laugh.

'You're the only one who is.'

'I know it. I feel it.'

'Then I hope to God you're psychic, my child.'

'Mr Maitland-Gibson will do something for you.'

Hew shrugged his shoulders: 'We'll see. Now don't stay down here and lose your beauty sleep. I'm quite all right.'

She wrinkled her nose.

'It feels dampish and quite chilly after all the rain. The fine weather has broken. What about a nice cuppa?'

'What—a tea-party at two a.m?'

'Why not?'

'I wouldn't mind a drink, I must say, and there's nothing like tea—hot and strong.'

'I'll get it in a jiffy,' said Briony and rushed into the kitchen, radiant at being allowed to serve her idol. She felt even happier when she was sitting beside his bed drinking a cup of tea with him. He was treating her like a human being. It was wonderful. He was being quite friendly. Not talking about his tragic condition but telling her of a fearful storm which he had once encountered in the Congo on an occasion when he and Dick had been out there. This little rumble of thunder, these flashes of lightning, were child's play compared to those tropical storms, he said.

'I've lain in a hammock and watched the lightning play all round me in a circle,' he said.

'Oh, Hew!' she exclaimed and fixed him with her big, interested eyes.

He thought how extraordinarily sweet she was and how kind to him. He had never felt more like taking her in his arms. The long bitter days of inaction—of despair—had been bad for his morale he told himself. Had made him feel dependent and in need of human companionship—of close contact with someone sweet and sympathetic and gentle—like his little secretary.

He set his teeth and turned suddenly from the altogether too alluring sight of that slim figure in slacks and jersey stretched over slight pointed breasts. She looked lovely, with no make-up and ruffled curls. Lovely and desirable. No, no, he thought, it mustn't be. She was just the type to *want* to offer her services because he was a helpless paralytic. He wouldn't accept any such sacrifice. She was made for love and life; those slim arched feet were meant to dance. She had had a failure with Clive Dormer. He was a bounder of the worst type. But there were plenty of other young men in the world—healthy, sporting and nice, who could make a girl like Briony very happy.

Suddenly the force of his own emotions pushed Hew back into his customary shell. Gruffly, he told her to leave him.

'I think I can sleep now,' he said, 'thanks for the tea. Run along—'

Reluctantly she obeyed him, said 'Good night', and walked out with the tea-tray. That hour beside him, while the rest of the world was asleep and the storm raged over Monks Farm had been exhilarating and full of happiness for her. She had not wanted it to end.

Another fortnight passed. It showed little improvement in Hew, except that he began to eat more and to put on some weight. His face looked less sunken. He managed to do a little more writing each day, too, which delighted Briony.

The whole household was even more delighted when the famous Maitland-Gibson came to see him and uttered the first words which contained any real hope.

'I think something *can* be done,' he told Hew. 'Carry on with these injections and then we'll examine you again and see how the old legs respond. We may even decide that an operation may be the final answer.' That was all he would say for the moment. But it was enough to rouse Hew out of his deep despondency. Besides which, the little doctor who came every day to give him his injections, encouraged him. Hew's was a bad case, he said, but he had known worse ones, patients with infantile paralysis, for instance, to recover. He would not allow it to be said that Hew Vanner would never walk again.

So Hew passed through one stage to another, alternating between hope and despair. And his moods fluctuated in parallel, Briony never knew how she would find him. Always at his best when they worked together—anxious that she should not sit too long at the machine, and tire herself out. Never again, perhaps, quite so friendly and close to her as he had seemed on the night of the storm. But obviously relying on her nowadays which gave her immense satisfaction.

When Aunt Caroline questioned her (deeply interested now in her niece's 'romance'), Briony had nothing to say. Nothing had really changed. The man she loved so passionately seemed as inaccessible as ever.

When her parents wrote to ask when she would be going home she said not until the book was finished. And now she began to be a little cunning and not type quite so fast because she could not bear the end to come. Hew was dictating all too quickly. She just couldn't *endure* it if there was no longer an excuse for her to stay on at Monks Farm.

At the end of September, Dick came up to Wasdale for the last time. He was very depressed about his friend. He shrank from leaving him still paralysed. But Dick had his commitments. He had arranged his trip to South America. His passage was booked. The expedition with Gonzola had been planned. But to embark on it without Hew—that was a tragedy. Dick, with the passing of time, had recovered some of his natural good spirits. But they failed him whenever he was with his old friend.

On his last visit—which was to bid Hew

and Briony good-bye, he had a long intimate talk with Hew.

'What are your plans, Van? Supposing this fellow, Maitland-Gibson, doesn't get you right—what'll you do, old boy?'

Hew narrowed his gaze and looked away from Dick.

'Damn it all—what *can* I do, but lie here like a log?'

Dick scratched the back of his head. His healthy face puckered.

'Look here, you and I have known each other a long time and been through a lot together. I feel privileged to talk to you on rather a personal matter—'

'What's on your mind, Dick?'

Dick cleared his throat. He felt hot and nervous. He had spent a good deal of his time whilst here, talking to Hew—but he had also had a walk with Briony and a long chat with her. The poor little thing looked so thin and drawn, he thought, and she seemed mad about Hew. Dick had abandoned all thoughts of getting Briony to look at *him*. He now had only one wish—to help her on the road to happiness and to make things easier for Hew.

He burst out:

'You're a bit of a darned old ostrich, Van. You don't seem to see what's happening.'

Hew, took his pipe from his mouth.

'Come on—spit it out—what's on your mind?'

'Why, Briony, of course.'

Silence. Hew changed colour. And Dick was swift to see it. He added: 'That poor kid's crackers about you. Absolutely crackers. Can't sleep or eat. I'm quite shocked at the amount of weight she's lost. No girlish giggles—always darned serious these days—not at all like herself.'

Hew said nothing. But his heart-beats quickened. This was what his old nurse had already told him. But he had discredited it. He felt the sweat break out on his forehead. Dick enlarged on the theme.

'Look here, old boy, she's the nicest girl I've ever met. And just the one for you. Why don't you marry her? It's what she wants and it's what *you* need. A nice charming wife to give you, shall we say, an *élan* for existence. Something to live for.'

He stopped, embarrassed by his own daring. Never had he discussed Hew's private affairs so openly. But he could see the effect of his words for Hew, looking equally embarrassed, answered his friend frankly:

'You fool, Dick! I'm no ostrich. I see it all. I *know* she's fond of me. It's been obvious since my accident. I've tried not to believe it, but I do now.'

Encouraged, Dick said:

'Well—you—you like *her,* don't you?'

'"Like"—is hardly the word. I adore her.'

As he uttered the words, Hew felt a kind of exaltation. He adored her, yes, every little hair of her head. If possible it was an even more absorbing kind of love than he had felt for little Anne. She had been his first young love but he had not known her very well and lost her almost before his love had had time to take root. After that he had cherished her as a dear memory. But Briony had become part of his life—just as she was part of this household. Without her there would be a decided blank. She had worked with him, lived under his roof, shared so many things with him for so many months now. And he yearned to tell her how he felt about her. But in a few firm words, he assured Dick that it could never come to anything.

'Do you think I could allow a lovely girl like that to tie herself down to a *log?*'

'But you won't always be a log, we hope, old boy.'

'That remains to be seen. They haven't cured me yet.'

'Well, I see your point. But, at least, you could let the girl know that you are fond of her. You do treat her "rough", you know, Van.'

Hew ground his teeth.

'I know! I know! I hate myself for it. But I've got to keep myself under control. I daren't let go. Can't you see that? I can't let her sacrifice herself for me, and if she dreamt what I was feeling for her she'd never leave me. And I'd never want her to,' he added in a low wretched voice.

The two men got no further than that. Dick felt little more encouraged, when he took his final leave of his friend. Things looked pretty hopeless, he thought. But when it came to saying good-bye to Briony, he found himself on the verge of betraying Hew's confidence. It was more than he could bear to see that hungry sad look in Briony's glorious eyes. He took both her hands and pressed a kiss on each palm in turn.

'Dear little Briony, if I didn't know what you feel for old Hew I'd ask you to come to South America with me,' he said.

Briony was touched. Impulsively she reached up and kissed his cheek.

'You're the nicest thing that ever happened and I do thank you for what you have just told me. It's sweet of you. But I could never, never leave Hew. You know that.'

'Yes, dear, and I know something else ... he doesn't *want* you to leave him.'

She caught her breath.

'I don't think *that's* true.'

'Oh yes, it is! I can't say more. But I'll tell you this much—stick it out, Briony—don't let him get you down or drive you away. You wear him down, my dear! He needs you as much as you need him. Stick to it. For both your sakes.'

Briony considered this—her pulses racing. Old Berry had said the same sort of thing, and she hadn't taken much notice. She looked up at Dick with eyes full of wild hope.

'Do you *really* think that?'

'I do. Hew is a queer chap—no matter how fond he was of you he'd never let you know it until he thought things were going to be all right with him—I mean—well, you know what I mean,' Dick broke off, then shook his head at her and added: 'Don't ask questions. I've no right to answer—I've said too much already. But I've done it because I'm so dashed fond of you both.'

She put her arms around his neck and hugged him as though he was a brother. Her eyes were full of tears.

'Oh, Dick, you darling, you've made me the happiest girl in the world.'

He dropped a kiss on her hair, then drew away from her, swallowing.

'I'm an idiot when I want you for myself. I'm off now. So long, sweetheart. Keep your pecker up and remember what I've said. I'll send you postcards from the Amazon and you might drop me a line. Hew's got my *poste restante* address. He'll never write but I'd like you to let me know how he goes on.'

Briony, sniffing into her handkerchief, nodded, and blew her nose.

'I'll write you once a week, I promise.'

After he had gone she stood outside Hew's door. She felt the pounding of her heart-beats shake her body.

If it were true—if it were only *true*—the wonderful thing at which Dick had more than hinted. And Berry, too. *If they were right.* If ... *if.*

She was in a welter of doubts and fears, threaded through with the maddest of hopes.

But suddenly she felt that she could not bring herself to go into the study and face Hew. She turned and ran up to her own bedroom. She shut herself in until she heard Berry calling her. When she went down again to see to the supper, she had regained her control. Time and time alone would show who was right, she told herself. But whatever happened she must not do or say the wrong thing and risk Hew sending her away. She must not lose his friendship and what confidence he had in her.

But she wondered how long she could go on under this strain.

TWENTY-THREE

October came. The Lake District was at its loveliest with Cumberland wearing the rich colouring of autumn—decked out in green bracken and purple heather. The trees were changing colour. The countryside was exquisitely painted in russet brown—in bright scarlet—in burnt gold. In the herbaceous border at Monks Farm, great old-fashioned clumps of Michaelmas daisies made a brave show of purple; chrysanthemums hung their heavy pink heads. The Virginia creeper on the walls of the house took on its own brave scarlet obscuring the grey stone.

Since Dick Forrester had sailed to South America, neither Briony nor the old nurse had had an easy time with Hew. But because they loved him ... they understood. If he had black, difficult moods it was because the man's very soul must sicken at the knowledge of his helplessness. In his mind, no doubt, he travelled continually with his friend. He thought in the small hours, while he lay sleepless, of that expedition which he had meant to take—dreamed of the great Napo, the volcanoes, the swamps, the lagoons he had hoped to navigate. Of the dense jungles he had longed to penetrate ... of the roar of those deep canyons and foaming cataracts. All now impossible. Everything that had made life worth living must have gone with Dick.

That was what the two women at Monks Farm imagined. And not since Dick's farewell had Briony allowed herself to believe that Hew cared for *her;* that any of his grief and despair was on her account.

What troubled her most now was the fact that he seemed to be getting no better. There was still no movement in those fine long legs which were getting wasted. A visiting masseur came regularly. Maitland-Gibson changed the treatment. On one occasion he swore that he saw an improvement and that he was more certain of ultimate recovery for that injured spine. But it was all slow and disheartening for the injured man. He was forced to learn the bitter lesson of patience which was so difficult for him, and to accept constant service which, again, he found repugnant. He could not bear his new dependence.

The day came when Maitland-Gibson reached an important decision and came in person to tell Hew Vanner of it.

Hew had been taken by ambulance back to Millom for further X-rays last week. Another man had seen the plates. A particularly brilliant surgeon from one of the big London hospitals who happened to be in the Lake District on holiday; staying with Maitland-Gibson.

Sir Phillip Morton had had special experience of infantile paralysis and spinal injuries. He had performed one or two outstanding operations during the war and since, Maitland -Gibson told Hew. The most remarkable case was a recent one—the small daughter of an American millionaire had been visiting London and was riding in the Row when her horse bolted and threw her. For months she had lain paralysed. The father had been on the verge of flying her back to New York, when Phillip Morton operated—and cured her. So complete had been that cure that she had since taken some training as a dancer. Didn't that give Hew confidence? It did, of course, Hew admitted.

On the other hand, both doctors had to point out to Hew that there was a certain element of danger attached to this particular operation. It was a question of 'kill or cure'. One little slip; any further injury to the spinal cord, and Hew's life might come to an end. It was unlikely but the risk was there.

Hew received this news grimly but calmly.

'I'll think it over,' he said. 'In all probability I'll decide to have the operation. It might be worth the risk. As far as I'm concerned, if I must stay chained to my couch like this—unless I'm operated on—I'd just as soon be dead. Kill or cure—eh? Not a bad idea.'

After the two big specialists had driven away Briony came in with Hew's lunch.

She set down the tray and looked at him anxiously.

'What did they say? Tell me.'

He gave her a grim smile.

'Kill or cure is the diagnosis, my child.'

'What *do* you mean?'

He explained.

'Risky job, you know, when these fellows start to cut you up in vital places. A spinal operation is bound to be tricky and—'

He finished with a sweep of the hand.

'And I might well end up in six foot of earth,' he ended, 'but as I told them, I think death is preferable to *this* sort of life. So I might as well take the risk.'

She stood quite still beside his bed. He could see that she had gone very white. Then she astonished him by being furiously angry with him.

'How dare you! How *dare* you want to die? You've no right to talk like that. You might want to die yourself, but what about those you leave behind? Those who couldn't bear to lose you—oh, you're the most selfish, *disgustingly* self-centred man—'

She broke off, doubling her hands, breathing hard and fast.

He looked at her in dismay.

'Briony!'

'Well, you've no right to want to die!'

He was silent in the face of her young frank fury. He knew by now how sensitive she was to anything he said or did and he was suddenly deeply moved. In a husky voice, he said:

'Briony, would you want to go on living in my place? Wouldn't *you* prefer to be dead?'

'Not if I knew that my death would bring infinite pain and grief to others.'

'Who have I got who would suffer that much on my account? I have neither wife nor mother.'

She started to speak but stopped herself. Now he saw that she was trembling violently. And suddenly he realized how cruel he was being. Not only to her but to himself. In a sudden agony of longing which temporarily weakened his resolve never to let her know what he felt, he held out a hand.

'Briony, *darling,* don't look at me like that, please.'

She neither moved nor spoke. Her eyes glittered resentfully at him.

'Oh, Briony, my little darling—my sweet, kind Briony, don't be angry with me. I can't bear your anger. I love you so much,' he said as though the words were dragged from his very soul.

Then she gave a cry, moved forward and flung herself down on the bed. She wound her arms round the big wasted figure, pressed her cheek to his as she had so often longed to do and with sobs racking her whole body, unburdened her love—passionately, unashamedly, at last.

'And I love *you.* Hew, I love you—I love you. I couldn't *bear* if it you died!'

For the moment the man had no more strength to resist. He was at the end of his own strength. His arms gathered her close. So close that he felt he must be hurting her. His lips touched her hair, drawing in the fragrance of it, and then kissed away the tears that were pelting down her cheeks.

'Briony, Briony,' he whispered her name.

'You're not to have the operation,' she sobbed. 'You're not to risk them killing you. Go on as you are. I love you as you are. Never mind if you can't walk again. I'll look after you. I'll never, never leave you. Hew, my *darling* Hew.'

He was staggered by the magnificence of

her young love and the generosity with which she offered herself. He could find no words to answer but went on holding her and kissing away those tears. She made him feel very humble, very ashamed of every act of unkindness he had shown towards her. She kept repeating:

'I love you, and you mustn't risk dying. Stay as you are, and let me look after you. Marry me. Yes, I'm going to ask *you* to marry *me*. Let me be your wife so that I can stay here and take care of you. And if you get well, you do, and if you don't—you don't, and I don't care. I *do* care, but I mean, I don't *mind*. Anything, anything rather than lose you altogether.'

Now his lips touched her mouth, and they clung together desperately. It was a desperate kiss. A kiss for which the man had hungered in secret and in torment and denied himself because he had felt it to be unfair to her. A kiss which she too had wanted with a pain almost beyond bearing. Eyes shut, her whole body one hot flame of passionate love and surrender, she returned his caresses. At long last she understood love in its deepest meaning. She knew now that she had never loved Clive. Never even come near to *this* amazing rapture. When the long kiss was over she drew back and gazed down at Hew with speechless admiration. Somehow he seemed to have changed—he looked so much more youthful, so extraordinarily happy—for him.

He shook his head at her with tender reproof.

'My mad, sweet, crazy little Briony.'

'I don't care. I love you.'

'Darling, I have done nothing whatsoever to deserve such love. You ought to hate me.'

'I don't. I love you with all my heart and soul. You're the only man that matters to me in the world or ever will.'

'Briony darling, don't. I'll never be any good to you.'

'You never were any good to me,' she said with a broken laugh, and lifted his fine long fingers and kissed them individually. 'But I adore you,' she whispered.

He stroked her hair—looked at her as though in wonder and amazement.

'I cannot imagine why. A hulking brute—a bad-tempered old misery like me.'

'It's only because you've been unhappy that you've been hard to get on with. When you're happy you're wonderful.'

'Briony, darling, how can you expect me to be happy with this ...' he tapped his legs.

The romantic feeling was fast fading ... the immeasurable delight of contact with her ... the thrill of her embrace. He was facing grim reality again.

'If I don't have that operation, Briony, I may stay paralysed always.'

'Then let me stay with you. I have no false pride. I am asking you to marry me, Hew.'

'Oh, my dear! You have nothing to be

ashamed of. I think it's wonderful. I bow before you. I'd like to be able to fall at your feet and kiss them, my dear, but I can't. I can't move. And if I can't move what use am I to any girl as a husband? You would be chained to an invalid's couch for the rest of your life. No, darling, no, a thousand times, *no!*'

She shook back her curls, her face hot and pink and wet with tears, her lips quivering.

'You can't turn me down now. You can't turn me down. You would not want me to feel ashamed of having asked you to marry me.'

'You've no need to be. You've every reason to be proud. Besides I love you, my dear. I love you every bit as much as you love me.'

She felt that her whole life had been worthwhile just to hear those words from Hew Vanner. Her very being thrilled. She said:

'Then, if you love me, you need me. You'll keep me with you.'

He hugged her close and groaned, his lips against her hair.

'My darling, don't tempt me. Please don't. I just couldn't accept your sacrifice.'

She strained against him.

'And what if I refuse to leave you? What if I just stay here for ever? What will they say in the district? Miss Moore living at Monks Farm with Mr Vanner—permanently? Think of the scandal—you'll have to marry me to save my reputation—' She broke off with a choked laugh and added, 'Oh, Hew, *Hew*, don't turn me down!'

TWENTY-FOUR

The hardest heart in the world must surely have melted before the passionate sincerity of that cry. And Hew Vanner was not by nature a hard man. He had become hard only because he had been disappointed and frustrated from his earliest boyhood. After the death of his mother he had never dared allow sentiment to rule him. He had been governed by his head. Until he met Anne Graham. But even that romance had turned into the ashes of disappointment. Since then—for years—he had lived amongst men, and women had not counted in his life. He had not wanted them.

The coming of Briony had changed all that. Despite himself he had felt the hard crust encasing all that was passionate and even romantic in his heart, gradually breaking away. She had reached right down to the depths. She had shown him all that was beautiful and sweet and tender in her sex. He could not help but love her. He had known just how much, on that night when he had held her in his arms and she had run away from him. He had known it, too, when he had met Clive Dormer and flung him out of the house in an access of jealous rage.

Since his accident—a dozen times a day or more—he had wanted to give way to this new and consuming love. More especially because he knew what she, herself, felt about him. That had made it even more difficult. Now that he had momentarily lost control and tasted the sweet intoxication of her lips and felt all the enchantment of her in his arms, he was tempted beyond words.

'Briony, Briony, what am I going to do?' he groaned.

'Marry me, darling—abandon bachelorhood and tie yourself to a nagging wife,' she said with a broken laugh.

'You would never nag. You would be the most adorable wife a man could want.'

'Then *want* me, darling.'

'Angel, I do. Isn't it obvious how much I want you? But it wouldn't be fair.'

'To whom?'

'To you, of course. Think of it, Briony—if I never walk again, it means that you would literally live your life waiting on me—being my nurse—year after year until I die—and that might be a long time if I don't have this operation.'

Her cheeks burned and her eyes flashed with the challenge that he had so often seen and admired. Briony was never defeated.

'I don't care! I wouldn't want you to die. I would want you to go on living until you had a long white beard. Even if I had to comb it, and tie it up for you!' She tried to laugh.

That brought laughter to his lips, and the sound was strange even to himself. He had so little time or cause for laughter in the past.

'Oh, you absurd child,' he exclaimed.

She threaded her fingers through his thick dark hair as she had so often done in her dreams and looked at him with deepest devotion.

'It isn't a joke. Honestly, it would be no sacrifice to me to nurse you or push you in a spinal carriage or—'

'Or be poor,' he broke in grimly. 'My private means are dwindling, and pray how would I support a wife?'

'You're an author. You have your royalties.'

'Not enough.'

'Then I'd take in typing—set up a secretarial bureau.'

'You're very sweet. I believe you mean it, but do you think I could lie here and watch my wife working for me when I ought to be giving her the earth? I would *want* to give you the earth. I couldn't bear to see you eking out an existence here with Berry and myself when you ought to be ... well ... enjoying yourself in Paris, with a young man who could take you down the Rue de la Paix and buy you wonderful clothes and ... and jewels.'

He ended rather lamely, his brows knit.

She tried to rub away the frown with her forefinger. She traced the contour of his face, which was too thin and bony for her liking.

'Oh, darling,' she said with a deep sigh, 'I'm not the sort of girl who craves for furs and diamonds. Those are the glamour type in books and films. I'm just an ordinary sort of person, and I was brought up very simply and I am used to the kitchen sink, and making beds and Hoovering and all the rest of it! I wouldn't mind what I did and I would think it a privilege to be able to nurse you, and to sit and listen to you talk.'

He shut his eyes. She was almost irresistible, he thought. So incredibly dear and brave and without a thought for herself. It was that which amazed him. He might have expected egotism in a girl as young and attractive as Briony. She was so completely unspoilt, which, of course, was one of the things which had first drawn her to him. He realized that she was offering him life itself, but he struggled to refuse.

'I won't let you do it. I'd be a blackguard if I did. Your parents would have every right to say so.'

'I wouldn't care *what* they thought—much as I love them. It's *you* I love and want. And when you talk about not letting me do this or that, you seem to forget that my whole happiness is at stake. If you send me away, *I* shall be the one to suffer. I think I'd wither up and die,' she added, in a low passionate voice.

He drew her back into his arms and their lips clung. It was too much for him. To kiss Briony was such a heavenly thing. Then he pushed her gently away from him. The sweat broke out on his forehead and he reached for a handkerchief and wiped it away.

'We can't go on like this, Briony. It just won't do. It isn't fair on either of us. I am grateful—more than grateful for your wonderful offer. That I love you is undisputed. But I would be a poor fellow if I accepted such a sacrifice from any woman. I shall never marry now. Unless, of course, some miracle happens and I recover my health and strength.'

She looked at him with an almost terrible intensity.

'Do you mean that you *won't* marry me?'

He turned his head from her.

'I can't, darling. I beg you not to ask me.'

'And do you admit that you would have married me if this accident had not happened?'

An instant's hesitation, then he said:

'Yes. When I was in that damned car I was on my way down south to see you. I was jealous of Clive Dormer and afraid that you might be going back to him. I knew that I loved you, then.'

That was some consolation to her but her eyes were full of tears as she said:

'Well, I think it's awful. Awful that I should

be made to live without you just because you won't accept what you call a sacrifice. I can't make you understand that it wouldn't be one and that it will be much worse for me to have to leave you.'

He felt a deep depression at the mere thought of her leaving him. A fresh anguish of resentment against the fate that had done this thing to him—and to her.

'I don't think I can stand much more of this, Briony,' he said under his breath.

Immediately she was all concern.

'Oh, how awful of me,' she said. 'Your lunch is stone cold and I've made you ill. I'm a fine nurse!'

He caught her hand and put it against his cheek in a tired way.

'You're a grand nurse. A wonderful secretary. And an enchanting creature, my darling little Briony.'

She fought back the inclination to cry. The feverish excitement and thrill of love—of his kisses—of his caresses—died down. The old misery came back—the old despair. Yet as she took that tray out to ask Berry to warm up the lunch, she seemed to hear Dick's voice echoing in her ear:

'Stick it ... wear him down for both your sakes ...'

And she would, she would, she told herself. She wouldn't take his 'No' for an answer. She would go on lowering her pride and propose to him regularly whether he liked it or not.

When she returned with his tray she was mistress of her emotions again.

'Don't worry about me—or about anything except getting well from now onwards,' she said coolly, 'but one thing I do beg you is not to have the operation and risk your life, whether you mean to share it with me or not.'

Hew gave her a brooding look.

'I'll think it over.'

'And you won't let ... what happened between us make any difference? You'll let me go on doing the book with you if I promise to be good, and you're good, too.'

He gave a short laugh and shook his head at her. His eyes were full of hopeless love as he looked at her determined young face.

'Oh, Briony, you're so sweet and incorrigible. And you know darned well that it will be the end of everything for me if you walk out now. But don't ask me to marry you. Not as things are, darling.'

And that was how it was left.

Later that day, while he rested, Briony took herself over to Seascale to see Aunt Caroline.

Looking and feeling exhausted, she poured out the story of what had happened between Hew and herself.

Miss Shaw really did not know what to say to her niece. It was so pathetic, she thought—poor little Bri—and that poor injured man. But she admired Hew for refusing Briony.

'No man worth his salt would have accepted you,' she told the girl.

'But he needs me even more than if he were not paralysed,' argued Briony.

'Yes, darling, but think of his mental outlook—watching you wait on him hand and foot, knowing that he ought to be taking you for walks or dances or—'

Briony broke in:

'Giving up dancing or travelling would be *nothing* and I can go for walks by myself. I'd have him for the rest of the time.'

Aunt Caroline shook her head.

'Briony, you're still such a child in so many ways. Don't you ever look ahead? Don't you see that now when you have this big heroic impulse for sacrifice, love means everything? But fevers die down and you're only human. You might not be able to lead a normal life with him. Perhaps you would never have children. You couldn't afford a family. He is older than you, and I expect he thinks of these things, poor fellow. He knows how hard it would all be on you. In time you might even meet some attractive young man who could give you all that you had forfeited, and fall for *him*. Yes—don't say "impossible". It *might* happen. And then think how unhappy you would be. And Hew would be much more unhappy than if you had never married him.'

Briony, who had just finished eating a rather poor tea in spite of the fact that old

Alice had made her favourite almond cake, had listened to what her aunt had said in a tense silence. Her face had grown white. Then suddenly she slipped on to the floor and laid her head on her aunt's lap.

Miss Shaw heard a muffled sob. Only that. No words came. But the older woman realized the hurt that was in the girl's soul. Poor little Briony! It was terrible to love so much and to have no outlet for that love. Aunt Caroline herself would have given a lot to be able to work a miracle and restore Hew Vanner to his old self.

She stroked the girl's hair in silence for a moment, and then said:

'It is hard, darling, but try and feel that it is for the best. Really you ought to go away. Go home. It does you no good being with the poor man.'

But here Briony protested, lifting a passionate tear-stained face.

'I shall never leave him while he wants me. *Never*. Whether he marries me or not.'

'Oh dear,' thought Miss Shaw, 'this is much worse than the Clive Dormer affair!'

It was a sad afternoon for the aunt who was so attached to Briony. She could not bear to see the girl reduced to such a state of unhappiness.

But forty-eight hours later a Briony in a much worse state rushed into the little house in Seascale, and flung herself into Aunt Caroline's arms.

'Oh, Aunt Caro! Aunt Caro! *He's gone!'*

Miss Shaw blinked and stared.

'Gone where?'

'To hospital—to have that awful dangerous operation—Sir Phillip Morton's persuaded him.'

'But when—and where?'

Briony, in a state bordering on hysteria, poured out the story whilst her aunt made her sit down, and sat beside her holding her hand. The girl was obviously in a state of shock.

'He didn't want me to know. He didn't dare to tell me that he was going to do it. He went while I was out of the house. He and Berry arranged it all between them,' she said in a strangled voice.

'But I don't understand. I thought Hew had decided not to be operated on.'

Briony shook her head. She had *hoped* that he would not take the risk, she told her aunt. He had said that he would think it over. He must have realized that it would terrify her and that she would try to stop him, because Sir Phillip, himself, had admitted the possible risk to his life. She had tried to make him believe that heart-breaking though his condition was, it was better than death. But obviously he had not agreed. And nervous of her reactions, he had sent her into Lancaster on pretext of finding a particular reference book about the Transvaal. Then, while she was away, the ambulance fetched him from Monks Farm.

He had gone back to Millom, Sir Phillip was operating on him there tomorrow morning

'Oh, it was cruel of him. Cruel not to let me even say good-bye,' cried Briony, the tears streaming down her face.

'Darling, it was very brave of him. And he had to do it that way. You see, he loves you and if you had tried to persuade him not to go you might have influenced his final decision. I think it was typical of your Hew. He is a man of great courage.'

Briony drew a hand across her eyes and pulled a letter from her pocket and handed it to Miss Shaw.

'He left that with Berry for me.'

Miss Shaw changed her spectacles and read the note at the end of which she had a decided lump in her own throat. There was something so pathetic about it. It showed her too what agony of mind the man must have gone through.

Forgive me, beloved Briony, for sneaking away. You've been so unutterably patient and kind and I owe you so much. If I hadn't found out how much I loved you I might have shirked this operation. But because I love you I am going to have it. It's my only hope of happiness. Of our happiness. For if I come out of it alive and walk again and can work for my wife as a man should, I shall come back to you. It will be my turn to ask you to marry me. Meanwhile help me by being brave and sensible. Go home, darling. It'll be too depressing on the farm and old Berry doesn't mind being alone. The thought of you and the memory of all your sweetness will be helping me. I shall try to live for you. God bless you, always.

Hew.

Blowing her nose, Miss Shaw handed the letter back to her niece.

'You're a privileged person, Briony, to have inspired a man to write in such a way,' she said.

'Oh, Aunt Caro, he mustn't die. *He mustn't.*'

'He won't, darling. I'm sure Sir Phillip will pull him through. He has had many successes. You said so. Don't look on the blackest side. I believe in thought transference. Remember your Shakespeare. "Nothing is good or bad but thinking makes it so." You must *think* that he is going to get well and go on thinking it, and he *will.*'

Briony sobbed as though her heart would break. But she nodded her head, and said that she would try. But she had, indeed, felt that her heart was broken when she walked into the house after she got back from Lancaster—not with the reference book, but another that she had bought for him as a present—and found what had happened. The deserted study; the empty bed; Hew's pipe lying on the table. The manuscript on the desk. And no Hew. *No Hew.* Just Berry with her guilty face, making excuses, saying that Master Hew had forbidden her to give Miss Briony any warning.

'Oh, why did he want to risk his life? Why did he not stay as he was and let me take care of him?' Briony had cried, in her first passion of grief.

But old Berry had tried to comfort her.

'There, dearie—it's for the best, Miss Briony. I know my boy. He could never have gone on lying there helpless. It was a risk he had to take. And we must just trust in God that he'll come home walking on his two feet again.'

TWENTY-FIVE

During the next few days, Briony lived in a world of agonizing suspense which very nearly destroyed any optimism or sense of humour that she had ever had.

Aunt Caroline was a tower of strength because she *understood.* She had quite altered her views on Hew being the 'mysterious stranger who might wreck Briony's life'. She had visited him so often now that she had grown to know him and to look upon him with respect. Even if he wasn't what she called 'a nice young man of the normal kind' with a nice job in a bank or solicitor's office (or something of the kind), she bowed before his mental qualities. He was one of the most clever men she had met, one of the most interesting to talk to. To her, also, he had always been courteous and charming. That he could be brusque and was difficult at times, she was sure. But she forgave him for that. She could forgive him anything now that she knew that he had turned down Bri's original offer. That showed that he was not a self-seeking egotist, willing to snatch what she offered, nor a young bounder like Clive Dormer.

In fact, Miss Shaw now approved of Hew. She *wanted* him to recover his health and strength so that Briony might eventually find happiness with him. So she took her niece under her wing during those crucial nights and days, and drove with her personally to Millom on the day of the operation. Briony felt that she could not even trust the telephone. She *must* be there on the spot. She and Aunt Caro went to spend the night in the same hotel at which Dick had stayed. She could not leave the district for the first crucial period following the operation by the great surgeon.

Poor little Briony! her aunt thought. She had certainly grown up. It was no laughing child but a young woman with grimly set lips and eyes full of consuming fear who waited with her in the hotel. Waited to see if her beloved Hew had survived that dangerous operation.

Sometimes when Briony looked back on that time, she thought she must have been a little light-headed. She did such silly things. She dragged Aunt Caroline into the saloon bar and, to that good lady's horror, forced her to play darts with two strange men. She took her out into the pouring rain (for it was a wild autumn morning) and induced her to walk miles looking senselessly into shop windows, until they had to go back and change their clothes—drenched to the skin.

She made her play poker patience with her in their bedroom until Briony could no longer see the cards and had to give up. She could only see Hew's face and hear his voice and feel his kisses on her mouth. Sick with anxiety she kept praying:

'Come through it, Hew. Hold on, my darling. Hold on for me!'

She had a trunk call from her mother. Lorna knew all about things, of course. And she, with Caroline to back Briony and assure her parents that he was really all that they could wish a son-in-law to be—was settling down to the certainty that if Hew lived, Briony would marry him.

Briony had written pages and pages home to Reigate telling them how much she loved him, and how wonderful he was. She had sent them a snapshot which she had taken of Hew in the summer. He had consented to that only when standing beside Dick, near the car, during their expedition to the Lakes.

Mrs Moore smothered her natural fears and came to the conclusion that Hew Vanner might in the long run prove rather a distinguished son-in-law. After all, he had a little money of his own and he had just written a book which would be the forerunner of others. And his father had been a don at Oxford. What more could a mother want? So Lorna gathered relatives and friends and showed them Hew's photograph and said:

'It's such a romance, you know. Bri was doing his secretarial work. He's a most *famous* explorer and so good looking, don't you think?'

Geoffrey Moore, who had all the way along believed that his daughter was a sensible girl who would eventually make the right choice, looked on with his usual placidity and even took the snapshot to the bowls club to show his best friend. He pointed, actually, in his vague way, to the figure of Dick, and said:

'Quite a good-looking fellow, eh?'

He discovered his mistake when he got home, but it didn't seem to matter. Hew and Dick were both good-looking fellows.

Now everybody who knew waited with Briony for the result of the operation. For truly it would be terrible if Hew died. Perhaps even more terrible for him and for her, if he lived—and was still paralysed.

On the telephone Mrs Moore sought to comfort her daughter.

'I've just seen old Dr Pinleigh—you know, who plays bowls with Daddy. He knew a case like this and it was just a question of releasing the pressure on the spine—I don't quite know about these things—but old Pinny is sure Hew will recover after this operation. He says Sir Phillip is absolutely wonderful.'

Briony, who had dark circles under her eyes and whose lipstick was smudged because she had done so much biting of her lips, exclaimed:

'Oh, Mummy, I hope he's right. You don't *know* what I'm going through. Oh, Mummy, I love him so much.'

'Chin-up darling,' said her mother, 'don't lose heart.'

Briony tried to laugh.

'I'm losing weight, though. My tartan skirt—you know the one—is much too big for me.'

'Oh, darling—do take care of yourself. Be sensible.'

'I can't be sensible. I don't think I shall ever be sensible again,' said Briony with another laugh which had a break in it.

Then she rang off because her watch told her that the operation must be over now. She *must* go along to the hospital.

When she got there, she felt so sick with nerves that her aunt had to take her by the arm and shake her.

'Pull yourself together, my dear,' the older woman said firmly.

Briony looked at her with large anguished eyes.

'I don't think *I* can ask. *You* go and ask them, Aunt Caro,' she whispered.

And so it was that Miss Shaw was privileged to carry the best news in the world to her cherished niece on that never-to-be-forgotten day. Looking quite youthful and radiant, Miss Shaw hurried into the waiting-room where Briony was sitting with a magazine upside down on her lap.

'It's all right, darling. Yes—everything has gone according to plan. Sir Phillip is delighted. Hew is going to be all right. When they got him on the table, apparently, they found things were not as bad as they thought. I have spoken to the theatre sister. She says Sir Phillip did the most wonderful and delicate operation and it is one hundred per cent successful. Already there is movement in one leg and the other will follow suit. And now it is just a question of lying quiet and having daily massage and electrical treatment, then learning to use his limbs again.'

Aunt Caroline poured out this speech breathlessly. Briony listened with both hands pressed against her lips and her heart plunging as though she were in a lift which was going down too fast. Then she seized her aunt by her hands. The colour poured back into the young face. She had to swallow several times before she could speak.

'Oh, how wonderful—how *wonderful*—it's

too good to be true!'

'It's perfectly true! And I hope I didn't do wrong, dear, but I told them Hew's *fiancée* was here and would like to see him. They said not now, he'll still be under the anaesthetic for some time, but first thing tomorrow you may have a peep. He won't, of course, be allowed up for weeks.'

The tears which had been hung up all day now began to pelt down Briony's cheeks. She cried and laughed as well, hysterical with relief.

'You're quite right. I *am* his fiancée. He's engaged to be married, is Mr Hew Gordon Vanner. Once he can walk again, he is going to step right into the spider's web. *I've* spun it for him. Oh, my *darling* Hew! Aunt Caro I could shout and scream, I'm so thrilled.'

'Well, remember you're in a hospital and control yourself, my dear,' said her aunt.

Briony wiped her eyes. Her whole being was flooded with a tremendous joy almost too great to be borne. The operation was successful. Hew would walk again. He had lived for *her*. He would come back to her. He had said so. He *wanted* the web she had spun for him. They would be happy—happy ever afterwards. Madly, gloriously happy!

She did not know how she could wait till tomorrow to see him.

She tore to the telephone. The first thing she must do was to phone old Berry who she knew had been waiting at Monks Farm, practically on her knees, praying for 'her boy'. And after she had given Berry the glad news, she would phone Mummy and send a cable to Dick.

Aunt Caroline tried to restrain her.

'Don't be too impulsive, darling, it's early days. I don't want to damp your spirits, but I think you ought to wait for a bit and see how he goes on.'

But Briony's spirits had soared beyond recall. All the weight of pessimism had lifted. She was the optimist now. She *knew* that he was going to get better and better.

When she saw Hew for that few moments, the next morning, she felt it even more. For although he lay white and still and rigid, his eyes smiled at her and the terrible look of strain, of brooding misery, of bitter resentment, had gone. He looked as though he had been through fire and come out curiously youthful and purified. He whispered:

'I made it. I wanted to be all right *for you.*'

She leaned down and touched his lips with hers. He thought he had never seen anything more beautiful than the expression on her face. It was so unutterably tender, so full of abiding love.

'Darling, darling Hew. You can do anything. You've never been defeated yet.'

For an instant the old cynical twist lifted the corner of his lips.

'I know somebody who wears rose-coloured

spectacles,' he jeered.

Her fingers smoothed his hair. He felt the sweetness of her lips on his again, then she said:

'Darling, they're only going to let me stay for a few moments. They think I'm your fiancée. Otherwise I wouldn't have been allowed to come.'

He pulled her hand against his lips.

'Here—I say—I'm being blackmailed. Who said you were my fiancée? I haven't asked you to marry me, yet?'

'Oh, darling, ask me, *please,* before I go away again. If you don't, I shall go out of my mind and be carted off to the local asylum.'

'Lord, I don't want a mad wife on my hands!' he said.

She giggled. It was a joyous sound which he had found enchanting when he first heard it. Now his own spirits soared to match hers. He was in pain. His back hurt like hell, he reflected. His legs had pins and needles in them. But that was good—*good!* That was worth all the suffering—for it meant that he was no longer a paralysed wreck.

'I'm a lucky chap,' he said solemnly. And whispered against her lips:

'When I am well enough and can totter into a church, darling, will you come with me? I haven't much to offer you, but anything I have is yours if you still want it.'

She drew a long sigh. This was the moment

that her young passionate ardent heart had waited for. She whispered back.

'With all my soul, darling, yes. I still want it ... and you, more than anything in the world.'

She made another telephone call—in fact, two—that morning. The first to Monks Farm.

'Berry, he's better—he can talk—he's had some food—and his back hurts and so do his legs, which is *wonderful.* It means the feeling is coming back—he's going to be able to walk again.'

Berry sniffed.

'Our prayers have been answered, Miss Briony. Now I can get down to spring cleaning the house.'

'You old duffer—it'll be autumn cleaning, but I know what you mean,' said Briony, and added: 'treat me with respect, please. I'm the future Mrs Hew Vanner.'

'Mercy on us—you don't say!'

'I do say. Master Hew and I are going to be married as soon as he can walk and let me tell you, Mrs Berry, the first thing I shall do will be to persuade him to *sack you.* You're too much of an old bully.'

Berry screamed down the phone.

'You don't mean it, Miss Briony! Oh, my goodness, you don't mean it!'

'Of course I don't, you duffer! We couldn't live without you. Would you like to be one of my bridesmaids?'

A croak of laughter from Berry.

'A fine bridesmaid I'd make. Oh, Miss Briony, how you do go on! But it will be a grand day for me when my boy comes home with his lovely young wife.'

Here Briony closed her eyes and grew solemn.

'It will be a grand day for me, too,' she said so softly that the old nurse could not hear it.

After that Mummy had to be told; a further cable was sent to Dick. How pleased old Dick would be to know that his friend was going to recover, that there would be a wedding for him, too.

'I shall make up to Hew for all he's suffered and he won't be half as difficult as before,' Briony informed her aunt as they returned to Seascale.

'I dare say you're right,' said Miss Shaw, and when she got home, she set to work to examine her bank account, and see what kind of cheque she could give those two to start them off. For the 'Treasure Shop' was doing good business, and as well as the little house in Seascale, Miss Shaw owned quite a tidy piece of capital. She didn't intend to die and see it all go to the Government. She planned secretly to give a very handsome cheque indeed to her niece on 'the Great Day'.

After that it was a question of time, and what time proved.

To begin with, Hew made a rapid

recovery—all the strength of his fine constitution behind him. The day came when a proud and radiant Briony, in company with the old nurse, fetched the patient from hospital and drove him back to Monks Farm. Not on a stretcher but on two sticks. Hew, looking a bit sheepish, calling himself 'the old crab'. But Sir Phillip had assured him that this was only the beginning, and early days. Before winter came, he would be walking normally again. He was another of Sir Phillip's triumphs.

It was Briony's triumph, too, for, as the car rounded the bend and they started to descend the hill within sight of Wast Water, Hew put an arm around Briony. He drew her close to his side and nodded toward the lake.

'Look, darling ...'

They all looked. It had been a stormy morning. A wild day of October with driving rain obscuring Scafell Pike. The screes frowned darkly. But just as they drove down the hill, the sun broke through the jagged clouds and touched mountain and lake with purest gold.

'It's a good omen,' muttered old Berry.

'*Our* lake, darling,' said Hew. He stammered a little because he was still not used to making pretty speeches, and added, 'welcoming us home, my darling.'

What fun they had, getting him out of the car and watching him move on his sticks by himself into the house. And what utter relief, to know that he need never lie immovable again, and fear that life had ended for him.

Mr and Mrs Moore were due to arrive at Monks Farm this evening. It had been arranged that they should stay here a few days and get to know their future son-in-law.

After that, *Bird and Beast* must be finished, that was only the question of a week because they were nearly at the end. Then Briony must go home. Reluctant though she was to do so, she must leave her beloved Hew and Wasdale, and return to Reigate.

But only for a short while, as Hew told her. To prepare for their wedding. They had fixed the date provisionally for two weeks before Christmas. By that time, Hew should be a good deal stronger on his feet. They were planning to spend Christmas with Briony's parents (a real old-fashioned Christmas which Hew looked forward to as much as anybody. Berry to be there, too). Immediately afterwards they were sailing for Rio de Janeiro. They were to tour Brazil, and possibly meet up with Dick and Gonzola on their return from the Napo expedition. Hew could not do any exploring now but he could at least hear about it all first-hand, and show his wife the wonders of South America—some of the loveliest and most exciting scenery in the world, he said.

It sounded so thrilling to Briony that she could hardly breathe as she discussed it with her fiancé. The chief trouble, of course, he said, was money. They would have to do things carefully. Then come back to Monks Farm and settle down to real economy whilst Hew wrote another book—this time about his adventures in China.

But they had decided that they would 'go a bust' for those first few months after their wedding. They would escape the English winter, and enjoy the sunshine of South America. Hew needed it after his illness and for Briony it would be a new and wonderful introduction to a world she had never seen and never really thought about until she met her 'darling explorer'.

The visit of the Moores to Monks Farm was a great success. Geoffrey liked Hew the moment he saw him, and Lorna Moore had no more qualms once she had talked with him. His was a curious personality, she decided. Obviously the man had inhibitions and repressions which were a legacy from his unfortunate boyhood and his tragic love affair. But even whilst she was at Monks Farm, Lorna saw him altering, expanding under the warmth and love Briony lavished on him.

Lorna thought that she had never seen anything sweeter than the way Briony fussed over him, and cared for him, and guarded his interests while he worked. Obviously he was good for Briony—he brought out all that was best in her. And for his part, he obviously adored the child. He could not take his eyes off her.

To her mother at their first meeting, he had said:

'I realize that you're going to hand over something very precious to me when you give me Briony, Mrs Moore. I can't thank you enough. I think she's wonderful. What that chap Dormer was about I shall never know. He must have been a lunatic. I may be less mercenary—but a first-class job wouldn't tempt me to leave Briony. I haven't much money. I'm a struggling author these days, but I can look after her, and we can work together. I hope you have no objections.'

To which Lorna answered that she had none and she was perfectly satisfied that he would make Briony the best possible husband.

'Besides which,' Mrs Moore added, 'neither Geoffrey nor I believe that it is a good thing for young people to start with *too* much money. Very few people *can* of course, as things are. It's an age when young wives live at the kitchen sink, so to speak. But it won't do Briony any harm to have to work—so long as she's happy.'

Here Hew smiled and said:

'For as long as old Berry is alive, Briony won't be allowed near the kitchen sink. But I think I can promise her an interesting life—we shall undoubtedly do a bit of travelling from time to time, because I have a nature that needs travel and change, and I think Briony will enjoy it too.'

Lorna laughed in the pretty way which was so like Briony's.

'Well, that's all right, so long as you don't take my child to some poisonous swamp to look for spiders!'

'I shall not do that. Travelling is one thing. Exploring another. However restless I am, I shall never want to leave Briony so I shall never go anywhere where I can't take her.'

So that matter was happily settled and the Moores returned to Reigate satisfied that they could not hand Briony over to a better man.

Now once again the little house in Reigate became a hive of activity preparing for another wedding to another man, and this time—as Mrs Moore said to her husband—please God it would not be cancelled.

Briony was staying up at Monks Farm for only a few days more in order to complete her job as Hew's secretary. Because they were engaged, Miss Shaw had deemed it right and proper to go and stay at Monks Farm with the young couple. This made Hew laugh but he gravely accepted the offer. It was then when Miss Shaw handed over her cheque, which made both Hew and Briony gasp.

It was for one thousand pounds.

Briony looked at it, and exclaimed:

'Oh, but Aunt Caro, I can't take so much from you—'

'You take it before the Chancellor of the Exchequer gets it,' said Miss Shaw grimly.

'I've plenty left to live on. And I dare say I shall have a few more dividends from time to time that I can hand over to you. And as you know, all my capital will go to you on my death.'

They were all three sitting in Hew's study by a roaring fire on a bleak winter's night, when this happened.

Hew, who was now walking with the aid of only one stick and could get upstairs to bed unaided once more, lit his pipe and shook his head at Miss Shaw.

'Now you've gone and done it, Aunt Caroline.'

'Done what, pray?'

She was beginning to be almost as foolishly fond of Hew as old Berry, herself. He had completely won her heart during his engagement to Briony. She loved the gentle way he treated the girl. The charming way he teased her, too. The way he considered everything from her point of view. And the taste he showed when he bought presents for her now and then.

Her engagement ring was beautiful enough to satisfy even the owner of the 'Treasure Shop'. It was a yellow solitaire diamond which Hew had got one of his friends in Brazil to buy and send over. A gorgeous thing which had made Briony's eyes open wide when she first received it.

'It's far too extravagant of you,' she had cried.

But he had kissed her and said:

'Take it, sweetness, and say nothing. I will probably never be able to afford another diamond like this. But it's for a very special occasion and a very special girl. You see, I owe so much to you. Anybody with less character and understanding would have run away from me when I was so hateful. But you stuck it and made me see where my real happiness lay. I owe you everything. You've made me the happiest fellow alive.'

Tonight, he grinned at Miss Shaw.

'You have come between me and my fiancée,' he said. 'I'm much too poor and proud to marry a rich woman.'

'Get away with you,' said Aunt Caroline and clicked her knitting needles at him.

Briony, who had been sitting on a hassock in front of the fire, leapt to her feet and rushed to him.

'You've *got* to marry me whether I've got a thousand pounds or not,' she said.

'But, darling—you're an heiress!' He had his tongue in his cheek. Gently he pulled one of the reddish-gold curls which he adored. He loved teasing Briony. He always got a rise.

With flaming cheeks, she said:

'I've just chosen my wedding dress. You *can't* let Aunt Caroline's money make any difference.'

Then, right in front of her aunt's very eyes, Hew wrapped her in his arms and kissed her and cried:

'Oh, my darling, *darling* little Bri, as if I would! I was only pulling your leg. It's a wonderful wedding present and it will give you something to spend in Rio, and I don't care whether you're an heiress or not, I love you—' (Which was infinitely satisfying to Briony. And to Miss Shaw, who thought it was time she went out to Berry and made a cup of tea.)

Alone with his love, Hew sat in front of the log fire; held her close and wondered why he had ever thought it a good thing to lead a life in which women played no part ... or ever imagined he would never want a wife.

'Tell me about your wedding dress, my poppet,' he said.

But Briony leaned her cheek against his sleeve and dreamily murmured:

'Wait and see.'

TWENTY-SIX

The eighteenth of December of that particular year was not really a fine day.

Briony woke up early—looked at her watch and saw that it was still only half past seven. Her little bedroom in the Reigate house was dark and chilly.

She shivered and pulled the clothes over her ears. Then as consciousness returned fully, her heart gave a tremendous leap.

'Good heavens! It's my wedding day,' she thought.

For a moment she lay breathlessly still and thought about Hew. He was staying the night in Reigate with Elizabeth Moore's people. Liz and her Derek—a blissfully happily married couple—were in Malta. Liz's mother had gladly offered Hew a bedroom. Old Berry was here in this house helping Mummy and the faithful Mrs Mellin. Aunt Caroline was down from Seascale, staying here, too. Seldom had the Moore's house been so full of guests.

What fun they had had last night! An intimate family dinner party, including one or two of their best friends. Only Hew had not been allowed to come, which Briony had resented. Following the convention that the bridegroom must not see his bride the night before! He, she understood, was having his 'stag party' in town with one of his own friends, who happened to be in England—another keen traveller, and also a friend of Dick Forrester's. This man, John Ripley, had volunteered to be Hew's best man in the absence of Dick. John had just come home at the right time, Hew had told him. And the answer from John Ripley had been:

'Who'd have thought you would ever get married, you old son of a gun?'

Nobody had thought it. Least of all Briony.

Flushed and happy, Briony pressed her warm cheek into her pillow, shut her eyes tightly, and conjured up a picture of Hew's face as she had last seen it. His smiling eyes when they lunched together in London just before driving with old Berry down to Reigate.

'I really think I'm fit for an asylum rather than a church,' he had grinned at her. 'I've gone quite crazy about my future wife. Can't concentrate on anything else.'

What a wonderful thing that had been for her to hear! And wonderful for her to see him walking with only the slightest drag of one foot, with the aid of a stick which he was shortly to discard. Sir Phillip's cure was complete.

Together they read a cable which had just arrived from Dick:

Heartiest congratulations stop good wishes for wedding stop idea of meeting in Rio tremendous stop wedding present awaits you new car for touring out here stop bless you both.

Dick

A car in which to tour Brazil! That sounded a magnificent gift. No doubt extra-magnificent because Dick still felt guilty about his friend. Well, old Dick was like that—hard up one moment and plenty of money the next—but it *was* a thrilling prospect.

'My whole life is a thrilling prospect,' Briony reflected in the little room where never again she would sleep as Miss Moore.

At twelve o'clock this morning she would become Mrs Hew Gordon Vanner (Gordon had been his mother's name).

Briony suddenly switched on her lamp, put on her dressing-gown and slippers and gazed with shining eyes around her room. At the new suitcase and trunk marked with her future initials. B.G.V. At the wedding dress on its hanger outside the wardrobe. A simple dress because Hew had wanted it to be a simple wedding. He so dreaded publicity. Briony would have been quite happy to have gone off with him alone and got married in some remote chapel in their beloved Lake District. But Mummy had done so much for them—her feelings must be considered. And like any other mother she wanted a 'little show', Briony was her only daughter. So here, the wedding and reception was to be.

They had invited only relatives and bosom friends. No bevy of bridesmaids, no page, as had been arranged for that *other* wedding, with Clive Dormer. Just Penelope to follow the bride.

Now it was growing light. Briony pulled back her curtains. The garden was caked with snow. In the bluish light of the early morning it all looked very cold, yet lovely—a pure glittering world.

'I shall be a snow-bride,' Briony told herself sentimentally. And was glad that she had chosen this particular material for her dress. Satin with a pinkish lustre to it; with long tight sleeves and a high collar. She was going to wear a Russian coronet of orange blossom and a cloud of tulle. She would not have the Limerick veil which Aunt Caroline had lent before ... she had felt adverse to wearing anything as she had been going to do for Clive. That was all so different—and seemed paltry beside this new tremendous event in her life.

When she remembered various little episodes between Hew and herself during his convalescence ... how tender and gentle he was with her these days—gentle even when they were sparring—she could hardly believe that he had ever been that other Hew. Bad-tempered and exacting.

'You're the lamb and you've tamed the lion,' he had laughingly told her on one occasion.

'I'm far from being a lamb—' she had answered, 'and I love my lion even when he roars.'

She looked now at the filmy lingerie laid over a chair in readiness. Creamy georgette, hand-embroidered; one of Mummy's extravagances in an otherwise modest trousseau. At sheer nylons and white *crêpe* shoes. At an old ivory and gilt prayer book which had come out of the 'Treasure Shop'. At a double row of pearls which were Daddy's wedding present (as well as a cheque). And finally at the short ermine jacket which was one among many presents from Hew himself. She had learned, since their engagement, how generous he was. He kept selling old treasures in order to buy her special gifts. She could not stop him.

They had received quite a number of useful presents from the Moore side. That good-looking Tartan travelling rug and pillow from Liz's parents. Useful for the coming voyage. That handsome pigskin handbag—ideal for a journey—from Penelope and her family. And then Briony peered inside the wardrobe, and touched tenderly the well-cut blue-grey tweed suit in which she was 'going away'. She was to wear it with an exquisitely pleated *crêpe* shirt, with a small felt hat to tone, and lacy veil, and a warm overcoat of the same tweed with a big fox collar. Everything had been chosen with an eye to the travelling Briony was so soon to do. There were cotton frocks and linens for a hot climate in that trunk. But it was difficult to think of heat and sunshine on a raw December day like this, she thought ruefully.

The door opened and Mummy put her head in.

'Oh, *Bri!* I told you to stay in bed and have breakfast quietly and rest,' began Lorna.

'Oh, Mummy darling, I *couldn't* rest. I'm much too excited.'

Mrs Moore sat on the edge of her daughter's bed and looked fondly at the girl's radiant face.

'It's just what I felt when I was going to marry your father,' she said and her memories brought sudden sentimental tears to her eyes.

How strange life was—one passed the torch on from one generation to another. One brought a child into the world to suffer or to be happy—as one had done before her. To love; to give birth, and finally to die. All in cycles.

Yes, she, Lorna, had looked and felt as radiant as Bri, when about to go to her marriage with dear old Geoff. The first thrilling raptures of love very naturally faded but there was so much left—such deep devotion and companionship. She prayed that her daughter would always be as happy as she, Lorna Moore, was today. Remembering that other man—Clive—Lorna could realize now that she had been far more unhappy at the thought of losing Bri to *him* than she was this morning, in relation to Hew. She had seen quite enough of Hew to know that she was about to give Bri into a pair of very strong, sensitive and gentle hands. He would never let her down. As for the girl—she was quite silly about him and what could be better? The only regret Lorna had was the thought that Briony would so soon be sailing away and it might be some time before they saw her again.

As for the practical side of this romantic marriage, it seemed that Hew's publishers were more than ordinarily pleased with his finished manuscript, which was to be published in the New Year. It would sell more than his first, they said. And Hew's contract was for two more books of the same quality.

Another head popped round the corner of Briony's door. Old Berry, bearing a tray and two cups of tea.

'I reckoned the bride would be up and doing and want this,' she said.

Briony drank the tea happily. Then she sighed.

'Oh, Berry, did you ever think when you were looking after Master Hew that you would make the early morning tea for his bride?'

'I never did,' said Berry. 'And I must say it's a great moment for all of us ...' (sniff).

'Now, Berry, I'll murder you, and Mummy, too, if there is a *tear* shed at my wedding,' Briony threatened. 'It should be the cause of tremendous joy and I won't have these conventional tears.'

Mrs Moore drew her dressing-gown firmly around her and echoed Berry's sniff.

'It's high time you had a big bully of a husband to keep you in your place, my girl. You're far too cheeky and dictatorial.'

Briony threw her arms round her mother.

'I'm so happy, Mum darling—you don't know!'

But Mrs Moore did know. And it was hard to remember Briony's threat and to restrain her tears when at length the moment came for her to see her Briony walking up the aisle on Geoffrey's arm. Dear Geoff, looking so distinguished and solemn and yet pleased. The Parish Church not very full, just the right number. The organ was swelling gently. Briony ... looked ... well ... Lorna's eyes were blurred over, so that she no longer saw her daughter.

But Hew saw her very clearly. Standing there at the altar steps without a stick this time, dressed in his morning suit and feeling rather stiff and self-conscious, he watched his bride approaching. And he was filled with sudden amazement and awe that the fates should have given him such beauty—such perfection—for his very own.

She was like a lily, his Briony, pale, slim and straight in that satin sheath of her pinky-pearly gown. Her eyes were huge and serious. He had never seen her look more lovely with her flame of hair confined in the floral coronet gleaming under a floating tulle veil! When she reached his side he put out a hand and took hers. He found that it trembled. He pressed it tightly and his gaze met hers in a quick reassuring look of tender love.

The officiating priest, who was an old man, smiled at them benignly and began:

'Dearly beloved, we are gathered here together ...'

Mr Moore stepped back a pace in line with Penelope, the bridesmaid, who had just taken Briony's bouquet. It was of deep red roses—an unusual choice, but the bride's favourite flowers.

Lorna Moore prayed silently for her daughter's happiness. Old Berry peered through her glasses and wept unashamedly as she thought how near 'her boy' had been to death, and how well he had recovered and what a great day it would be when the young pair got back from South America and she could get Monks Farm ready to welcome them.

The ceremony went on. John Ripley, the best man, did his part and handed Hew the ring. As Hew slipped it on to Briony's finger, John caught a glimpse of the bride's face and the expression in her eyes. And he thought:

'I'm not surprised old Hew fell. She's not only as beautiful as a dream—she's a darling. He's a lucky guy!'

And that was what Hew himself thought, when, finally, to the triumphant lilt of Mendelssohn's *Wedding March,* he walked down the aisle with Briony on his arm. They stood for a moment for the inevitable photographs. It was a snow-white-covered world outside, but the sun had suddenly broken through the clouds and shone upon them. The snow looked dazzling. Hew and Briony looked into each other's eyes, smiling, and they, too, were dazzled. One of the photographers said:

'Just one more, please.'

But Hew thought that he had had enough and that it was high time that he got his wife back to the hotel where they were having the wedding breakfast. At five o'clock they were catching a train up to London. They were going to spend the first few days of their honeymoon there and, they had agreed, 'abandon the wide-open spaces' for the 'bright lights' and do all the shows and go to restaurants, and even dance. Yes, Briony was determined to make her husband dance with her if only once, she declared.

After that, Christmas at home; then Southampton and the liner which was to take them to Rio.

Hew gave another ravished look at his exquisite bride who was laughing and kissing her hand to one or two of the women who had never seen her in her life before, but had gathered there at the church door to wish her luck.

'This,' Hew said 'is where I exert my authority as your husband, Mrs Vanner.'

And he picked the shimmering lovely laughing girl up in his arms and held her there a moment. Her tulle veil drifted over his arm down to the snow and became one with it. They smiled into each other's eyes.

Then he carried her into their waiting car.

The publishers hope that this book has given you enjoyable reading. Large Print Books are especially designed to be as easy to see and hold as possible. If you wish a complete list of our books, please ask at your local library or write directly to Dales Large Print Books, Long Preston, North Yorkshire, BD23 4ND, England.

Other DALES Romance Titles In Large Print